The Crooked Knife

A Nell Munro mystery

JAN MORRISON

BOULDER
BOOKS

BOULDER
B O O K S

Library and Archives Canada Cataloguing in Publication

Title: The crooked knife / Jan Morrison.
Names: Morrison, Jan (Jan Anne), author.
Description: "A Nell Munro mystery".
Identifiers: Canadiana 2022019002X | ISBN 9781989417461 (softcover)
Classification: LCC PS8626.O7595 C76 2022 | DDC C813/.6—dc23

Published by Boulder Books
Portugal Cove-St. Philip's, Newfoundland and Labrador
www.boulderbooks.ca

Design and layout: Tanya Montini
Editor: Mallory Burnside-Holmes
Copy editor: Iona Bulgin

Disclaimer: Although places such as North West River, Sheshatshiu, and Happy Valley-Goose Bay are real places, this is a work of fiction. Names, characters, businesses, events, and incidents are the products of the author's imagination. Any resemblance to actual persons, living or dead, or actual events is purely coincidental.

Printed in Canada

We acknowledge the financial support of the Government of Newfoundland and Labrador through the Department of Tourism, Culture, Arts and Recreation.

Funded by the Government of Canada · Financé par le gouvernement du Canada

Canada

For the kids of Sheshatshiu
who taught me so much
with their love and humour

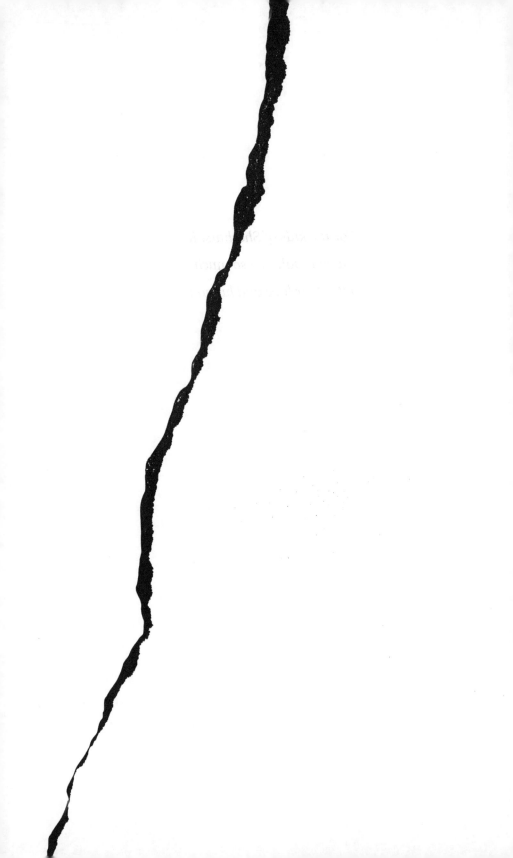

He woke within the dream to the sound of an uapineau drumming. The rhythm the grouse pounded out with its feet was simple—an ever-increasing thump until the sound was continuous. It reminded him of two girls from the north coast he'd heard throat singing, the rhythm quickening and rising until it could no longer be contained and the girls collapsed in laughter. While he watched, he heard another drumming. It was atikuat—caribou. The drumming of the herd and the drumming of the uapineau increased, and then shifted, and he went with the dream to another place: his grandfather standing by a skin tent in nutshimit—the land. The rhythm of the hoofs and the claws met with the rushing of Otter Falls. He felt it come up through his feet, felt it in his blood: three beats, interwoven.

His grandfather held out a drum, and the boy knew that he was supposed to take it, but there was something in the way.

He woke again, this time in his own bed.

This was his third dream with that rhythm. Where was his grandfather's drum? It was time.

Sunday, November 1

+++ Chapter 1

We'd been having the best kind of Sunday morning. A lovely lazy time in bed until a different hunger moved us into the kitchen, where Nick made the kind of breakfast you only have time for on a weekend, and I worked the crossword puzzle. The second pot of French roast was brewing and we were making our way leisurely through our bacon and eggs when I asked Nick what he had in mind for the rest of the day.

I'm no idiot. Just because I had the day gloriously off didn't mean he did. His life as an investigative journalist doesn't allow much room for conventional Sundays. Nick was working on a piece for a magazine that he'd then parlay into many more pieces for various media. It was how he supported himself while he was working on his book. For the last three years, he'd been researching, interviewing, and writing about the debacle called the Lower Labrador Project. Between the magazine piece and the larger book project, I held out little hope for company today.

The mess began with the first dam, Labrador Falls, which was built on the Upper Labrador River in the late 1960s. Now we were fighting this new dam (an extension of the project) at Otter Falls on the Lower Labrador, which was about an hour's drive from where we lived in North West River. Otter Falls had been a main portage for the trappers who'd worked along the Labrador River or travelled it to get to their lines, and it was an area traversed by the Indigenous of the area: the Innu and the Inuit. The building of the dam in this spot was a blow to any who cared about the history of Labrador or maintaining its wild beauty. And that was just one of the problems.

Nick tore through yet another slice of toast and reached for the coffee pot. "I'm not doing anything but hanging out with you, Nell. I'm at a standstill till I get an interview with someone from Sauvage." Sauvage was the French firm in charge of constructing the dam. "I think they're stonewalling me, but there's only so much kicking against the pricks I can do. So I thought we'd take Beany and hike up the Max McLean Trail till we get tired."

Beany, our dog, was a five-year-old rescue from Natuashish, a descendant of the dogs that had spent centuries travelling North America alongside its original peoples. They were known for their affable character and sly humour. Beany, called that for his pinto-bean-shaped body, appeared to have some husky and beagle in his heritage. He and I agreed that going out in the woods with Nick was the very best way to spend a Sunday. The trail wound along the Lake Melville shore, and we'd walk until we found a nice beach to have a boil-up. Until you've had one, don't think it's just boiling water to make tea. No. It is all about the contrast between hot and cold, wild and domestic. First, there's rustling about for windfallen branches and wood for kindling. Then, making a tripod of sticks to ensure that the water in the little boil-up kettle comes quickly to a boil. Finally, the payoff: sitting and sipping the hot tea while gazing out on a landscape few in this world have ever seen, or ever will. *Heaven.*

Then the phone rang: Sergeant Matt Renaud. I groaned. I worked rotating shifts at the detachment, and a Sunday off was a treat.

"Constable Munro. We need you to come in. We have a situation."

I work for the RCMP but I'm not a regular member. I'm a community constable—a CC. Basically a means of meeting the needs of a diverse and fractured community with a little neutrality, since police officers are widely regarded here with mistrust. The detachment is on the Sheshatshiu reserve, and I was hired because I made them hire me.

By "situation," Renaud meant that a youth was in trouble. I'd been a youth counsellor before I realized that I could do more good in the community as an RCMP officer. I did all the regular police work, but I was always called for anything regarding young people on the reserve. I didn't bother asking for details.

"I'll be there in a shake."

As I hung up the phone, I turned to Nick. He shrugged. "You get changed. I'll make you a bacon sandwich and fill up your thermos. Oh, and Nell, you might want to run a brush over your hair."

I pushed my fingers through my short, white-blonde mop and grinned at Nick. He knew that I didn't care much about my appearance. A few minutes later I emerged from our bedroom in my uniform, and he handed me the grub with a kiss to last the day.

✦

Our jack-o'-lantern had been kicked into a snowdrift by some kid— probably after I had turned off all the lights. It looked at me from its upside-down position, smiling fearlessly. We'd greeted the young trick-or-treaters (all bundled up for the cold with glittery crowns, capes, and masks jammed on top of their winter coats) who thrust their bags at us, looking so pleased with the evening ahead of them. Then we had gone early to bed, like we do every year, choosing to avoid the older kids demanding their due. I liked Halloween, but I had my limits. I jumped in my ancient car and warmed her up. She needed encouragement on cold mornings.

One of the nice things about living in North West River (population 543 on a fat day) and working in Sheshatshiu (population 1,873 and rising) was the short commute. I was at the reserve in minutes. I rode my bike when the weather permitted, but today, the first of November, it was snowy, blowy, and cold. I flicked on the radio to hear if I could glean anything about what I was about to walk into and was just in time to catch the end of the news:

Several environmental groups will present the Government of Newfoundland and Labrador with a document tomorrow outlining what measures they threaten to take if Bountiful Energy Corporation continues with its hydroelectric dam project at Otter Falls.

The dam is part of the Lower Labrador Project, which scientists believe will cause a significant increase in methylmercury levels in the water supply as the reservoir behind the dam fills, the cumulative effects of which would pose a severe threat to the surrounding communities and ecology. Yet Innu leaders insist that the Innu people are still supportive of the Lower Labrador Project, despite rumours to the contrary.

One resident of Sheshatshiu, who declined to be named, said that it is clear that the Aurora Agreement between the Innu Nation and the Government of Newfoundland & Labrador, which includes a sizable payout to each Innu in Labrador, was signed without prior knowledge of the possible methylmercury contamination issue. Protests have been increasing as the proposed date to begin flooding approaches.

BECorp refused to comment, except to say that their scientists are not in agreement with the findings of those commissioned by environmental groups, and protesters found at the construction site will be met with the full force of the law.

I refrained from yelling at the radio. It made no difference. I was glad that, as a member of the Sheshatshiu detachment, I at least wouldn't be expected to spend time threatening Land Protectors. Leave that to the detachment in Happy Valley-Goose Bay—the closest town to the site. It occurred to me that Nick would be busy as soon as he heard about this. Not that he wrote quick news items; his kind of journalism was a long game. But the long game was made by following the story as it unfolded, to see how it informed the longer piece. It did mean that our plans for the day were doomed even before I received my call and, selfishly, that made me feel better.

A few minutes later I walked into the office, my fragrant bacon sandwich in one hand and a mug of good coffee protecting me from the station's dreadful brew in the other. Sergeant Renaud was standing at the reception area.

"What happened, sir? Halloween party get out of hand?"

"No. It's Jay Tuck."

"The teacher?"

"Yes. He's dead."

That was bad. Jay was one of the good guys. The kids at the school loved him. He had been at the Innu Sheshatshiu School (kindergarten to Grade 12) for the past seven years and at the older, now defunct, school a few years before that. He taught English to the high-school grades. He was funny and sharp and he didn't suffer fools. He helped the students write and put on plays. He lived on the reserve, which was unusual. He said that it was stupid to try to connect with kids when you didn't share in their community woes. I admired him for that.

He was Irish, although he never talked about it—he was private about his past. I remembered him speaking at a diversity lecture put on at the school a few years back when I was a school counsellor. "When people put you in boxes, even ones many believe to be true, such as our ethnicity, parentage, gender, or nationality, they are being lazy and stupid. Anyone who points a finger at you and says you're a queer, a spic, a come-from-away is simply suffering from a lack of imagination."

I understood that the kids saw him as an authentic cheerleader for their lives. He refused to care about labels, and these kids, slapped with racist and institutional labels constantly, understood that he had no mask. He was simply there for them, whatever was needed. He was kind. He let them run with crazy ideas, sitting with them long enough for them to see that they didn't need to believe their own destructive thoughts. The loss of him was terrible.

"How?"

"Looks like his throat was cut with a crooked knife. He was found in his classroom."

I swallowed. "Looks like?"

"His throat was cut, and there was a crooked knife beside the body. The case where Tuck kept them looked to have been forced open."

"Who found him? And, uh … why bring me in?" I was cautious. I had gotten my knuckles rapped a few times for blundering into areas beyond my purview. Renaud often had to remind me that I couldn't have an opinion about everything, or at least I couldn't always be *expressing* my every opinion. I've learned to shut up about almost everything except when it came to the youth. At least I've learned it theoretically, if not quite in practice yet.

"One of the teachers went in to get something she'd forgotten. She noticed that his door was open and the light was on. We need you on the investigation because it was done in the school." Renaud looked cautiously around the office. "And because we think Pashin Rich might have something to do with it."

I took a deep breath. There was no way. Pashin was a lovely kid.

Seventeen, in his last year of school. Pashin was a rainbow kid. The First Nation peoples call them two-spirit.

I tried to keep my voice level. "What makes you think he's involved?"

"Two things. Jay was teaching Pashin how to make crooked knives, apparently. And someone heard them argue last week." Renaud looked stressed.

"Well Jay Tuck has taught a slew of kids to make crooked knives. He's been doing that for years." I watched him closely. "Who heard them argue?" I was aware that I was being a tad pushy and defensive, so I tried to keep my tone soft.

Renaud raised his eyebrows in a subtle show of frustration. "I did. I gave a talk to a class on intimate violence last Tuesday. I promised that I would bring Jay the money I owed him for the Timberline Marathon fundraiser when I was finished. When I reached the door of his classroom, I heard the two of them fighting."

"Oh." That was very bad news. I sat down at my desk and threw my bacon sandwich in the garbage. My appetite was gone. "What about?"

"I didn't hear the first of it. All I know is it was to do with some piece that Pashin had written. Jay told him that it wasn't going to work. Pashin exploded. I don't know what he was saying, but he sure sounded furious. I left them to it. Didn't think anything of it till now."

"Well, good. Doesn't sound like much of a motive."

"Normally I'd agree, but under the circumstances I'll have to take what I heard seriously, which includes hearing Jay say 'Over my dead body,' and Pashin answering, 'Your choice, sir.'" The sergeant raised his eyebrows as if to enforce how his hands were tied.

I relented. "Have you brought Pashin in, sir?"

"No. We aren't sure where he's residing right now, and I don't want the whole community in an uproar. Constables McLean and Hind are at the scene now, and we're expecting a crew from the Goose Bay detachment."

It was making sense to me now. I liked Sergeant Renaud, but we didn't always see eye to eye. He's older than me—43 to my 41—but he's years ahead in conventionality. He likes to do things old school, and I'm anything but. I was hired not only because I'd hectored the force but because it appeased the Band Council. I'd put in years convincing them that I would work on behalf of the Innu kids, not the whites, and they respected my approach and commitment to doing that. Moving from being a youth counsellor to being a cop wasn't that much of a leap, and I was sure Renaud had no cause to regret my being part of his staff, although he'd be one of the first to say that I didn't make his job easier. As a community constable with a strong allegiance to justice for Innu youth, I was trained, uniformed, and armed, but my allegiance was always in question. I was happy to have the job, but I needed to watch my step.

I chose to be transparent. "I believe Pashin is at his aunt's, Rebekah Pokue's. Here on the reserve. At least that's what he told me last week. Do you want me to bring Pashin here, sir?" It would be better to see Pashin early on, before any rumours could gather and swell.

Renaud softened at my offer. "No. I don't want the community alerted just yet. How about you just visit and talk to him there."

"Sure thing, boss."

"Just try and keep it friendly. If you think something is amiss, let us know and we'll handle it from there. Come on over to the school when you know something."

I grabbed my coat off the hook. Was I ready for the long, cold winter? I wasn't ready, but I was looking forward to it all the same—the first place I ever lived where I could make that statement. Yes, winter was long, with plenty of snow, but compared to the black ice and freeze and thaw of Nova Scotia, a Labrador winter was a dream. It got cold quickly and the snow was dry. Nearly every day was sunny and everyone loved to see the white stuff piling up. For old-timers, it had always meant the freedom to get around; it was much easier to snowshoe across the lake than tramp through mud and muck in the woods the long way around. In modern times, it also meant easy transportation. Rivers and lakes and the inland sea of Lake Melville became roadways for snowmobiles, and people trekked out to their cabins. As summer was bug season, winter was for recreation.

✦

Snow also covered up the trash that littered the reserve. When I first came to Labrador, seven years ago, my white sensibilities had despised the fact that everywhere the Innu lived or played was a thick layer of garbage, but after a few years I got it. I understood, if I still didn't like it, that the Innu were masters of passive rebellion. Just because theirs was the type of garbage that could be seen didn't mean that whites were any better at keeping the earth pure. Our garbage was just more subtle: the poisoning of lakes and streams with industrial waste, the hiding of our massive consumer culture in landfills far from our refined eyes, fracking, mining, and forestry. These were much more polluting than what a small community did with Cheezies wrappers and pop cans.

The plow had been through town, and I saw a few kids bumping over the roads on their rundown bikes. The only other life was a pack of wandering dogs. Dogs were autonomous in Sheshatshiu. They didn't so much live with humans as visit them from time to time.

Rebekah lived in a house near the water. There the houses were slightly older and in better shape, and some had gardens or grass poking through the snow. Most front lawns on the reserve had old bikes and broken appliances strewn across dusty patches, but Rebekah liked to keep her place tidy. Her bungalow had been painted this past summer, probably by one of the many kids she'd brought up—her own or not. It was sunny yellow with white trim and a view of Lake Melville and the Mealy Mountains across the water. Her house had four bedrooms, most with practically wall-to-wall beds in them, except for hers, which had a double bed and two cribs. All of Rebekah's own five kids were grown, and three of them were gone: one to St. John's, the other two in Sept-Îles, Quebec. Two remaining daughters lived in Sheshatshiu, but their kids came and went to their grandmother's house, as did an assortment of nieces and nephews, Pashin among them.

Since I'd known Rebekah, she'd been earth mother to a brood. There were always extra chairs to be brought to the kitchen table and plenty of warm clothes for kids in distress. Kids flowed freely all over Sheshatshiu, whether they were kicked out for bad behaviour, looking for a change of scene, or hiding from those who might want to put them in care. It was easier to let them go than try and keep them in one place. Innu kids, on the whole, were resilient and able to bounce back from bad situations and times of high stress such as holidays and elections.

As it was a Sunday morning, I knew that Rebekah would be going to Mass, at noon, so I didn't have long before she'd need to get ready. When I knocked and entered at her shout, I found her sitting at the table with a mug in front of her and a cigarette burning in the ashtray. It was unusual to see Rebekah sitting. She was usually on the move: cooking, wiping up messes, helping a kid with homework. There were no kids in sight.

"Hi, Nell."

Hmm ... not the warm, fuzzy greeting I'd hoped for. "Hey. I was hoping to see Pashin. Is he around?"

"He's not here. And a good thing too. He'd probably have flipped off the social worker that came last night. He doesn't have much patience with white people these days."

That didn't sound like Pashin. "What was a social worker doing here last night?"

"Someone from Family Services came and got two of Kanani's kids. She and her sister took the rest of the kids and headed out. I'm not saying where, because I don't trust anyone." She gave me a hard look.

I nodded, taking the hit. Kanani was Rebekah's eldest daughter. Maybe Family Services were just doing their job, but with their high-handed ways they sure made life difficult on the reserve. "Did they say why?"

"No. They don't have to. If it's not them, it's the Band Council. The kids always get the short end. How can we keep kids in Sheshatshiu from doing drugs when everything seems so hopeless? Kanani never did anything to cause Family Services to grab her kids. She doesn't drink or use drugs, and she tossed out that no-good, skinny man four months ago."

"You mean Leonard?" Kanani had had a rocky start, but she'd gotten clean, and I believed Rebekah when she said that she still was.

She nodded and stubbed out the cigarette. "I heard that he went back to Nataushish, but now I'm thinking he never did. Would be just like him to get someone stirred up to make some complaint to a social worker—not because he wants those kids either. Only one of them is his, and he never paid her any mind. No. He's just pure mean." Rebekah got up from the table. "Want a cup of tea? I've gone through one pot, but I'm going to put another on."

"No, thanks. I do need to talk to Pashin though. Isn't he staying with you?"

"She went to his older sister's a few days ago, last Thursday I think. Said he was working on a big project and needed a quieter place to work. It's plenty quiet here now." Rebekah talked as she put the kettle on the stove. "Why? What's she supposed to have done?"

The Innu never worried about using the correct pronouns. They were interchangeable, with no system whatsoever. A sentence could easily go: *My mother is coming today. He is tired of where she is staying.* It was a constant reminder that they held a different world view than we settlers did. Gender wasn't important—relationships were.

"Jay Tuck was found dead last night and—"

"Eh! Mr. Tuck is dead?" Rebekah moved back to the table and sat down heavily.

"They think that Pashin may have some information. I guess he and Mr. Tuck were close."

"Yes, Pashin liked Mr. Tuck. What's going on?"

"I need to find Pashin and see when he last talked to Tuck. The sooner the better. Can I find him at his sister's? Do you have her number? No. Forget that. I'll just drive over. What's the address?"

"Three doors down. The white bungalow with the wrecked red truck in the yard. She's a slob, that niece. My brother never taught her nothing."

"Melissa? Oh, I didn't know she was related to Pashin. Is she his full sister?"

"Nah. They had the same father—my brother, Gerard Rich—but different mothers. But Melissa's about 10 years older than Pashin. He was already on her own when Gerard died."

"Okay. I'll try to keep it straight."

Rebekah laughed, the first one I'd heard from her today. I thought of how much pain she must be in to have her grandkids taken by Family Services.

"Thanks, Rebekah, and I'm sorry about the babies. Can I help with that in any way?"

She hoisted herself up. The kettle was boiling. "Maybe later, but if we all start complaining, they'll just make it worse. You know what they're like … give people with no smarts all that power. Stupid."

She had that right. The longer I lived the more I saw the same thing. People who were paid shit wages with basic training in specialized jobs were somehow in charge of the world. Petty officials, customs, and border protection agents, and bureaucrats who got to boss around and determine the fates of the most disenfranchised of this country.

"Don't worry. I'll keep my nose out of it till you say." I hugged her hard.

+++ Chapter 2

At Melissa's, I knocked and waited. There was no way to disguise this as a friendly visit. Rebekah and I were friends, but to Melissa I was just another cop. After about four minutes longer than I wanted to wait, Melissa came to the door wearing those pyjama bottoms that people wore at any time of the day or night and a stained, long-sleeved T-shirt with a kitten on the front. She looked bigger than I remembered from the last time I saw her, but it might have just been the schlumpy clothes. Melissa's home had none of the cheery chaos of her aunt's. It was smaller and rougher, although the furniture was newer and, if not fancy, large. She had a humongous television on the wall and two leather couches with raggedy throws on them. The room was dark, the blinds closed.

"Uh ... oh, hi, Nell. Come in. Come in." Melissa wiped her nose with her sleeve and gestured to the table. Then she waited to see what I would say.

"Melissa. Haven't seen you in ages. Not since the Beach Festival." I remembered seeing her there hanging with her friends, loaded or stoned—hard to say which. My heart sank. How was I going to help Pashin in this situation? I had hoped I'd been wrong about Melissa back in the summer, but she was obviously still using. I was pretty sure that Melissa didn't work, but what she said next had me checking my assumptions.

"Ya, sorry I was so slow getting to the door. I finished up a seven-day cycle at Otter Falls last night and I'm trying to catch up on my sleep. And I think I caught the lousy cold that my boss has."

The new dam being built at Otter Falls came with a juicy deal offered exclusively to the Innu, in which BECorp agreed to hire Innu for unskilled labour before anyone else. Big whoop. The Innu were made flag people, cleaners (of the movable ratholes they offered up as residences for workers), and basic dog bodies. They'd work a week on and leave flush and without much to do their following week off. Not all, but many spent their money on booze and drugs. Sometimes my friends tell me I sound cranky. I am.

But maybe Melissa was different. I looked at her again and realized that what I'd first thought was weight gain was actually pregnancy. "When are you expecting?"

"Middle of January."

"This is your first, isn't it? You must be excited."

"Yes and no. Heard last night that the damn social worker scooped my cousin's kids for no reason. I know you'll think I'm paranoid, but they've been targeting the Rich family lately. They'll probably snatch this one before I meet it proper."

"That doesn't have to happen. Any help you need in making sure it doesn't, I'd be happy to give. Right now, I'm looking for Pashin. Do you know where he's at?"

Melissa was leaning on the table, and when I mentioned Pashin, she looked at me quizzically. She took a while to answer, but that was fairly normal for people on both sides of the river. Labradorians were never in a rush.

"He's gone. I have no idea where. He left yesterday. Left me a note for when I got off the work bus. Said he needed to stay somewhere else. I don't know why. I'm surprised he left a note, to tell you the truth. I figured he was at our aunt's. Did you try there?"

"Rebekah? I just came over from there. She hasn't seen Pashin for days."

"Well, he had some big deal going on. He was going on about something he'd written, and he was mega-tripping on it too. At least, he was before I left for this last stretch of work. Had something to do with those Land Protectors or whatever they're called."

This was definitely strange. Whatever Pashin had been writing had got Jay Tuck's back up and caught Melissa's attention. "Any idea what it had to do with the Land Protectors?"

She shrugged. "I got the sense he was working with them on something."

The Land Protectors were a local environmental-activist group led mostly by old-timers. Some of the ringleaders were Metis, some were Inuit, but the bulk were settlers (white folk). They were gaining some credibility but the problem, as always, was that the different groups—the Metis, the Inuit, the Innu, and the settlers—had been effectively polarized by the Government of Newfoundland and big corporations like BECorp. The Innu had been bought out years ago, back when the Upper Labrador Dam was being built. It was one of the most painful aspects of modern life here: the Innu, who could force change, had given all their rights away for next to nothing decades ago.

Hearing that the Land Protectors were reaching out to Sheshatshiu for young members was very interesting. I'd better look into that. I knew one of them, a white woman named Roberta, who was an old-time activist who really knew how to organize. I wondered too about Melissa's comment about Family Services picking on the Rich family. Anyone who worked or lived in Sheshatshiu knew that a hierarchy of families existed, but the Richs were considered to be, if not a top family, a solid middle one. They mostly kept out of the kind of trouble which would have their children removed.

"What do you know about him making a crooked knife with his teacher, Jay Tuck?"

"Huh? Nothing. Why would he do that? Stupid kid. He doesn't know anything about carving." Melissa's tone was slightly scoffing, but her face betrayed fondness. "Tuck was always trying to get us making those things. What does a white guy know about crooked knives?"

"Lots. Jay Tuck has a huge collection of older ones, and he's made several extremely beautiful ones over the years." I refrained from telling her that the crooked knife was claimed by many cultures. It had become a futile disagreement about appropriation over the years. One of the arguments against the notion that the crooked knife was wholly designed by North American Aboriginals—both Inuit and First Nations—was that there had long been a similar knife used by European farriers to work with horses' hooves. But this long-standing dispute meant nothing to most people.

"Any idea why Pashin would be interested?"

"Beats me."

This was going nowhere. "Okay. If you see him, could you tell him I need to talk to him? He's not in any trouble—make sure you tell him that." Was that true? I hoped so.

"If you find him before me, tell him that Shirleen called to tell him there's a meeting later on tonight and to make sure to be there and to do nothing about anything till he'd talked to all of them."

"Our Shirleen?"

"Shirleen who used to work with the doctor. Shirleen Gregoire."

That would be our Shirleen. She worked at the detachment as an administrative assistant and she was excellent. But why would she be calling Pashin? "Uh ... when did Shirleen call? Just in case I do see him?"

"She called yesterday, but she was talking about tonight. I don't know what it's about. She said he'd know. Probably some group for kids on drugs, most likely. Pashin likes hanging out with Elders. He's always been weird that way. Shirleen and him have been close since Pashin's mother died."

That made sense. Shirleen didn't have any kids, at least not yet, but was a big sister or aunt to a pack of them. She was Innu but chose to live in North West River. Maybe Melissa was right. Maybe it was a drug-intervention group. Pashin had done some training as a youth leader, so maybe she'd recruited him.

I walked slowly, pondering what I knew, back to the car. It was time to head over to the crime scene.

+++ Chapter 3

The Sheshatshiu school is a beautiful building made up of three wings. Because it sits on a hill, you can see out over Lake Melville, all the way to the Mealy Mountains. Even though the community tries to keep the school in good shape, it's a losing battle.

Word had obviously gone around; a crowd of people were gathered near the entrance of the school. As I passed through the front door, one of the officers told me that the team was in Jay Tuck's room. I walked into the lobby, where large glass cases displayed Innu handicrafts, clothes, and other items, past the beady eye of the school mascot, a large eagle suspended from the ceiling, and into the hallway that led to Jay's classroom. I could hear the subdued but cheerful voices of a team at work. Homicide scenes have a certain air—a formality—but most police workers and pathologists try to maintain an opposing atmosphere of joshing and banter. I don't mind it. I'm not squeamish about a dead body. Unless it's a hanging. I'm not sure why, but the sight of a hanging triggers such a terrible loneliness in me.

The room had the metallic smell of fresh blood. It's always weird how a person known in life becomes, in death, simply a body. This body was propped in a semi-reclined position in the far-right corner from the door, legs splayed awkwardly. Jay didn't look as if he'd been in pain, although his eyes were open. Honestly, he looked beseeching in a surprised way, as if he were saying, "This isn't what I expected at all." The most outrageous feature was the ring of red around his throat, from ear to ear. Crooked knives can't be used for stabbing, since they don't have a sharp point, but the edge is like a razor. On the floor, by Jay's right hand, lay a crooked knife. I could not see if it was bloody. An officer was dusting the glass cabinet where Tuck kept his collection of crooked knives. If the lock had been forced, it hadn't taken much effort; nothing looked broken.

I wasn't sure of the chain of command at the scene, so I didn't ask any questions. I couldn't imagine that there would be any surprise about the cause of death, but you never knew what would be revealed.

I went over to talk to Constable Pete McLean, my colleague at the Sheshatshiu detachment, hoping that he might tell me something. Pete was young, in his late 20s, but he'd been a cop longer than me. He went right from high school to do his training. Word was out that he was in line to be promoted to corporal. We were short-staffed in Sheshatshiu, and our one corporal had been transferred a few months ago on compassionate leave. Pete was a local boy, born and raised in Goose Bay, and proud to be a son of Labrador. He was easy to work with, even if his naive attitude irritated me from time to time. His major failing was a shyness at taking initiative. Sometimes I had to still my own impatience with his lack of zip.

"Who's going to be in charge?" I asked quietly. Every investigation has a chief investigating officer, and everyone else sorts themselves out into the chain of command. There was no Major Crime Unit at the Goose Bay detachment, and none in Sheshatshiu. They wouldn't wait for a team to be sent from the Newfoundland and Labrador head detachment in St. John's. Sergeant Renaud was head of the detachment in Sheshatshiu, but that didn't mean as much as it should have.

Pete gestured toward the door, where Sergeant Al Musgrave caught my attention for the first time. Too bad. I'd hoped that Renaud would be given command of this case. I didn't know Musgrave very well. He'd been in Labrador longer than I had, but we didn't cross paths often. I found him officious, and word was that he was exceedingly ambitious. Having the lead on a murder investigation wouldn't hurt his resumé. He was one of those cops who had a military air, with his posture and his ginger hair in a buzz cut.

He must have felt me observing him. He tapped Renaud on the arm, nodded in my direction, and said, "What's with CC Munro?" That seemed rude, but I supposed he was curious about who would be on the team and why.

"Community Constable Munro is the youth liaison, Sergeant. I thought she'd be the best one to communicate to the youth but, of course, as the chief investigator of this case, it's up to you." Renaud spoke in his usual quiet voice. I could see Musgrave considering this, his mouth almost forming a sneer at the words *youth liaison.*

"Yes, good idea. We're short a few officers right now because of all that stupid protesting, so fine. But tell her to keep all of this to herself. Damn crowd already knows too much."

Renaud looked at me and raised an eyebrow, while Musgrave turned back to talk to someone (the doctor on call I thought) and nodded. I nodded back. Warning received. Unnecessary, but received. It was also unnecessary for Musgrave to act like a community constable wasn't a real constable. I'd had the same training as Pete. It was an old bias in the system. The only reason it was unusual for me to be here was because it was my day off. I had all the same duties as a regular constable, but I also could be brought in if it was deemed sensitive to the community culture—such as a youth being a suspect.

Renaud sidled over to me, speaking low. "Let's just handle this as gently as possible. I thought I'd get the lead, as it happened in our detachment area, but I didn't reckon with the fact that Musgrave just tidied up a very long investigation. He's the shining light right now. However it pans out, I want you to keep your opinions to yourself."

I smiled and shrugged. "Got it, Sergeant. So, what have they found out so far, sir? Estimation on time of death?"

"Sometime before midnight last night. The keypad entry system shows that Tuck used his personal code just after 10 p.m. and someone, presumably the murderer, left around 1 a.m., using Tuck's code. So we have a three-hour window of opportunity. Trouble is that he could've let the perpetrator in. There's no way of knowing. There's also a side door that teachers use as a shortcut and to smoke, so there's that, too. The doctor agrees with the estimated time of death for now but can't confirm it till the autopsy proper. The last time anyone saw Jay alive was at 8 p.m. or so. Some kids came by his house trick-or-treating, and he answered the door. Gave them candy."

We were interrupted by one of the forensic team.

"Sergeant Renaud? When we moved the body, we found several items. A page from some book—looks torn out, with blood on it—and strands of a bright pink synthetic material."

"Thanks. Make sure it goes in the kit for analyzing." He paused. "Wait a minute—I'd like to see the page."

The constable brought a piece of crumpled paper over and placed it in Renaud's gloved hand. It had blood on it, like he said, and I saw with surprise that it was a page from a playbook: *Hamlet*.

"Sergeant, may I see the page? I won't touch it."

"Damn straight you won't. Why do you want to see it? Know your Shakespeare, do you?"

Great. Shakespeare geek now added to my list of peculiarities. "Yes, Sergeant, sir, I know my Shakespeare and I for sure know my *Hamlet*." I couldn't help myself. "Why? Does being literate not fit into the correct police way of being?"

Thankfully Renaud met my sass with indulgence. "The lady doth protest too much, methinks." We grinned at each other. "And that's act 3, scene 2, in case you need to know."

Well knock me over with a feather; the man knew his Shakespeare. Okay, simple re-evaluation needed. "Sorry for my boorish assumptions. But truly, what page is it?"

He squinted to see the print on the blood-soaked top of the page. "Act 3, scene 4. Says Gertrude and Hamlet on here."

The closet scene. "Hamlet has come back from school to find his father dead and his mother married to his uncle. He's reproaching his mother for her haste in remarrying, when he accidentally kills Polonius, thinking it's his uncle hiding behind the curtain." Renaud and I looked at each other. "Maybe they were going to do *Hamlet* for the school play? It may have been what Pashin and Jay were arguing about."

Renaud lifted one eyebrow. "Maybe. Or maybe the page just happened to be there. The man was an English teacher. Let's not leap to conclusions, Constable. It'll go for prints, but I'll leave you to figure out if there's anything more to it than that." He turned his head to see if anyone was listening. "Did you find our person of interest?"

"No. He's not at his aunt's or his sister's. They don't know where he is, but I have a few ideas."

I was intrigued by the cloak and dagger approach he was taking to Pashin. I guessed he hadn't shared much, if anything, about Pashin with Musgrave. I was thinking that was a good thing, when Musgrave came up to Renaud.

"We found something of interest, Sergeant. It's a photo of a young man, almost nude. It was in Tuck's shirt pocket. Know who this is?"

I looked over Renaud's shoulder as he examined the photo Musgrave held out. My heart sank. It was Pashin, coming out of the water somewhere—a river? A lake? I didn't recognize the place. His long hair was in a topknot, his body shining with water, undeniably gorgeous. He was laughing at whoever was taking the photo. He looked maybe 14 or 15. I wondered at Musgrave calling someone in a bathing suit "almost nude." Seemed overly dramatic.

Renaud sounded sorry. "It's Pashin Rich, Sergeant. A student of Tuck's."

Musgrave looked intently at Renaud. "Is that the same student you said you heard arguing with the deceased?"

Renaud gave me a don't-even-dream-of-speaking look, then answered carefully. "Yes. Nothing mentioned about a photo."

Musgrave didn't respond, just took it over to the other evidence.

I decided I needed to renew my interest in finding Pashin. "I'll go and talk to the students out front before the body comes out. They might know something about what play was in the works. Okay, sir?"

"That's fine, Constable. And I'd like you to take some time to go over and check out Tuck's apartment. I've told Pete to go over as soon as I clear him from here. I'll tell him to send you a text when he gets there, okay? Is your cell charged?"

Fair question. I hated my cell. It's true I always forget to charge it, but the other reason is that it hardly ever worked once I was over the bridge and in North West River anyway. I sighed. "Yes, sir, it is charged. And I'll pay attention to it."

Renaud waved his hand in dismissal, so I made my way out of the school.

Since I'd been inside, quite a crowd had gathered. They had grouped themselves, as people will, into their own particular subcultures. There were the mothers, looking tense, nervous that one of their kids might be considered a suspect. A low murmur of chatter punctuated by the occasional eruption of laughter. As a people, the Innu are prone to much jocularity. I've never been around a group that liked to laugh more. Near the women was a group of men wearing an air of bravado but who were definitely uneasy. I was surprised to see several men that had been considered *of interest* to the RCMP lurking about. One of them was a cousin of Chief Anthony Montague. He was a young man who'd had several brushes with the law but always managed to come out unscathed, and he was talking to Frank Andrews. I'd never had any dealings with Andrews, but it was generally known that he was a dealer. It would seem that he was in possession of enough nerve to not mind being around a gaggle of police. To one side stood the chief and some of his closest people. He was not paying attention to his cousin Anthony or Frank, and in fact had his back to them.

Then there was the group I was most interested in talking to—the kids. They were gathered in the playground on the other side of the parking lot, sitting on the swings or leaning against the chain-link fence, smoking, laughing, and talking.

"Hey, Miss, what's going on? Tell us what's going on, Miss." No matter how long I'd been here I couldn't break the older kids from calling me Miss. It drove me nuts. I'd explained that I hadn't been a *Miss* since I was 17 and, even then, as a stalwart feminist, I'd been a Ms., but they wouldn't hear that. No such word to them. And they wouldn't call me Nell, because that was disrespectful to adults. The younger kids called me Nelly Jelly Beans quite happily, but as soon as they hit Grade 7 that was over and I was *Miss* to yet another kid.

"There's been a death. It's Mr. Tuck. Very sad."

"Ya, but Miss, how did he die? Did she kill himself?"

"Hey, you guys all watch CSI, you know I'm not allowed to say what happened. And, anyway, I don't know. You'll just have to wait till they make a statement. What have you heard? How come everyone's gathered?"

"Smoke signals, Miss."

"Very funny, Tony. I guess you mean Facebook, eh?"

"Miss, we want to know what happened. Is there a killer around?"

"I hope not, Mary-Louise." There were about nine kids, mainly from the third level (Grades 11 and 12 in white schools). I didn't see Pashin or Zann, but two of the other kids involved with the theatre gang were there. Zann was one of Pashin's closest friends, and I'd hoped to find her. A smart cookie, she would've known how important it was to find him quickly.

"Hi, Kaitlyn. Hi, Jeremiah. Pretty sad, eh?"

They both nodded, although they looked more excited than sad. Normal for teens around this type of tragedy, and the truth was that they'd seen too much death in their lives already.

"I heard you guys were going to put on a play with Mr. Tuck. Which one were you going to do?"

"We were gonna do *Hamlet*, Miss. Only then Mr. Tuck said, 'Nope, we're going to do *Romeo and Juliet*.'" Kaitlyn was always a help. I had a soft spot for her.

Jeremiah kicked the dirt at his feet. "Don't matter because now we won't be doing any play. None of the other teachers can be bothered."

I thought about that. Maybe it wasn't true that most teachers couldn't be bothered—more like they felt out of their depth—but it amounted to the same thing. "I'll help you, if you want. I worked on a few plays with Mr. Tuck and he'd want you all to go ahead, I'm sure. Have you had auditions yet?"

"No. We're supposed to have them tomorrow after class."

"Okay. I'll meet you at the school. If it isn't open for some reason, we can go to the Mary May Healing Centre. I'll give them a heads-up. Say 7 p.m.? Will you guys post it on Facebook for me?"

"Yep, no problem, Miss."

It felt good to see their faces soften. "I wonder why he decided against *Hamlet*?" Just thought I'd put that out there.

"Mr. Tuck said *Romeo and Juliet* was perfect for us: kids our age carried away by their great love, bossy adults who don't know squat, and like that," Kaitlyn said.

Jeremiah shook his head. "I'd rather we did *Hamlet*. I wanted to direct with Mr. Tuck, and we'd already started going through it. I think that's what Mr. Tuck and Pashin had their fight about."

"Do you mean an argument with shouting or a fist fight?"

"No—just yelling. Pashin came out of Mr. Tuck's classroom totally pissed off the other day after class. Said Mr. Tuck was just like all the others and didn't believe in the truth. Said she was really really fed up, and he was going to deal. Whatever that meant."

We were quiet for a moment, then Kaitlyn spoke up. "Pashin don't hang out with us like he used to. He's become really ... you know, protest-y? Like he's always angry at the colonizers. He has friends not from here now—older. It's like, he went away in the spring to an Indigenous youth conference on the environment, and he came back different." She looked worried when she said that, and I thought maybe she felt like she was betraying him. "He's still a good guy, Miss. I get it. I just don't want to be mad all the time like he is."

"Do you know where Pashin is?" I saw Kaitlyn's eyes cut to Jeremiah.

"No. Haven't seen him since class on Friday."

"What about last night? No Halloween parties?" I could tell by their facial expressions that they were holding back. "Come on. Pashin's not in trouble, but we need to talk. If you saw Pashin last night, let me know and if you know where he is now, let me know that too. The sooner I speak to him the sooner we can clear this up."

Kaitlyn started to open her mouth but I saw Jeremiah's hand press up against her leg. Her mouth slowly closed.

Instead, Jeremiah spoke. "We didn't see Pashin last night. Didn't see Pashin since Friday. Don't know where she is. Didn't go to any Halloween parties. We're in our last year, Miss. We want to make it through and get out of here. You understand that, don't you?"

I did.

+++ Chapter 4

Just as I was about to leave, I saw everyone's attention swing to the school door. An ambulance that had been sitting there started up and two guys rolled out the body on a stretcher. The people didn't move any closer as they might have tried to do in a city, but stood as they had been, but much quieter—all looking toward the body.

I went back to my car and waited until the ambulance pulled away and the crowd started to disperse in fits and starts. I didn't drive straight to Lonesome Johnny's. I didn't want Pashin alerted by cell. So I drove as if back to the station and then swung around on a lower road and looped back behind. I parked down the street from Lonesome Johnny's just in case anyone was looking. Sheshatshiu is a nosy place. As people are always asking me where I'm going and what I'm doing, it's second nature to cover my tracks. I went to the side door, again for concealment reasons, knocked hard, and walked in. Pashin was sitting on the couch talking to Johnny. He leapt to his feet and made to go, but Johnny put his hand on his arm. "Come on, man. Settle. She's not the enemy."

How had I known where Pashin was? When I talked to Kaitlyn and Jeremiah, I realized that they wouldn't tell me where Pashin was hiding out. Too much like squealing, no matter what their common sense told them. On the other hand, because Kaitlyn wanted to tell me, I knew that she knew. She'd looked over at the street in front of the school and up the hill. Several streets there had newer houses. Not exactly charming ones, but rather more kept up, as if they haven't been around long enough to be totally trashed. I knew that at the top of the topmost street was a house owned by a strange dude: Lonesome Johnny.

Johnny Tuglavina was not an Innu but a coastal Inuit. He'd come to Sheshatshiu in the 1990s and had fallen in love with an Innu woman. They'd lived together for a few years until the house they lived in burned to the ground. Rumour had it that the fire was caused by kids or adults sniffing gas. Sadly, not an uncommon story in the north. The woman, the two kids they'd had together, and another child of hers died. But Lonesome Johnny survived and, for some reason, decided to stay. He'd just been Johnny in those days, but as the years rolled on and he stayed by himself in his little house, he became Lonesome Johnny.

Johnny carved beautiful things in bone and stone, like many Inuit artists, but he also carved in wood. Over the years, artist reps and gallery owners had approached him, but the gossip mill said that he would have none of it. He said that his work was between him and God and no one else need interfere.

Lonesome or not, some of the edgier kids hung out at Johnny's. Apparently, he would not allow any drugs or booze or anyone high to come in but offered good meals and a honest interest in their lives—something in short supply for these kids. Probably for kids anywhere. Every once in a while, some parent or official would say that he was a perp or a sexual deviant or a cult leader, but the accusation would blow over when it became obvious that it had no grounds. His place was a refuge, and I should have thought of it before Kaitlyn's tell gave it away.

"Hi, Pashin. I wanted to talk to you about Mr. Tuck. A few people heard you two arguing and I'd like to hear from you what it was about. Let's talk, and if you agree then we'll go down to the detachment and you can make a statement. Okay?"

"I don't have anything to say."

"Pashin, don't do this, man. You got lots to say. And this woman, she wants to hear it, so give it to her." Johnny's voice was soft.

I sat back and prepared to wait. I looked around the room. It was plain and comfortable with two couches, two easy chairs, and, over against the wall, a big, round table. There were also several things you didn't normally see in Sheshatshiu homes. Bookcases and books, for one. The other, an absence—no television. Television was usually always running in the background of every conversation in this community. It was quiet here, and I liked it.

"Do you want tea, Nell? I just made a pot." Johnny rose and moved toward the kitchen.

"Sure, that would be good, as long as it hasn't steeped too long. I was just up at the school and that wind is cutting. So early."

"No. Just on time. November is a reminder for us to get our wood in. To get ready, put some food by. I like it."

I could see and feel Pashin relax. He sat back in his chair, and I gave myself permission to look at him. Pashin was big, about 6 foot 4, with long hair that he sometimes wore in a braid or a topknot. Today it was loose, and he was dressed in jeans and a Tribe Called Red T-shirt. His face was neither overly masculine nor feminine and had sensuous lips like those of so many Innu people I had met. His eyes, espresso with streaks of caramel, usually kept a steady gaze, although today they flicked here and there, betraying his anxiety.

Johnny, in contrast, was short and stocky with a wide, flat face, broken into a perpetual grin. An old scar ran down one side of his face. He brought over a Brown Betty teapot, three sturdy diner cups, and a pitcher of milk. We sat in comfortable silence as he poured tea into the cups and handed me one. It was pleasant to sit and breathe in the warmed air rising from the cup, to hold it against my chest and feel its warmth spread out, to smell that familiar smell of a million kitchens and as many conversations. I sighed. I was tired. I thought this was going to be one kind of day but it had turned into entirely another.

"How's that man of yours, Nell? What's he working on? He's a good fella, eh?"

Everyone liked Nick. He was constantly in both communities, talking to the people who might help him make his stories good and true. And not just those who might agree with his politics but also those diametrically opposed to his own values—that was his job.

"He's working another angle of the Otter Falls story. Frustrating, but he persists."

"Good. Someone must. You're both good people. You must be

patient with this community. It appreciates those who are willing to tell the truth, but it doesn't always tell them so."

I nodded. Johnny was encouraging me, but I had to step carefully. I had to look patient, even if I was a burning ball of irritation on the inside. My mind flickered to a friend back home in Nova Scotia who was teaching me to meditate. When I complained that I lost my temper too easily, she told me to consider the lotus: "Thich Nat Hanh says that the lotus grows out of the mud. Without the mud, there is no lotus. Suffering is a kind of mud that we must use to grow the flower of understanding and love." She taught me that I could transform my anger into compassion. I took calming breaths and realized that I appreciated Johnny's way. To bring my family into this meant that he was seeing me and asking me to see the truth here too.

Finally, Pashin spoke.

"How was Mr. Tuck killed?"

"I can't tell you that, Pashin. And no one has said he was murdered as of yet."

"I'm not stupid, you know."

"I know. And I also know that you're aware that I can't talk about the crime scene." I sighed and sipped my tea. "It would be good if you could just tell me what you two were arguing about. Before you say anything, I know that you did. Someone heard you."

"Well, why don't you ask them, then?" Pashin's voice was cynical and mean. I'd never heard him speak like that.

I waited, and finally he spoke again.

"We argued because I wanted to do my version of *Hamlet* and he didn't want me to. He said it was too hot a topic now."

"What was your version?"

"It's about the environment and how Aboriginals always end up losing their land to big corporations. Tuck said we should take it slow. That there was no need to poke the snake with a stick."

"It sounds like you are really pissed that Tuck had given up the fight. And I can see how others might think it puts you in a bad light, you know."

"I can't help that," Pashin added quietly. "Do you expect me to lie? After all, I'm just another lying Indian, right?"

I looked at him in surprise. He knew better, at least from me. But Pashin looked different than I'd ever seen him. His face twisted in anger. He got up and in two strides was at the door. "You think I should talk to the sergeant, but you don't know shit. I don't trust any of you. Not anymore." And he wrenched open the door and left, while I sat there with my mouth open.

"He's not going anywhere, Nell. Just let him go. He'll be back. He's a real hurting unit."

"I know. I'll move slowly, but I can't be positive that the sergeant will do the same."

Too late, I remembered Pashin's sister's message. "Johnny, if you do see Pashin later, will you tell him that Melissa said that Shirleen phoned and there's some kind of meeting tonight. Pashin would know what it is."

Johnny was quiet. He seemed to be pondering something. He

must have reached a resolution, because he turned to me. "I know about the meeting. I'll tell you what, Nell. You come with me tonight and maybe I can get Pashin to talk to the sergeant."

"Where is it?"

"I'll pick you up."

"Nah, not sure where I'll be."

"Well, if you want to come to this meeting, I'll have to pick you up. The fewer cars seen going to where we are going, the better. And keep it to yourself. Them's the rules. Are you in? Oh, and another thing—you aren't on your moon time are you?"

"No, I'm not. Why?"

"Because we're going to a sweat. You good with that?"

"Sure. I love a good sweat. Call me when you're ready. I'm not leaving my car unattended this side of the river, so can you pick me up at my house. It's the old—"

"The Wheeler place on the beach. Yep, I know. Good. It'll be between 7:30 and 9."

"This is going to be one long day."

"Not for Mr. Tuck," said Johnny, and sipped his tea.

✦✦✦ Chapter 5

"Did you find out where Pashin Rich is at?"

Renaud had come up to my desk where I was going through some files. I kept my head down, although the truth was that I was avoiding his direct gaze. I make a terrible poker player when the stakes are quarters and dimes. No telling what my face registers with real lives in the balance.

Renaud picked up a report on a fracas that had happened at the rink last Thursday. I should have filed it already, but I had wanted to check out one of the statements. I saw him slowly read down the file as if it were a vital document.

With his attention elsewhere, I took my chances. "Nah. I tried every place I knew but couldn't find a thing. I have an idea for tonight though. There's some gathering that I'm going to this evening."

"What sort of gathering?" Renaud raised his gaze from the file and looked intently at me. So much for my casual approach.

"Oh ... I told the kids I'd help them with the play they want to put on. It's scheduled for December 14, so they have to move on it. They were worried because they thought that it might seem disrespectful, but I told them that Jay Tuck would want them to go ahead. Especially for the Level Three kids. They're supposed to graduate and some of them have been doing bit parts and makeup for several years just so they'd get a chance for a meatier role come their last year. The spring is too crazy, and, plus, they're supposed to enter something into the province-wide contest."

Not bad, and all true except I hadn't made the arrangements for tonight but tomorrow night. Ah well, the best lies have a line of truth in them. And it worked. Apparently just the thought of a bunch of kids doing Shakespeare caused Renaud's eyes to glaze over. He dropped the unfinished report on my desk.

"Deal with this tomorrow would you, Constable? Shirleen was bugging me about it on Friday. It doesn't look good when the administrative help is complaining about one of my officers. Filing reports is a boring but necessary part of this job. Okay?"

I nodded but before I could make excuses or apologies, the sergeant asked me another question. "What did you find out from the crowd outside the school?"

"I talked to some kids who'd been at the play meeting. They were tight lipped. They said that they hadn't seen Pashin since Friday, but I'm not so sure about that. Oh, and apparently they'd been set to do *Hamlet* but Tuck changed it to *Romeo and Juliet*. Not sure why. Okay if I continue to poke around, or will Musgrave get up your butt if I do anything that might resemble actual police work?"

A laugh escaped Renaud's mouth before he could settle on a serious expression. "Where'd you get that idea? Don't let Musgrave get under your skin. He's old-fashioned, doesn't quite get what a community constable is. Report to me and I'll report to Musgrave."

I felt relieved to hear him say it, but I still had something more to say.

"How come Musgrave was put on this detail, Sergeant? I know he just tied up that big investigation but don't they get that you'd be the best here on the reserve?"

"Don't underestimate Sergeant Musgrave, Constable. He's been the lead on several important investigations and he is a thorough, meticulous investigator. Also, Constable, this might have been a decision made by the higher-ups based on the detachment and not the personnel. It may be considered a political necessity to keep the investigation based in Goose Bay and not in Sheshatshiu. Keep your eyes open and your head down and learn as much as you can. An investigation like this on the reserve, if not handled properly, could have repercussions for years."

I took a long look at the sergeant. He looked harried in a way that I hadn't seen him before. An important community member was murdered. I would do as Renaud said, but I still wished he was heading up the investigation. Maybe Musgrave was good but it was clear that he wasn't ever going to listen to me because I was a woman or because I was a community constable. Or both.

"Is Sergeant Musgrave going to set up the incident room here?"

"That's under question right now." Renaud shook his head. "It can't be in the detachment, not enough space. I thought the school, but Musgrave is talking Goose Bay. He wants everything handy. Till he decides, we'll keep working at the school. We've taken over the Place to Be room since it has enough space and computer hookups.

I'm supposed to organize the details." He shook his head as if to shake off the thought. "Let me know if you find Pashin. I'm sure the news is out in the neighbourhood, so tell anyone you see that it would be very good for Pashin if he volunteered to come in for questioning. I'm not sure how long I can keep Musgrave from issuing a warrant and starting a manhunt. It's only because of the political pressure that I got him to slow down, as it is. And I'd like you to head over to Tuck's place now. Pete's there, but another set of eyes wouldn't hurt."

✦

Tuck's apartment was in a house not far from the Sheshatshiu detachment office. It was a grubby place from the outside, but the times I'd been in it I'd been surprised at the order and beauty Tuck had managed with such few materials. It had a separate door around the back. I remembered that the main part of the house was not lived in at the moment. The house was owned by a family that spent time in Nataushish, the reserve on the north coast. I saw that Pete was already at work inside and so I just hollered from the door and went in.

Tuck's apartment was a largish open-plan room with a small bedroom and bathroom at one end. The living room was wall-to-wall bookshelves with an eclectic set of books: an extensive collection of modern and ancient poetry, many well-thumbed art books, books on religion, race, and, more oddly, gardening. Everything seemed to be in an established place, but what that order was I didn't know. Christopher Hitchen's *God Is Not Great* leaned on *A War against Truth* by Paul William Roberts. A well-worn leather chair was placed by the window. Beside it was a table on which sat a pair of reading glasses and an empty glass. Other than that, the room held a scrubbed-clean pine table that doubled as desk and dining table. I suppose guests could bring one of the two wooden chairs over to join the leather one if needed, although it seemed obvious that this space was designed for one. The kitchen had a single counter with a small stove and bar fridge with two pine shelves above it holding the minimum of kitchenware: a plate, a cup, a bowl, a teapot, and some pots and pans. There were no rugs on the floors or paintings hanging on the walls, but the overall feeling was peaceful. As I scanned the room, Pete came out from Jay's bedroom.

"Geez. The man was a monk. He owns nearly nothing but all these books."

I checked out the bedroom. It was functional, with a single bed and a small set of three drawers, which was also his night table, the top of which had a black-and-white photo of a woman. It looked as if it was taken in the 1940s—the woman's shoulder-length hair featured the rolls and curls of that era. Lipstick darkened her lips and accentuated her cupid's bow. She wore a flowery wrap dress, and the photo had caught her laughing, holding up a shoe with a broken heel.

I called back to Pete. "Did you find anything here?"

"Nothing. Socks and underwear. Bathroom just as bare. But go ahead and look. You might find something I missed."

I opened the drawers, and it was as Pete had said: everything neat and tidy, socks rolled up, boxer shorts folded, five T-shirts, and a few pairs of chinos and jeans. The small closet held seven shirts, all neatly ironed and hung up, and a basket with a few soiled items. I almost missed something in the space behind the laundry basket. A small, old-fashioned suitcase. I called out to Pete. "Did you look in the suitcase?"

"No. I never noticed a suitcase."

I took it out and saw that it was locked. I pulled out my Swiss Army knife and opened the suitcase. The interior smelled like attics and trunks and the olden days: musty, yet exciting. Inside was a much-folded piece of black cloth. I gently removed it from the suitcase and unfolded it. A cassock, a Catholic priest's robe. I instinctively held it to my face. It contained a whiff of age and mothballs. It was fine, thin wool but not ancient by any means, with a small discreet label: *McCreaths, Dublin, Chandlers since 1910*. Below that was a small sewn-in laundry tag: *Father James Tully, Blackwater College for Boys*. James could easily change to Jay, and I'd always wondered at the name Tuck. It is not an Irish name that I've ever heard of. Maybe his past has nothing to do with his death, but Jay had been secretive. Maybe he had a reason for it.

I took the robe in its suitcase out to show Pete.

"You weren't far off the mark. Not a monk—maybe a priest."

Pete shrugged. "I heard a rumour like that years ago, but I never gave it much thought. He was never at Mass."

I'd forgotten that Pete was Catholic. "Maybe he went to the one here in Sheshatshiu."

"Maybe, but the only time I saw him at either church was for weddings and funerals, and anyone could go to those."

"Lapsed?"

"I guess," Pete said painfully, as if he were talking to a simpleton. "If he left the Church as a priest, he is probably lapsed."

"I think you should talk to the local priests and see what they know, and I'll check this Blackwater College."

"Yes, but so what if he is? I mean, it seems like it was Pashin who killed him. And just because he was a Catholic doesn't mean he was murdered for it."

I ignored the Pashin comment. "Right, that's true. But you say that you heard the rumour years ago, and that means that other people did too. Why did he leave the Church? Let's just talk to Sergeant Renaud and he can tell us what next. Are we finished here?"

Pete pushed the side of his mouth out with his tongue—a sign of deep thinking, I knew. "I've taken a few prints, but they'll all be Tuck's, I'm sure. How about I run the kit back and talk to the sergeant and you see if you can find anything else? There's a little pile of papers tucked into the bookcase, near his chair. I was just about to pull it out, but you can while I run this back. When you're finished, you can go back to the detachment and see if there's anything else that needs doing."

I took the pile of papers and letters over to the pine table and sat down, handling them carefully, gloves on. It was the regular stuff everyone accumulates, no matter how you live. No bank statements or bills (they must all be online), a few notices from teacher associations, a book catalogue from a small publisher that specialized in history and philosophy, an order form for music

CDs, and an unaddressed envelope. I opened the envelope, which appeared to be one he'd had for a while. It was filled with photos. Just a handy place to put loose photos? Why had he taken it out, and where did it live normally? It contained several photos that appeared to be of a graduating class. The same woman that was in the photo on his night table (his mother?) was in one photo standing proudly beside a young man looking like a much younger Jay Tuck in cap and gown. All the photos were taken on the lawn of a large cathedral. Maybe it was a seminary graduation. In one, four young men, all wearing caps and gowns, arms linked, smiled at the camera. The third from the left was clearly Jay Tuck. Knowing that Jay was in his early 50s, I would think it was the mid-1980s. On the back, in pencil, were four names; the one third from the left, *James*. The others: Michael, Luke, and Aiden. I checked out the other photos, but there was nothing written on any of them. I put them back in the envelope and decided to take them back to the detachment. Maybe I could find out the name of the seminary from the college and try to track down the other men. It was a long shot, but it was something.

✦

Back at the detachment, Renaud had already been briefed on the existence of the priest's robe and sent Pete off to talk to the local priest.

"It's a strange time in an investigation. It's hard to know what's important and what's gumming up the works." Renaud looked up from a report that he was filing. "I know you want to get at finding out some answers, but I want you out in the community right now, Constable. Tomorrow I'll get Shirleen on the photos that you found.

Right now, I'd like you to keep talking to the kids and anyone else who might give you some idea of what is going on."

"Okay, Sergeant. I'm going to talk to Shania about getting the word out about the Place to Be room being off limits. She might have some background on Pashin that could be helpful. I'll see you tomorrow."

"Just make sure that you are looking at what you find out without bias."

I raised my eyebrows.

"Your job is to find out as much as possible without making your mind up about who is innocent and who is guilty in this investigation. The facts will do that. Get it?"

My head nodded a yes, but my heart beat a maybe.

+++ Chapter 6

Shania lived on the edge of the reserve, near the bridge to North West River. Her house, which I'd heard she'd inherited from her aunt, was older and felt more solid than most on the reserve. Like an old-fashioned hunting lodge, it had a large enclosed porch with plenty of room for firewood, pegs for hanging up outdoor clothes, hooks for snowshoes, and even space to overhaul an engine without mucking up the living room. The floor was plywood, but the walls, or what could be seen of them, were a warm shade of yellow festooned with retro hunting calendars and pictures of dead creatures and grinning guys wearing plaid or camouflage. I entered the porch and gave a solid knock on the inner door. Shania opened it and gestured me inside without speaking. She was talking into her phone. I kicked off my boots, grabbed a pair of slippers off the shelf and entered the house proper.

"Just a second," Shania said to the person on the phone before turning to me. "Nell, I have to finish this conversation. It's work. Make yourself at home."

I tried not to listen but that's hard for a snoop like me.

"I don't care. That was totally overkill. There's a procedure and the numbnuts didn't follow it. Those kids were taken in the middle of the night like we are a pack of wolves descending. I don't care if she's related to a premier, the prime minister, or God. She messed with a very sensitive issue, and now I'm going to have to straighten it out. Now, if you don't mind, it's Sunday and I have a guest."

I'm glad that it wasn't me on the other end of that phone. Shania Penashue was fierce when she was pissed off, and she was steaming. I inferred that the person she was talking to worked at the Goose Bay Family Services. Shania herself was a social worker for Family Services in Sheshatshiu. She went over to her desk and started writing, so I did what I was told and made myself comfortable. It was easy, since we had a friendship going back several years. She and I had set up the drop-in centre at the school, Place to Be, when I worked as a youth counsellor. I'd liked working with Shania. She was smart, direct, and knew her people.

The porch and a bathroom off the other side of the house were the only distinct rooms. The rest was one big area, about 30 by 20 feet, which included a large wood stove, big old chairs, and a table in one corner that held an open laptop where Shania was finishing up whatever report the call was about. A four-poster bed covered in furs was out in the open and a bathtub near the wood stove had only a screen for privacy.

Shania gestured to her cookstove. "I just put a pot of moose stew on. It's not caribou, but anything wild is better than beef. Want some?"

I knew that it was pointless to protest that I hadn't meant to disrupt her dinner. She didn't care, and it was a waste of perfectly good talking time. Not to mention that it smelled fantastic. With all the running around today, I hadn't considered anything for dinner. I nodded and grabbed my phone to text Nick. As he usually had hockey practice on Sunday nights, for dinner we usually fended for ourselves. Nonetheless, it was only polite to let him know what I was up to. I texted *At Shania's eating good, and you?* and got an answering chime in moments. *Spent the day doing research. Heading for the rink, see you in bed.* That made me laugh. He knew me so well.

"This must be about Jay Tuck's death. Or did you know I had moose on the menu?"

"Yes, it is. Just thought you could use a heads-up about Place to Be. The detachment is using the space as the incident room. I don't think the school will be open for a few days, anyway."

"Yes, the principal phoned me. They'd do that for the death of any teacher or student." Shania paused. "Or for any Elder." She looked at me. "Or for any event, anywhere else that would be of no interest to the school."

We shared a grin. It was true. The school was always closing, and for those unused to the culture it could be mystifying and irritating. Shania was being funny, but we'd both fought long and hard to ensure that the school stayed open as much as possible. It was understandable, if frustrating, that they closed for every funeral. This was a tightly knit community and everyone who lived in it was part of an extensive family web. It was closure for the other events that bugged us. Last year they tried to close the school during Band Council elections. The reserve was a terrible place for kids during electioneering. No matter who was running or how hard they tried to run a clean campaign, there were those who believed that it wasn't a real race unless you were carting in truckloads of beer and hooch from Goose Bay. We made a strong defence for keeping it open, arguing that most of these kids have only one safe place during those two weeks, and did they want it to be taken away? I was happy to let Shania spearhead such fights, because when it came right down to it, I was a crazy-ass white woman and she was a respected member of the Innu community.

"Let's see if we can set something up at the clinic. Or maybe we can convince Renaud to let us have another space at the school for Place to Be. We could stay out of their hair, right?"

"Yes, but it isn't Renaud. It's Musgrave."

Shania stopped what she was doing, which was making us both a drink. We shared taste in beverages: sparkling water with a splash of grapefruit juice. Sometimes I liked a splash of tequila in mine but Shania didn't drink.

"Oh? Why him, when Renaud is right here and knows all the players?"

"Beats me. I never understand chain-of-command stuff. I guess Musgrave just handled some big investigation and so the powers-that-be want him in charge."

She handed me my drink, and we moved over to the soft chairs and cozied up close enough to the wood stove so that our feet rested on the hob. Heaven.

"I haven't had much to do with Musgrave. Seemed slick every

time I ran into him. The kind of guy that looks over your shoulder while he's talking to you in case someone more important should show up." We both laughed. "I heard that his wife finally left him, though. Never thought she had the gumption to blow out her own birthday candles."

"Oh, I didn't know that. It's hard being a cop's partner—just ask poor Nick. Did she stay in town?"

"Yep. Their daughter lives in Goose. Married with a baby. She's not going anywhere."

"Well never mind him. I've got other stuff to talk to you about. I have to ask you some questions. Can we keep it unofficial?"

"Sure. I figured that's why you were here. Go ahead."

"I'm worried about the kids in Tuck's drama group. What do you know about Pashin or Zann? Noticed anything going on with that gang lately?"

I looked at Shania while I squished down into the chair. The heat coming off the wood stove was perfectly divine and if I didn't have this crazy case and worries about the kids who might be involved, I would've closed my eyes and dozed in the pleasure and warmth of it all.

"Well, seeing as you brought it up, yes. I have noticed something with Pashin. He's not the softy he's been since he was a baby. He's getting harder than I like to see. I don't know why. Kinda figured it might have something to do with the fact that he's out of his aunt's house again. His sister doesn't really make a home. I know that Rebekah probably bugs him about his homework and Melissa doesn't. I don't think that it's good for kids his age to hang out where there are no adults. Or at least no adults that care. And I know Zann is still friends with him, but I think her patience is getting thin."

This was quite a speech for Shania to make. We were careful. She had her people and I had mine, and both came with problems that were too obvious to discuss, even between pals. What was the point? Shania knew I didn't agree with most of Family Services' policies, and she agreed with me. But she was a social worker and that's who she worked for.

It had been a coup for a community member to not only go through six years of university but to have tasted the outside world and still decided to come back to her own troubled community. When Shania came back, she did make changes. She also avoided having a family of her own. She wouldn't date any man. I believed that she thought that the best way to avoid the trouble that her extended family and most of her friends were in was to say "no" to men and to kids of her own. Although I'm sure she—the trifecta of smarts, humour, and good looks—has fended off suitors.

"Speaking of Rebekah, any reason why her daughter Kanani's kids were taken?"

Shania shook her head, looking beat. "I can't really speak about that, Nell. Let's just say that's the issue I was complaining about on the phone when you came in. What's it got to do with Jay Tuck's death, anyway?"

"Nothing. I was at Rebekah's on another matter and she was fuming mad. I thought it was odd, because Kanini has been clean for ages."

Shania sighed. "Okay, I know we both have political issues in our workplace. Can we leave it at that?"

I laughed and agreed.

"But still, I'm wondering why you're asking me about Pashin and his family. Is he connected somehow to Tuck's death?"

"I can tell you that the sergeant wants to ask him a few questions and that, from my point of view, he's not a suspect. But the more I know, the better I can make sure that he doesn't become one. Sorry if I'm being circumspect, but I know you understand. I figure that the more I know of anything going on in his life, romantically or socially or with his family, the better."

"Okay. I can't think of anything else about him. You know he's LGBTQ. A two-spirit, if not three." She smiled fondly. Two-spirit was a perfect word for Pashin. He was simply more than male or female. "As for romance, I'm not sure. I thought he liked this young guy that came to Shesh from Sept-Îles a year ago, but now I hear he split with him. Not sure what that was about."

"Was it the Sept-Îles guy that got him interested in culture all of a sudden?"

"You got it. They were in the sweat lodges every second night. They tried to start up a drumming circle but that got shot down. Pashin's grandfather on his father's side was a drummer and Pashin was learning real pride about that, but that didn't make a difference. Letting just anyone drum is okay for some of our people, as in the Mi'kmaq and Black Foot, but in the Innu Nation you have to be called to it. It's totally shamanic, not just kids playing games."

Shania knew very well that neither the Mi'kmaq or Black Foot were "kids playing games" when they drummed, but I decided not to quibble with her on this point. I understood that a strict protocol is to be followed if you are to become a drummer in the Innu tradition. The potential drummer is to have a drumming dream at least three times before they can be taught by a drumming elder in the community. Traditionally, there would be animals in the dream and the beat would be given to the dreamer. I've seen drummers come into the community from other traditions, the Maliseet for instance, and suggest a drumming circle as a way to heal youth, but the Innu took a hard stand on the issue.

"Did anyone give Pashin a tough time about being gay?"

"No!" Shania looked at me in surprise. "There's never been much of that sort of bullying—not with his age group anyway. I don't know how his family handled it, though none of them are in any position to cast stones."

"Ya, I never heard anything either. I just wonder about his level of anger lately." I thought of him calling himself a "lying Indian." So strange.

"Yes, well, it isn't my business, but I wouldn't be so quick to rule him out as a suspect. I don't want it to be him, but the way he's been acting lately, I can see how he could fly off the handle easily. Maybe Tuck was in the wrong place at the wrong time."

That was too horrible to contemplate. I thought of one of my old teachers when I did my RCMP training. He told me that the biggest problem I'd face when moving from therapist to cop would be that my habitual allegiance would no longer be the client but the law.

Shania broke the silence. "Hey, if you don't have any more questions, I think that moose stew should be ready. Let me put another log on the fire, and we'll each grab a bowl. Mind if we don't eat at the table? I've got a case all spread out there. Terrible story. No place to put the kids and it's a family of nine kids. I think they'll have to go to Roddickton."

That was an old bugbear for both of us. Roddickton was a town in northern Newfoundland that seemed to have replaced their dying wood industry with fostering kids from Labrador. Too many times kids were taken out of their familiar culture. Kids that spoke Innu-aimun as their first, and sometimes only, language were dropped into a community in which only English was spoken. They were put into single-family homes, when they were used to extended families.

"What a drag. How do those people sleep at night?" That wasn't exactly fair. Most Roddickton folk probably felt that they were doing something righteous and good. They probably didn't realize that they were causing whole communities in the coastal and central areas of Labrador to be gutted. For about the millionth time, I pondered what it must be like to know that people were watching your parenting and could swoop down at any minute and take your kids from you. At one end of the spectrum, you had social workers and other community types saying, "Tut-tut, why do those people drink?" At the other, you had Innu saying, "I might as well drink. No matter what I do, they take my kids and I can't get them back. At least it dulls the pain." The whole situation seemed unsolvable.

Shania handed me a bowl full of beautiful stew. It smelled

delicious: tender fragrant moose, mushrooms, potatoes, carrots, and herbs that Shania grew in containers on her kitchen windowsill.

"Do you want another drink, or shall we wait and have tea afterwards?"

"Tea after. Hey, are you going to the fifth festivities?"

"You betcha. You white people have some really gruesome rituals. I wouldn't miss it for the world."

November 5, Guy Fawkes Day, was celebrated with great fervour in Newfoundland and Labrador, unlike in the rest of Canada. There was always a community bonfire up on Sunday Hill Road at the brush dump, followed by more private events. People made and dressed up effigies to burn on the bonfire, and prizes were given to the best one. I started going with Nick a few years back. It was fun to be around a roaring bonfire with neighbours that you might not see that often.

"Good. You can join Nick and me afterwards when we go to Upalong for the usual yee-haw."

"I hope to. I like that husband of yours, Nell. If I were into husbands, that's the sort I'd like. Is he still a lousy hockey player?" Shania, who had been making a pot of tea while she talked, brought out homemade oatmeal and walnut cookies to go with it.

"Yep, but don't let him know. He thinks he's Guy Lafleur. God love him, but he just can't skate. He's good for other things though. Makes a great bouillabaisse. And he brings me coffee in bed."

"Ya, he'd do anything to keep you there. Jeanie Blake was after him when he was in school here. She must have been burned up when you two sashayed into town." Shania chuckled. There was no love lost between her and Jeanie. "You never told me how you met him."

I didn't talk about it with anyone. Nick came into my life when I was at a very low point and he was instrumental in delivering me from a grim situation. Was I ashamed? Yes. Plus, it was hard enough being a come-from-away around here—never mind one with a sketchy past.

"Uh, I met him when I was a teenager. He was kind enough to wait till I grew up to pounce. He was already a journalist, albeit a cub reporter, and I was a nothing then. Just a dumb kid."

"Well, I'm glad you found the right guy so young. I fell for a lot of losers."

So did I, I thought. And I was one of them—a loser, that is. Luckily Nick saw the gold shining through the tinsel. I was about to make some smart-ass comment when my cell chimed. A text from Johnny telling me he'd be at my house in 10 minutes.

"I hate to eat and dash, but it's work. Some day off. See you on the fifth." I pecked her on the cheek and headed out to the car.

+++ Chapter 7

I drove home, got out of my uniform and into a hoodie and yoga pants. I grabbed the string bag that held the skirt, sleeveless T-shirt, and towel I'd need for the sweat. It still held the smoky smell of the last one I'd been to three weeks previously. Johnny picked me up at the bottom of the driveway, and soon we were heading out of town. We left North West River, crossed the bridge and passed the reserve, and headed toward Goose Bay. I broke our companionable silence with a question that I'd been pondering.

"Why do you meet around a sweat?"

Johnny paused before speaking. "You know, Nell, we're in a painful situation. We think there are some folks who don't like it when we meet to discuss what we might do as a community outside the Band Council. This is one way we can meet without anyone being curious. It's just a precaution."

That made sense. A sweat was a great way for those who needed to meet to do so without any interference.

We took the turn halfway to Goose Bay that led to Caribou Lodge: a collection of old buildings that had been built as a fishing lodge for folks from away. At one time, there'd been a small community out this road, so there was a network of branching roads that led mostly to cabins or Innu tents. Caribou Lodge was right on the lake, its buildings lying helter-skelter around the shore and into the woods. Johnny carefully parked behind one of the larger buildings, where I noticed there were several others, not visible from the road.

"Okay, Nell. Time to get out."

"Sure thing. This is your rodeo." A woman I knew came up to the truck. Lucy Goodeye was a young, active member of the community. She worked with Social Health on the reserve and had been mentored by one of the most revered Elders in Sheshatshiu. That Elder had died several years back, but she had passed on much of her knowledge of the old ways to Lucy.

"Hi, Lucy, nice to see you here."

She nodded and motioned for me to follow her to a large ramshackle shed. A few feet from the entrance was a fire pit where a young man tended the stones on a large bed of coals. Inside the shed I saw the dark shape of the lodge itself, like a turtle shell or woolly seed pod, with a blanket covering the entrance.

"You can change into your skirt behind the curtain. Make it snappy. The sweat's already started."

I got into the skirt quickly and peeled off my sweater and long-sleeved shirt. I piled up my clothes and took off my rings and my watch, putting them neatly into the boots I'd removed. You can't have a sweat on a whim. It takes hours to gather stones and heat them to the right temperature. The fire that I could smell on the cold air had probably been burning since mid-afternoon. You need at least two people to hold a sweat: a sweat lodge Elder and a fire keeper. The fire keeper takes care of the mechanics of the sweat—creating the fire to heat the stones and setting up the lodge. The Elder takes care of the spiritual rituals. Sometimes the young people, or unknowing whites, thought they could just show up, do a round or two, and go back to whatever party they had come from. But you weren't to be under the influence of any substance when you were at a sweat lodge. Women were invited, but if it wasn't an all-woman sweat, called a *moon sweat*, no woman who was menstruating would be allowed in. It has nothing to do with them being unclean, as most whites assume. A menstruating woman was considered to already be in a state of being purified and, therefore, was not in need of a sweat.

"Come now. They're waiting."

It was cold in the drafty shed with hardly any clothes on, even though I had a large towel draped over my shoulders. I followed Lucy into the lodge, bending low and moving to the left, where the women sat.

My senses were immediately bombarded with the sweet, intoxicating smell of the spruce-bough floor and the warmth rising from the bodies collected in such a tight space. Before my eyes could properly adjust, I could see only the sparkles that lit the edges of the stones in the centre pit. I had been told at my first sweat that it was like a mother's womb: warm, protective, the sweat like amniotic fluid, cleansing and purifying our bodies and spirits.

I couldn't see who was there, but I felt the presence of bodies all around me. I settled and felt the atmosphere grow unbelievably intimate. I was wedged into the kind of space, light, and warmth that is usually shared only with lovers and children.

The Elder picked up a spruce bough and dipped it into the bucket of water. He slapped it onto the stones and a billow of steam filled the space. I remembered to dip my head, breathing through my hand. The water is followed by aromatic botanicals that smell like cedar and sweetgrass. When the herbs hit the stones, they sparkled and crackled—the only light in the room except the crimson glow of the stones themselves. I loved that part. Some sweat lodges are quiet affairs, with one person offering prayers and everyone else just *unh-uhing* along; some sweats are very unquiet, with each person telling a story, saying a prayer, or voicing a wish as they sit. Sometimes someone plays the drum or sings a song in different rounds. I liked those best. The offering up of various stories—*This is my truth and this is my medicine*—could also be terrifically moving. Sometimes there was laughter and sometimes tears. At the best sweats, both were offered to the ancestors.

Someone with a drum was across the fire pit from me. I guessed by the sound, and then by his voice as he sang, that it was Pien Nuna, a favourite drummer and singer in the community. The heat was starting to build and no one had spoken but Pien, who drummed, sang, and said prayers in Innu-aimun. For about the tenth time, I wondered why Johnny had brought me here. My eyes were beginning to accept the dull, soft dark of the lodge. I couldn't see much but I could distinguish forms across from me as vaguely human.

Pien said something in Innu-aimun and everyone made to go out. The first round was completed. It had seemed such a short one, but I had come in late. Time got squishy in a sweat, and of course, I had no watch.

Outside of the lodge, but still in the shed, a wood stove kept us warm. There were benches where you could sit and a big stainless-steel bowl full of orange quarters. Sometimes, in such circumstances, I could be quite shy. Shirleen was talking to Johnny, but I held back from approaching her. Lucy had slipped off somewhere and so had Pien. I had hoped that Pashin would be there, but I didn't see him. I didn't know the others that were talking and smoking quietly in the corner. I decided to go outside for air.

Other than the glow from the fire outside, it was well and truly dark now, but I walked away from the lodge toward the shore. The water glimmered in the starlight. It would be frozen soon. The sounds of people chatting and laughing inside the shed kept me warm as I stood in the crisp air, looking up at the canopy of stars. I loved the night sky in Labrador—like a swathe of black velvet with precious stones scattered across it. I thought about Jay and how he had loved the night skies here too. I felt a great sadness come over me and I let it.

About 10 minutes later, Pien and Lucy came back from wherever they had gone and motioned to me that the next round would be happening. I crawled into the lodge just before Lucy. Pien started with prayers, again in Innu-aimun, and then said that this round would be a chance for everyone to say anything that they were carrying that needed to be purified. We would go around clockwise, starting with him—no talking stick. People usually finished their outpouring by saying *Ho*—the Innu version of *So be it*, or *That's it for me.*

The first person to Pien's left was a man I didn't know. He started in Innu-aimun, and then I heard Johnny's low voice, and the man changed to English.

"Sorry, I forgot that we have a guest." Everyone laughed, and he went on. "I'm worried about my kids. There's nothing for them in Sheshatshiu and they're losing the language and the ways. They won't go out into *nutshimit* with me unless it's for something big—like travelling by helicopter or to go to a cabin with their friends. They won't learn to hunt, and, anyway, there's no caribou left. They get crazy with wanting everything. I know it's my fault. My wife and I drank and drank when they were little. And there's something worse. People are pushing drugs on our kids. They feed them lies with the other shit they give them. Then the kids won't listen, and they won't tell me who it is." There was a long pause while everyone digested this. Then the man said, "Ho."

Next was Johnny. "I've heard of this too. I think it's a group of people trying to cause pain in our community so they can do the evil they do. Jay Tuck stood up against those who threaten our kids, and now he's gone. Some of you are wondering why I brought Nell here. Those who know her will know that she has only done things to keep our community strong and safe. Things are getting worse, and we need her help."

Whoa! This is why I was here. They had something to tell me. Who were the bad people? I had also heard rumours of something that seemed more organized, more malevolent, than the usual selling of dope around the school. My mind caught for a moment on how normal it had become to hear of the everyday selling of dope in an Aboriginal school, but I brought my attention back to the present.

The man to Johnny's left murmured a few words that obviously meant that he was passing. Fair enough. No one was forced to share. Next I heard Shirleen.

"Thank you for coming here, Constable Nell. You honour us with your presence."

This was Shirleen at her most formal, and I listened for what else she might say.

"The death of Jay Tuck is very serious. Someone has killed our friend—a protector of our children—and is trying to point the finger at one of the kids he protected. This is wrong. Who would do this? Our community must take action. I will not rest till this person is dealt with. Ho."

Shirleen was a woman of few words, but these words left no room for confusion. I had known her since I first moved to Labrador, but, apparently, I did not know her at all. At the detachment, or before that when she had worked at the clinic, I had found her to be pleasant and quiet, focused on the job at hand. She baked cookies and went to visit the elderly and the sick. Sure, she had proved fiercely protective and loyal to those she worked for, but I had never figured her for an activist. Now there was no mistaking her passion and resolve.

Lucy spoke next. "My heart is sad today. I'm scared for our community. There's an evil loose here, and we must find it and contain it, or eliminate it. Will the police, the judges, and the government ever understand what they have started and where it goes? Our community made a short-sighted decision years back—a decision that costs us more every year. Our land and our water are in danger. Do we listen to our leaders or listen to our own wisdom? The evil that runs through our community feeds on our chaos. When our kids are threatened, we can't think of anything else—that is, when the thieves come in and take what is not theirs. I do not disrespect our sister, Nell, but maybe it's time for the Innu people to take their destiny into their own hands. Ho."

I knew that Lucy represented the more radical of the Innu who wanted changes. They were done with white solutions. It was hard to blame them. Nonetheless, I had to speak my own truth in this sacred space.

"Thank you all for bringing me here to your sacred sweat lodge. It's an honour each time I'm invited to do so." The Innu liked formal gratitude and I knew the drill—besides, I meant it. "My heart, like that of so many others in this community, is heavy and sad, but also I'm angry to hear that someone has dared to come to the school and sell drugs to your children. I believe that Sergeant Renaud wants the same thing all of you do: to make Sheshatshiu safe for everyone. I don't know what happened to Jay Tuck, but what you say leads me to believe that many others here must be in danger, and if the drug dealers are behind his death, then we must discover it quickly. I don't know what you wish of me, but I'll work as hard as I can to find out what's going on. Jay Tuck was my friend. The loss of him is vast. Ho."

A few others spoke after me but in Innu-aimun and very briefly. When everyone who was going to speak had spoken, Pien drummed. Another round was over. It had heated up—in every way. We had three more rounds, but there would be no more English or sharing of any kind. I fell into my own reverie as I sat there sweating from every pore. I was wondering about the whole thing, but I also went to where I did at any sweat; I thought of all the young people who were making decisions based on fear or hopelessness and how they were our only future, no matter their ethnicity. I also wondered where Pashin was, when it seemed that he was part of this group. I imagined myself at his age at this gathering. *Too slow*, I would've thought. *Too slow by far.*

+++ Chapter 8

I got a lift back to the bridge at North West River with one of the young men at the sweat who had not said a word. I suspected that the others stayed to discuss the next plans.

It had been a long and terrible day, and I was happy to crawl into bed next to Nick. He was snoring lightly but woke when I touched his flank with my icy hand.

"What the hell ... oh it's you."

"Who were you expecting?"

"I don't know. I was dreaming about this mermaid. So frustrating, mermaids. They look all come hither and then they've got this fishtail from the belly button down. What's a horny, old land-guy supposed to do?"

I loved how he always turned the dial down and helped me get calm. I scooched up against him, an attentive audience of one.

"So I was asking her, quite pleasantly I thought, what I could do, you know, intimately with her, when this big cowboy comes up and punches me in the arm. Only it wasn't a punch. It was more of a slap, because it wasn't a normal hand: he had this half-frozen fish attached to his arm. But it was you, and now you're here and you aren't a cowboy. I'm so confused."

I grinned into the muscles of his back. "How lovely. My hands are cold because I got dropped off at the bridge. I wanted to walk home from there. The sky is so beautiful, I thought maybe I'd catch sight of some northern lights, and I wanted to clear my mind a little." I sighed. "Lucky for you I'm not a mermaid, and I think we could finish what we started this morning."

"But we did finish." Nick stopped. "I mean ..." He realized what he was turning down. "I mean nothing. You are so right. We weren't near finished or else I wouldn't have been dreaming about mermaids and cowboys. Which do you want to be? And by the way, your hair smells like smoke. What were you doing?"

And then we didn't talk for a while, because he knew that I wouldn't answer that question and, besides, we were busy. I like to clean my mind of images seen over a day like today, and sex usually does it, but this time it didn't. It just seemed beyond unfair that Jay should be looking bewildered and so dead while Nick and I were having such fun with our very alive bodies. It was hard to turn my thoughts and the pictures off. I still managed to have a good time, but it wasn't the obliteration of images that I'd been hoping for.

When we finally rolled away from each other, it was nearly midnight, and I should have been thoroughly and completely ready for sleep. I wanted to think about all the things that I had heard from kids, adults, cops, and social workers today—to find the pattern, the logic in it all. I knew that it was there somewhere. Maybe I needed more, but I bet I'd find on the day that it was figured out that I'd had all the knowledge I had needed that very first day. This day.

I fell asleep while thinking about *Hamlet,* so it was perhaps no surprise that in my dream I was at a rehearsal. Only it wasn't the school kids, but me as Hamlet at the top of act 5. I take the skull that is Yorick, except it isn't Yorick but Jay. The skull wears a jester's cap, and I say the famous lines, "Alas, poor Jay! I knew him, Horatio, a fellow of infinite jest, of most excellent fancy. He hath borne me on his back a thousand times. And now, how abhorred in my imagination it is! Where be your gibes now? Your gambols, your songs, your flashes of merriment, that were wont to set the table on a roar?"

The skull becomes Jay's very head as it looked when I last saw it in the afternoon. His face is vacant and terrible, left behind when Jay's most alive aliveness had fled for good. To my horror, Jay's head falls from my hand, and as it does, its eyes fly open, begging me for something, although his mouth stays, thankfully, quiet.

I awoke with a terrible start, my body nearly levitating above the bed, and got up as quietly as possible. The clock beside Nick's side of the bed flashed 3 a.m., so I made my way to the kitchen for hot chocolate. Beany woke up and padded out to see what I was up to. Was there a possibility of treats, he wondered? I gave him a head scritch, but with nothing else in store he padded back to his bed, and it wasn't long before I heard his little doggy snore.

That was all I could hear, though. It's quiet at our end of the beach. I sat in my favourite spot, an old-fashioned and well-padded chair that had belonged to Nick's mother. It was right by the window that looked out toward the water. There was only a sliver of moon, so that all I could see were the ghostly spruces and the line of fence that divided our yard from the beach. While I sat there, I thought about my dream. Why *Hamlet*? Why not *Hamlet*? The dream reminded me of something that wasn't making sense. Pashin had told me that Tuck had given up and wanted him to give up too, but that isn't how it sounded at the sweat. Why the difference?

I hauled out *Romeo and Juliet* and *Hamlet*, skimmed them both, and considered the basic plot lines. *Romeo and Juliet* was always a no-brainer for a high-school crowd to stage. Why not *Hamlet*? Hamlet was a student himself who felt as if people around him were making poor decisions. These people were in control of him, and the decisions seemed based on their gaining more power and money. Yep, I could see how that might work in the community. When I read *Hamlet*, I always get antsy. Was Hamlet crazy or brilliantly cagey? Oh, and something else nagged at me: Tuck doing the deciding. It simply wasn't the way he usually did things. He might coax the students into examining their choices, but he was never, in my experience, high-handed about it. It went against his ethics to cheat kids out of their autonomy like that.

I sat sipping and thinking and waiting for the tardy, old November sun to come up.

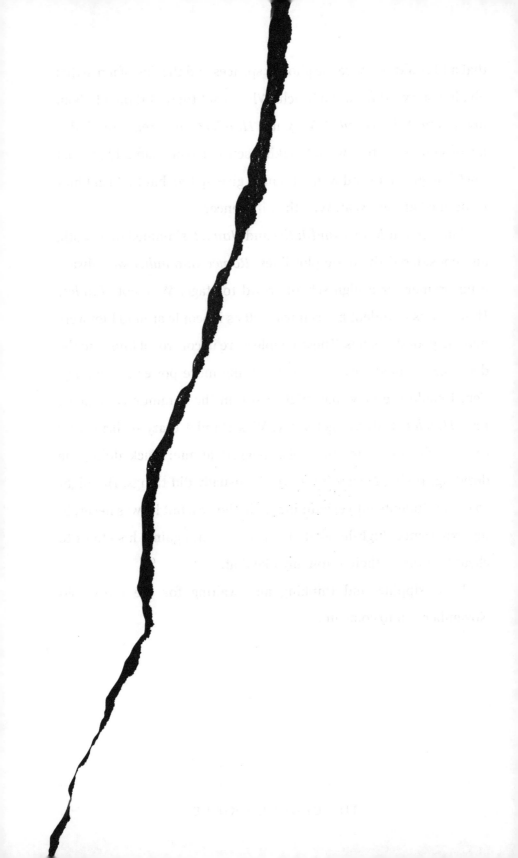

He had gone looking for the drum in the house his mother moved to when she'd hooked up with that creep. He remembered that she'd brought the old wooden box his father had kept his few treasures in. He thought his grandfather's drum would be there. There was no one home when he arrived. He knew the door would be locked, but he remembered a window in the back that was easy to jimmy; he'd used it when he'd go out at night rambling. That was before his mother died and he'd left for good. He found the box under a bunch of useless junk. In it he found the drum: it was about two hands wide, the skin bare of ornament. Just like his grandfather: useful but not beautiful. Only, to him, it was beautiful. He hated that all his grandfather and father had come to was in this place where not even his mother could watch over it. Later he'd realize that his grandfather had led him to this house for a reason.

Monday, November 2

✛✛✛ Chapter 9

I tried to put my thoughts of *Hamlet* and Jay Tuck away as I got ready for work. It was early, and Nick wasn't stirring. He made his own hours, and we didn't do breakfasts together during the week, so I quietly prepared for another long day. We constables took eight-hour shifts, starting at 6:30, 9:30, and 11:30 a.m., to take us up to the night shift that began for the night dispatcher at 7:30 p.m. and went for 12 hours. This week I had the 9:30 shift.

Usually, I'd go in and ask the duty officer and anyone else who'd been around on the weekend if there were any kids I needed to see, but today was going to be different. I already had my assignment and a list of people I wanted to talk to. I was sure that the rest of the detachment would have their own, too. Plus, I needed to make sense of what I'd found out last night, while avoiding questions from Renaud about it. Maybe I'd swing by the school to see what was going on there. Although if the sergeant was right, it would be closed to staff and kids alike. Then I had minor issues unrelated to the murder to see to. A young woman had been in a fist fight with another girl and the cops had been called. She'd been put in the drunk tank on Thursday night, and I wanted her to talk to Legal Aid about a charge that had been laid. I was also part of a wraparound care team for a

13-year-old who'd started down a dark path. Wraparound care is a way of working with youth that involves people from every part of their life. This one had a teacher, two relatives, a hockey coach, a clinic nurse, and me. I needed to check in with my teammates to see what was happening there.

Pete McLean was working at his desk when I came in. No Renaud. No Shirleen.

Pete filled me in. "Sergeant Renaud got called into Goose. They aren't happy."

"Pardon? Who are *they* and what are they unhappy about?"

"It's Musgrave. He thinks that this whole thing would be better handled entirely from Goose Bay—that it needs distance."

I frowned. Already this day was more than I'd bargained for. "That doesn't make sense. We're the ones that work right on the reserve. How's the sergeant?"

"He doesn't seem too bugged by it. You know him. He says that if the higher-ups say hands-off then it's hands-off. It's turned into a—what do you call it? A political hot potato. That's what Shirleen said."

And why wasn't Shirleen here? She worked from 8 a.m. to 4 p.m. every day during the week. "Where's Shirleen?"

"I don't know. She got a call and said she had to go take care of something. It was right after all the turmoil about the situation."

I swallowed my frustration at McLean's pathologically vague communication skills. "What turmoil?"

"The whole lot of them were at the school protesting the fact that Musgrave hauled in Pashin. He's holding him in Goose for questioning. Took him in on a 503. The Innu are saying that we have no cause and that they're tired of their youth being—what was it?" Pete picked up a report from the desk. "Racially profiled for every crime that happens in Labrador."

Oh my sweet Jesus, this was going to be a mess. A 503 meant that Musgrave took him in without a warrant, which is not unusual here where you might not have the ability to talk to a judge right away, but incendiary at the best of times, and this was a murder investigation. It meant that Musgrave could keep him for 24 hours. Then he'd need to have a judge sign a warrant, or let him go.

"When did they pick up Pashin?"

"Oh. They didn't. He came in here this morning. Lonesome Johnny brought him. Said he was willing to talk. 'No problem,' said the sergeant, 'we'll talk.' Only then Musgrave came in and said he'd be handling it. When Pashin heard that, he tried to leave. That's when Musgrave arrested him. Put him in cuffs. That's why the Innu are pissed. That gang across the road waiting for a ride saw him leaving in cuffs. Word spread and soon there were a bunch of them at the school. It's a mess. Shirleen says it's a crying shame. Whole thing could've been avoided if only they'd just let the sergeant do his job."

"Why didn't they put him in the holding cell here?"

"Toilets still leaking since last Thursday. The whole cell is a mess, and Ernie Plouffe said he couldn't come in to work on it till Friday at the earliest."

Oh, the joys of an isolated community: one handyman, always in demand, who could decide any day he liked that he'd rather go fishing or on a drunk than work when he was needed.

"Right. Did the sergeant tell you what I'm supposed to do?"

"Nah. He just said we should all hold tight till it got straightened out. Oh!" Pete paused as a light bulb went on. "You're to go see what's-her-name—Pashin's aunt. She's got something for you, sergeant said."

I moved toward my desk. "Is it urgent? I have a few kids I need to check on first."

"No, he said to do it sometime today. He was distracted."

So I sat down and dealt with a few half-finished tasks that could be dealt with handily. I found a Legal Aid lawyer for the girl who'd been put in the drunk tank and sent off emails to everyone on the Wraparound Care Committee to let them know when I could next meet with them. Then I decided I'd check in at the school before heading to Rebekah's.

✦

When I got to the school, I saw that the parking lot was full. Many times when the Innu got their dander up about a child snatch, they'd get in their cars and trucks and fill up the parking lot of the Family Services building so that social workers couldn't get in or out easily. It was a particular form of passive protest that I rather admired: no signs, just a solid block of vehicles with folks sitting in them smoking and talking to whoever they had come over with.

I parked on the road and walked up the long sidewalk to the entrance, waving at anyone I knew. They didn't see me as the enemy, or I didn't think that they did. School is an important part of life in Sheshatshiu. It's hard to explain to those who live in other, more urban areas, where, unless we have kids who are in school, we don't give it that much thought. Here, if the school went down, the community would be in trouble. It was like the kitchen of the home called Sheshatshiu. It was where people went when their hearts were broken or they had major questions. It was where people felt safe and sane or free to not pretend to feel safe and sane. It was like a good-enough mother. When it started to get disorganized (which it did over the years when the staff mix wasn't quite right), when there were too many kids not attending, or an issue arose that made the parents distrust the school, then the whole community felt like it was wobbling and about to spin off its axis.

In North West River, a desire for a school for trappers' kids had formed the village. In Sheshatshiu, the building of a school had been both a carrot and a stick. There were those Innu who wanted their kids to have an education, but as well, the government had used the school as a way to force the Innu from their nomadic lives and onto the reserve.

There were, of course, mixed feelings about schools in general. It was only a few generations back that many of these same people had been brought to residential schools—the shame of which still reverberates through all of Canada. It had been different in Labrador, where most schools were residential for all kids—settlers, Inuit, and Innu—but there was no doubt that the Aboriginal kids had not fared as well as the settler kids. They might have shared a dorm and a classroom, but they were not treated as equals. This meant that, even now, it was sometimes challenging to get parents or grandparents into the school for meetings or activities. Understandably, they didn't feel comfortable with institutions.

The new school tried to ameliorate this mistrust in both its architecture and human structure. The building itself felt open and warm, with many reminders that it was a special place within a special culture. Large photo-murals depicting Innu people and the land covered the cafeteria walls. Banks of glass cabinets displayed skin boots, Innu hats, and baskets. The staff included a strong Innu component, with an Innu vice-principal, Innu culture teachers, and as many Innu teachers as could be found.

I pushed my way gently through the group of men outside the front door of the school. They weren't trying to get in; they were just standing there, solidly blocking the way. They weren't aggressive with me; in fact, they were more respectful than I expected. Perhaps there'd been some word of my experience at the sweat lodge and they knew I was working to keep Pashin out of jail. Hard to say. Whatever the reason, they parted as I entered. Some greeted me by speaking my name.

Inside, I saw a constable from the Goose Bay detachment standing by the door. He had seen me approach and unlocked the security system.

"What's going on? I thought the incident room was here. Has it been moved? Where's everybody?"

"Incident room was moved to Goose. Nobody here but me and Neville, who's down at the door to keep the crime scene protected."

"So why secure the whole building?"

"Sergeant Musgrave said we were to secure the premises because the situation is too volatile, and there may be more forensics coming down this morning."

"I'll be on my way then." Looked like there was nothing for me to do here. "Is the group out there behaving?"

"Yep. No problem so far. I'm to call in if they try anything."

"They're feeling terrible. They've lost a positive force in the community and a young man whom everyone admires has been hauled away."

"Oh, I don't know about that. That Pashin. I hear there may have been some sort of gay club operating down here and that he was a ringleader."

"Really? This isn't the 1950s. It isn't illegal to be gay in the first place, and Pashin is out and accepted. What sort of gay club do you think operated here?"

I should've shut up. I should've nodded and walked away, but it got so blessedly tiresome to hear this sort of thing all the time. The constable just shrugged, so I turned and left.

✦

I found Pashin's aunt at home. Rebekah seemed more like her old self today, and at least little kids were running around. When I entered, she pointed to the kitchen table where a mug was waiting for me as well as a plate of Innu doughnuts. They are my favourite guilty indulgence: fried hunks of dough, sugary and crisp. They are basically a sugar- and raisin-enhanced bannock. Rebekah made them the right way. I didn't know what that was, scared to find out actually, but some people's doughnuts just didn't have the right texture or taste. I had learned over the years that Innu doughnuts are like martinis: one is not enough and three are too many. Actually, two were too many, but worth it nonetheless. I savoured a bite before I got into the hard stuff.

"I heard that Pashin was taken in. You okay?"

She dropped into a seat opposite me and broke open a doughnut without eating any. "No. I'm not okay, but I'll deal. I know that it isn't your fault. Stupid cops from Goose are always ready to put us in chains. But right now I need you for something else. I phoned Legal Aid. I want to make sure we get Penny Leap. Can you help me with that? He's the only lawyer I trust right now."

Before I could answer, she was on to the next thing. "First, I want to show you something I found in Pashin's room and you can tell me what you think."

Rebekah brought out a piece of heavy felt called *stroud*, the kind local folk use to make slippers. She unrolled it, being careful not to touch the contents: a crooked knife. The handle was a piece of white wood, birch maybe. It looked new. It hadn't even been oiled yet, although it was sanded. The steel shaft looked sharp enough to shave a fox, if that's what you wanted. And it had blood on it.

My voice stuck on a lingering bite of doughnut. I swallowed. "Where in Pashin's room was it?"

"The windowsill. Just rolled up like this and set down on the windowsill next to his bed—like it was nothing."

"And what were you doing in Pashin's room?"

"Looking for a photo she said he wanted last week. It's been bugging me because she asked and said it was for some school project. It was a photo of Otter Falls that he took last month and printed out at the school. I know he can never find stuff, so I thought I'd look, but I couldn't find it."

"Has he been here since the murder happened?"

"No." She looked at me long, making sure that I understood. "No, he hasn't, and he hasn't been at her sister's either. I know he's okay because I've been told so, but I haven't seen him once since the day before Halloween, Friday. And that was at the rink."

"The last time you checked his room ... was that knife there?"

"No. He told me that he was working on making one but he usually shows me stuff when it's finished. He didn't. And if he wasn't here, and I know he wasn't, how did that get here?"

I sipped the bitter tea, wincing a little at the taste. "Who's been here since Saturday?"

"Just the babies. They were brought back yesterday, late. And that's another thing. How come? How come my grandbabies were brought back by Family Services two days after they'd been taken, with no comment or explanation? I asked that social worker assistant to tell me why, and she had no idea. He was just told to pick them up from the foster family in Goose Bay and bring them back here. They aren't allowed to live with Kanani, yet they are okay to stay here. I don't understand."

Neither did I.

I tried to untangle it all, thinking that when Rebekah was upset like this, her pronouns really sprang free. I remembered something I'd heard back when I was doing social work and one of the workers, a man from Toronto, said something about the Innu being so ignorant that they didn't know one gender from another. He wasn't aware that he was talking to an Innu. Shania hadn't leapt down his throat like I'd wanted to do. She'd looked at him and said, "English isn't their first language. How many languages do you have? Furthermore, we don't care about gender as much as you white assholes do."

As I considered the possible implications of the moves made by Family Services, I contemplated the crooked knife in front of me. A crooked knife, skilfully made, is a beautiful thing. It's traditionally a woodworking tool with a curved end. *Crooked* refers to its strange shape, as the handle is set at an oblique angle to the blade. The blade itself can be straight or curved, long or short, and is typically made from a piece of repurposed, hardened steel. A straight blade could be used for all manner of whittling wood and a curved one for anything that needed to be hollowed. This one was straight.

I rolled it back up and, glancing briefly at Rebekah for permission, placed it in one of the plastic bags in the evidence kit I had with me.

We made our goodbyes shortly thereafter. I told her I'd be in touch with her as soon as I had any news and headed back to the detachment. I hoped that Sergeant Renaud would be back and that all would be shipshape. But no, it was not to be. Only Pete was there to greet me, and he was in a state.

+++ Chapter 10

"No. Renaud isn't back yet. And before you ask, I don't know where Shirleen is either. I wish I did." Pete looked wild. "Jordan is up at the arena about someone breaking in and ripping off the canteen, and I have to deal with those frickin' dogs again. That woman from North West is furious that they're running free—like that's police business. I know Shirleen got called away, but I don't know what for." The phone rang and Pete answered it.

Dang! I'd been hoping that the sergeant would be in so that I could discuss the crooked knife with him. Truth was, I wasn't sure what to do with it. I knew that it would have to go to Goose eventually, but the chain of command seemed fractured. Or that was the excuse I was telling myself.

"Nell? Would you mind checking Shirleen's desk to see who was going to go to the municipal office to meet about the fifth? I don't know who's supposed to be there, and Ed at the municipal office wants to know."

Shirleen's desk was like her mind: orderly and focused. She had a file holder with files labelled for various pieces of police business that she dealt with daily—vulnerability checks, complaint files, citizens with current charges outstanding, and the like. As well as that, she kept a planner front and centre on her desk and was meticulous about keeping track of everything of import in it. She kept the petty-cash list there and noted any calls that came in. Sergeant Renaud had told her time and time again that it was a duplication; the computer had systems for tracking every call and interaction. Shirleen would always say, "That's all very well till the system goes down. I'll keep all that up, but this is my own little backup." Hard to argue with. I checked her notations for today: three calls for Renaud from the town detachment (all probably Musgrave), then a notation for 10:30 that read *me—town office—bonfire detail.*

"Pete, I see in her book that she was going to be at the town office at 10:30. Is she there?"

"No, that's why they phoned. It's 11:20, and no show. I thought maybe it was supposed to be one of us, but she never said."

"Well, she must have gotten held up somewhere. I bet she'll walk in shortly."

I went back to looking at her planner. I noticed that there were four calls from various citizens that she must have taken off the machine with little notes beside each one written in her own code. Any emergencies after hours went straight to the dispatcher in Goose Bay, who would then decide who needed phoning. I took a look:

Jacob Panash: msg snowmo fr. Trtmnt Cntr

I was almost sure that that pertained to the ongoing problem of a snowmobile gone missing from the treatment centre across the road.

Ren McWilliams: bear again!

School: open or closed?

Plouffe cancelling again. Look elsewhere?

✦

I scanned down to the last one on the list, the others all making some sense. The last one looked like she was writing it as she was on the phone and then broke off. The word *Terrington* appeared, crossed out.

I had no idea what *Terrington* referred to and none of this explained why Shirleen would have missed her appointment at the town office. Shirleen, unlike the dogs of Sheshatshiu Pete was still arguing about on the phone, was not a rambler. If she was supposed to be somewhere, she would be there.

Before Shirleen worked at the detachment, she'd worked across the street at the clinic. Her work ethic there focused around Doctor Jenny Black. Jenny had worked assiduously to change things for the Innu community, but in the end she had quit to start a catering company. Some said that it was Jenny's futile fight against the methylmercury contamination from the Lower Labrador Project that caused her burnout. Whatever it was, when Jenny quit the clinic a few years back it wasn't long before Shirleen left. She applied for the admin job at the detachment, and the force became the beneficiary of her loyal hard work.

It was time for me to stop procrastinating. I had to take the knife to the Goose Bay detachment. Shirleen would fetch up somewhere and this business wouldn't solve itself. No problem if I stopped into her house before I went to town though. I wanted to find out what had been said after I left the sweat, and I was sure that Shirleen would share.

Shirleen was Innu, but she preferred, along with a few other Innu families, to live in North West River. She didn't see the benefits of living on the reserve. She was quietly vocal about the fact that taking the dole for living in Sheshatshiu was like staying with your parents and taking an allowance long past reaching adulthood. I'd heard her tell Pete once that the reserve was a curse. She lived in Upalong, which was what the first settlers had called the part of North West River along the river. We lived closer to the area called Downalong. Upalongers were known for being party types; Downalongers were a quieter, book-reading sort. But Shirleen wasn't a partier, or not so I'd heard. Her place looked out over Little Lake and got the sunset, whereas Nick's and mine looked out over Lake Melville and got the sunrise. We joshed sometimes about which was the better deal. Shirleen's house was immaculate: a wee perfect home nestled into a woody spot. It was a bungalow, which had probably been much smaller at one point, with a proper Labrador porch. The door to one's porch was always left unlocked, but the door to her kitchen was locked up tight. It didn't seem as if Shirleen had been back to her house since she'd left early this morning. No footprints in the snow going up to the porch, just the ones she'd made as she left the house.

Well, I'd done my best. As Renaud would say, "the woman is an adult." I had to get to Goose Bay and hand in the knife. I called Pete and told him that I was headed into Goose since I had something for the forensic team. He asked me what, but I brushed him off with something vague. No need for details. I had this small awareness that I was holding back about it, but I put that thought aside. As much as I didn't want to implicate Pashin with this piece of what I hoped was false evidence, I couldn't put it off indefinitely. Besides, I wanted to know whose blood was on the knife. As I left Shirleen's place, I decided I was hungry. I'd head to the Goose detachment once I was fed. I agreed with myself that I was only trying to be judicious about when I offered it up. Darn knife.

+++ Chapter 11

The drive to Goose Bay was about 40 minutes. I was forever glad that it wasn't where we lived. Yep, I was a North West River snob. Happy Valley-Goose Bay began in 1941 when the Americans and Canadians decided to build an air base. The need for workers to build the base drew civilians from other parts of Labrador. At first, they camped close to the base location, but when authorities decided that civilians were living too close to the fuel storage for the air base, the workers moved to a nearby location, one that would become the town site of Happy Valley. To me, the town was akin to a long commercial strip. There were attractive neighbourhoods, but most places—banks, the Co-op, restaurants, churches, the community college, gas stations— were strung along the main road.

The detachment was at the farther end of town in what was the original Happy Valley. I decided to head to the Big Eat for a quick lunch. No point in getting to the detachment when everyone in the office would be on their lunch break. Plus, there was the added benefit of possibly finding out what the local gossipers were saying, since the Big Eat was a focal point in the community, and the folks weren't shy about talking over eggs and bacon. The Big Eat was that odd mixture of fast food and greasy spoon that Labrador seemed infatuated with. They did make a half-decent burger though, and I ordered one along with onion rings and a Dr. Pepper as I leaned on the counter looking out across the restaurant. Bingo! The end booth was empty. I grabbed my food, paid up, and headed to it. The high sides of the booths made it possible for me to slide into the side nearest the only other free booth and become nearly invisible to folks coming in. I took out my crossword book and put in my earphones to complete my camouflage.

Soon the booth next to me filled up with the usual gossipers. The first two to sit down were Dick Freemantle, the owner of the lumberyard, who loudly and regularly attested that Labrador was the last outpost for men who were men, and Fred Goudge, the owner of the Big Eat. Fred was also a councillor at the municipal level and rumour had it that it was the local good old boys who put him there. Nick said that he was a bully on the ice, but today I heard in his voice the sound of an anxious puppy trying to please. Scrunched down in my booth, I strained to hear who was joining them. When Fred called out, "Murph, we're over here," I knew it was Murph Lee. All I knew about him was that he had something to do with a bunch of companies involved in the Otter Falls dam project. Rounding out the bunch was Chesley McMaster, a lawyer who had a reputation as a thoughtful considered leader, although I never found him that bright. In the kingdom of the blind, a one-eyed man is king.

A few other characters came up to the booth to say their hellos, but these four were the stalwarts. I'd heard that they ate most every day at the Big Eat, with occasional forays over to the Labrador River Hotel dining room when they wanted to drink too.

What were they talking about? Nothing much at the beginning, but I figured they'd come around to the murder sooner or later. They loved to be men in the know, especially among each other. They'd talk about things they weren't sure of just to get the upper hand in the conversation. That was good news for me. A bit here and a bit there could add up. There was more to my visiting the Big Eat than delay tactics and onion rings.

It was interesting to speculate on the pecking order of the group. Freemantle, in his mid-60s, was the eldest. I believed McMaster and Lee to be in their 40s, and Goudge was the baby of the bunch, probably in his early 30s. Judging by what I could hear of the conversation and what I'd observed in the past, they deferred to McMaster, probably due to his being the one professional in the bunch. Lee also seemed to garner respect, although I wondered if that was based more on fear than respect duly earned. He didn't engage in the same way as the others, who seemed careful not to tease him as they did each other. Collectively, they wore the righteous pomposity of small-town leaders. So far, the conversation was mainly puerile, but I listened more diligently as they exchanged stories of what they'd done on the weekend.

"I was out to Lab City. The wife wanted to go to WalMart, so I had no choice. She's the boss." Freemantle chuckled ironically and it came back to him in the round. "Driving 530 kilometres back and forth to buy something that's on sale for 20 bucks cheaper than we could get here at the Co-op! With the gas and the wear and tear on the SUV, plus staying the night at Chippy's, it's a small fortune. No matter what I say, she still thinks we're saving." His voice dripped with derision, but if he felt that way about her, surely he wouldn't have gone. Probably just more show for the lads.

"You're lucky. I went to a Halloween dance in North West River."

"What did you go as, Goudge? A successful businessman or a crooked politician?" That was Lee.

Much laughing at this hilarious jibe. Fred sounded defensive when he answered.

"The *bubble-gum slut* it was called on the pack. I had boobs out to here and a pink wig. I looked great."

Everyone split a gut on that one. Just imagining that big dope with plastic hooters was enough to kill all sexual desire in me forever.

"You looked right darling, you did! I nearly pissed myself when I saw you come in." That was Lee again.

"You mean both you guys were at a party in S'triver that the rest of us weren't invited to?" Freemantle joked. "Jeez! What's that about?" S'triver is what some Goose Bay types called North West River.

"No one was invited, Freemantle," Lee growled with barely concealed derision. "It was a community dance. My cousin's in The Grand River Stompers and it was their gig. I left early but the bubble-gum slut stayed on till the bitter end. And I suppose the slut went in the first place cause he's always after hot S'triver broads. My cousin told me that slutsky here danced something awful till 2."

I stopped listening to their puerile humour for a while and attended to my burger. At the word *murder*, my ears perked up.

"So, fellas, what have you heard? What's the scuttlebutt about this murder? Eh, Lee? We know you have spies in the department." That was McMaster. There was less laughing at this than I expected. What did he mean by spies in the department?

The voices dropped, and I prayed they wouldn't look over the side of my booth.

"Oh come on now, b'ys, you knows I don't know nothing, you don't." The laughter this time around was there, but thinner, maybe put on. I felt the adjoining seat push back as if one of them was stretching out his legs, but I didn't dare look. Freemantle spoke. "I think the Pashin kid has something to do with it. He's funny anyway. Probably got caught putting something where he shouldn't have."

I was impressed and horrified at how quick the rumours had spread.

"Nothing to do with what we were talking about the other day, was it? With the deadline?" That was from McMaster. Now those were interesting and mysterious questions, I thought. Why would the murder of a teacher in Sheshatshiu by a young Innu have anything to do with deadlines pertaining to these fine upstanding men?

It was at that moment I got caught. Murph had stood up to stretch or get another coffee, I don't know what, and glanced over the side of the booth. His eyes went all slitty and his mouth made a grim line across his face. I did my best to recover, pretending I was caught up in the music I was supposedly listening to and acted startled to see him glaring at me. I made a point of removing my earphones and asking him a question.

"Were you asking me something? Couldn't hear anything with my earbuds in."

Murph looked at me suspiciously but just shrugged. I put my earbuds back in and, without, I hoped, appearing to rush, finished my meal. Then I gathered up my belongings and walked across the room toward the exit. I stopped to talk to an acquaintance from North West River.

"Are you going to the bonfire on the fifth?" I asked her.

"Ya, of course. I heard they arrested someone from the school for murder. Is that true?"

How could I pass up the chance to muddy any suspicions the men might have? I shrugged. "Not sure. I'm just a lowly community constable."

I didn't know if my subterfuge was going to work. Oh well, nothing I could do and it wasn't likely any of them would accuse me of eavesdropping. After sharing a few more pleasantries with the woman, I cleared out. I had evidence to deliver, whether I wanted to or not.

✦

When I arrived at the Goose Bay detachment, Musgrave was hanging up his jacket and heading for the interrogation room. He stopped when he heard me ask the receptionist if she'd heard from Shirleen. They were often on the phone to one another, as would be expected. Musgrave slowly turned on his heel and looked at me with a distinctly odd expression.

"What is it exactly that you *do* to earn your paycheck, Nell?"

Calling me Nell was a not-so-subtle way of putting me down. Even the lowest of recruits got the full measure of respect by means of being called by their rank.

"Sergeant, sir. I'm the community constable with the Sheshatshiu detachment, sir. In charge of youth liaison, sir." He couldn't reprimand me for using too many *sirs*. He was my superior but not my boss, and those of us who worked with Aboriginal specialties held a cachet that was protected by the service.

"I'm well aware of what job you are supposed to be doing, Munro. What I want to know is what you are doing here in town. I'd think that you'd be pretty busy with the Sheshatshiu youth and their parents right now. This detainment of one of their own has them upset, as I understand it."

The man was like cheap margarine: smooth and tasteless.

"Is it the usual 24-hour detainment then?"

Musgrave looked at me with a penetrating stare. I had developed a Teflon coating working with youth, so I kept my composure and my eyebrows lifted.

I guess he wasn't going to deign to answer such an obvious question. If he wanted to hold him longer, it would be a matter of getting a judge to sign a warrant and that would depend on there being more solid evidence than I thought there was. He could not be sure what a judge might do with his request.

Was I to take his attitude as a threat or was this just the way Musgrave rolled? I didn't know, but I knew better than to rile him any further when Pashin was under his watch.

"I'm not trying to meddle, sir. It's just that I'm supposed to be informed as the community constable and youth liaison, sir. And I need to talk to Sergeant Renaud. Is he still here?"

"No. He headed back to Sheshatshiu."

"I have some evidence that was handed in to me this morning. It's a weapon that may or may not have been used in the murder." I handed over the plastic bag with the cloth-wrapped crooked knife rolled up in it. "It's a crooked knife."

Musgrave looked at me. He moistened his lips as though he were thinking this through.

"Tina, call Constable Sinclair and tell him we have something that needs to be properly bagged and sent to forensics." Although he spoke to Tina, his face remained trained on me. "And where did this piece of evidence show up? And why didn't you just hand it over to Sergeant Renaud?"

"Sir, I was going to but I remembered you were leading the investigation."

"I understand that this is your first murder case, but I know that you know how the chain of command works. If you'd given it to your superior officer, he would have known what to do with it. Why do I get the sense you're using this as an excuse to check up on that kid? I sure don't want to be hearing about anything to do with *insensitive handling of Innu youth* or any of that shit on CBC. Since you're green, I'll give you a pass."

Anger flared in my gut. "Are you suggesting that I would tell Nick privileged information?" I couldn't keep the outrage out of my voice. "I'm a professional and so is he—so *no*—you won't hear about it on CBC, sir." I tried to keep my eyes cast down in the penitent position but I flicked them up at the end to see how he was taking my mea culpas. He had an amused look on his face.

"Oh relax, CC. I was just giving you a jibe. I know you wouldn't tell Nick anything. Besides, he's on my hockey team. Though I'm not sure why."

Everyone felt that it was okay to rib me about Nick's hockey playing. Everywhere I went in this hockey-loving land, someone was sure to remind me that Nick couldn't play for beans. I just smiled and shook my head in what I hoped looked like a jolly fashion. I did wonder how he knew that Nick was my partner. Yesterday, the sergeant didn't even seem to know who I was.

"What about Pashin? Has he been in touch with a lawyer? His aunt?"

"Penny Leap from Legal Aid has been notified. He's not talking, anyway."

"Will you let me know what they say about the blood on the knife?" A person could ask.

"No. I won't. Where did it come from anyway?"

"I found it in Sheshatshiu." Like it was on the road.

"Right. *Where* is what I'm asking—no, demanding."

"At Pashin's aunt's house. In his room. But it arrived there when she hadn't seen him at all. Seems someone could've opened his window and stuck it there. She's been there the whole time."

"Right. Well, I'll be out later this afternoon, and you and I can go there and you can show me. I need to talk to Pashin's aunt about the photo anyway. Doesn't look good for this kid. Too bad, I know he was liked. I heard rumours that Tuck might have been playing for the other team. Maybe it was a lover's quarrel."

I opened my mouth to respond and thought better. He was playing me. I nodded and left.

+++ Chapter 12

The drive between Goose Bay and Sheshatshiu was quiet for the most part. Sometimes there might be a moose, or in the early spring, bears and their cubs. There are also six shrines strung out along the road made by the relatives of folks who had died in road accidents. Brightly painted wooden structures featured holy statues of Mary or Jesus with various doodads that had some significance to the victim, often with a plexiglass front that could be opened. Each was a different colour and the relatives would come out and freshen up the paint every few years. I particularly liked a large, bright blue one that, partly because it signified that I was only 15 minutes from my destination and partly because the blue was the colour that you crayoned the sky with when you were six. Some days, time permitting, I'd stop to see if anything had been added. The blue shrine held a statue of Mary, about 2.5 feet tall. Around her were bouquets of faded, plastic flowers. New ones were added, but none removed. Besides Mary, this shrine held a plastic lamb, a hockey puck, a package of black tea with the label all but gone from sun fading, a bottle of hot sauce, and a pair of small slippers of worn, thin, caribou hide trimmed with what may have been rabbit fur. The slippers, the size that fit an eight-year-old, had been chewed either in the shrine or before the owner had grown up and died. I never knew the man whom this shrine honoured; he had died years before I came to this area, but I felt that I'd met him. I always found consulting the shrines tremendously touching, much more so than the sterile gravestones of my people with dates and familial roles their only signifying items.

I didn't stop today. I wondered what a shrine for Jay Tuck would look like. It was odd to know now that he'd not only been a Catholic, but a priest. I thought back to the only time I saw him lose his shit. It was at a funeral in Goose Bay for a woman who had killed herself. The funeral was to start at 2 p.m. but the kids and the father were late. They'd had to buy pants for one of the kids at Reitmans. It was a bitterly cold day in February and the front entry held the crowd that couldn't be jammed into the pews. I was inside, just barely, sitting with Shania. She'd been in touch with the family by cell and knew they'd be late, but apparently the priest didn't care. He started the funeral Mass before the family entered. I noticed Jay rise. He quietly walked up to the priest and told him to wait. The priest tried to wave him off, but Jay didn't move, just stood there, vibrating with suppressed fury until the priest stopped. Then he went back to the pew, sat down, and we waited.

I wondered who would officiate at Jay's funeral.

Finally, my mind turned to Pashin. In the days before becoming a police officer, I often spent this drive considering some question about a client. It might have been to wonder how I could get a youth to pay attention to something positive in their life—hockey, a girlfriend or boyfriend, rock and roll—it didn't matter what it was, only that *something* was there. Obsessive interest in sports, art, theatre, music, or any weird hobby had saved many a youth, here and elsewhere, from a downward spiral. But this was a different problem. I had a youth that I thought was fundamentally a good guy, who had passions and intellect and respect in his community—and he was being implicated in a cold-blooded murder. I was missing something: some nagging detail that kept floating in my mind just out of sight. The more I tried to look directly at it, the more it eluded me.

I returned to Shakespeare and *Hamlet*, not simply for the sake of an intellectual exercise, I assured myself. I would let my intuition have its way. Hamlet was grieving his father and hadn't fully separated from his parents when his father died. He was mistrustful of his mother, who had moved on quickly from the death of her husband, and had not been sensitive to her young son's emotional state at the discovery. How was that true of Pashin? Who was running roughshod over his feelings? Didn't seem like I could plug in Jay Tuck and have it make any sense. Sure, Jay had challenged Pashin, but he had done so in positive ways that Pashin appreciated. In this case, it seemed like Tuck had disappointed him. But I didn't think that would have led Pashin to killing him. What was I missing? And why wouldn't Jay have wanted the kids to do *Hamlet*?

Jay, who had always been one for telling the uncomfortable truth to whoever needed to hear it, had, it appeared, decided to take a more tactful route. He had changed his tune. That would totally piss off an idealistic young person who'd adored him, wouldn't it? Maybe

I was wrong to think that Pashin couldn't have done it. Maybe I was wilfully choosing to ignore certain facts. They had argued; Renaud wouldn't make that up. They were working on crooked knives together. There was a photo that seemed, at the very least, inappropriate for Jay to have on his person, although the killer could have planted it. I needed to find out why Jay had shut up. Who was telling him to be quiet? And why had he gone from boldly speaking his mind to silencing himself and Pashin? I considered what one thing would shut me up regarding injustices I was witnessing: the threatening of someone more vulnerable than me.

I couldn't help but ponder if there was any concealed reason why the investigation was being handled out of Goose Bay. Renaud's inferring that it may have been a *political necessity* was a trick turn of phrase used often in these troubled times. Sure, it was going to be a madhouse in Shesh for the next few weeks, that was a given. And why shouldn't it be? This was a deeply dysfunctional but tightly knit community. They were fed up with the powerful telling them how it was going to be, just like Hamlet was tired of his advisers lecturing him on the correct way for the Prince of Denmark to act when his father mysteriously died.

One thing was certain: the meeting at the sweat lodge was not an unrelated incident. Who was the person or people that the Innu considered an evil influence? What did they have to do with Tuck and Pashin and Hamlet? And why hadn't the Innu I'd met at the sweat gone to the police or political leaders to get things changed? There was a story there and I wasn't getting all of it. I needed to be patient and it would come. I hadn't spent all this time building bridges in this community to not trust that they'd hold. When I'd first moved to Labrador and began working with the Innu, I was always in a state of outrage about how they were being treated. I used to wonder why there was only ever the mild and expected gathering of trucks and cars at the school showing that the community cared about the latest act of oppression they'd experienced. I used to rail at anyone who would listen (in those days it was just Nick and, occasionally, Shania). They were both patient with me. What was it that I had to learn? That the Innu didn't go to the authorities when things went wrong. They weren't going to fight for their family members or tribe members or selves—not in that way. They would make silent protests, but they wouldn't write up complaints. Over many decades—no, *centuries*—they had developed a strong aversion to the criminal justice system, and no matter how much the police or the government or the schools tried to capture their trust in the system, it wasn't there. That isn't to say that some of them didn't try to change things through white channels, but mostly they endured until they didn't.

Like a free-wheeling dragonfly, my mind landed on Shirleen. She was usually willing to fight the system with the system. Where was she? This silence was so unlike her. Shirleen lived alone. She loved her solitude, but wasn't shy. I thought of her cabin. Could she have gone there? How would she get there this time of year? It was tricky, as the bay could freeze up at any moment, but it hadn't yet. There wasn't enough snow down to drive a Ski-Doo around the shore. She could've taken a boat. It'd be damned cold—not fun but doable. But whose boat? She didn't have one and I'd heard her say often enough that it was hard to find anyone willing to take her out. Going any distance was arduous this time of year with not enough snow for snowshoes or cross-country skis.

A few years back, I'd been out to Shirleen's cabin, in an enclave of other cabins in the old settlement of Butter and Snow. A perfect place, and if at first I hadn't truly understood why folks in a village of 500 felt the need to flee the hurly-burly for their sylvan cabin life, I had started to get the idea. Enough of that. I would see if she was back at the detachment, check in with Pete as to whether Sergeant Renaud had returned, and find out what was happening with the Innu protest.

✢

A crowd had gathered outside the detachment, but ... it didn't look too fierce. They probably knew that Renaud hadn't taken Pashin away. I saw Renaud's police vehicle in the lot, so I knew that he was at least back in Sheshatshiu. Good. I walked through the crowd, saying hello to those I knew. It was the usual crowd that came out for any protest, with a few more youth than usual. They weren't aggressive. Innu usually weren't, and other than a few mutters in Innu-aimun that I chose to ignore, everyone was polite. Inside, no Shirleen. Sergeant Renaud was talking to Pete when I came in and he looked at me with one eyebrow raised.

I decided to take his glance as an invitation. "No word from Shirleen, Sergeant?"

"No, but she's a grownup. I'm sure she decided to take a mental health day."

As if.

"So, what's the scoop on the murder investigation?" I thought I'd play dumb.

He looked at me with what seemed a theatrical level of disapproval. "I think you know. I heard you were talking to Musgrave."

"Yes, I brought in a knife that Rebekah found in Pashin's room. Not that Musgrave seemed that interested."

"Watch it, Constable."

"Sorry, sir. It's just a pain in the ass on top of everything else to have to go back and forth between here and Goose."

"I told you to report to me. I'm guessing you wanted to go for some reason of your own, but I don't care to get into that right now. Just tell me about this weapon."

"Yes, sir. It was a crooked knife that Rebekah, Pashin's aunt, found on the windowsill in his room. Thing is, sir, she found it, and he hadn't come home. Someone opened the window and stashed it there. I think someone's trying to frame him. Choice of weapon, and now this. Pashin wouldn't have put it there—he wasn't even staying there—but I bet whoever did it didn't know that. What I really don't get is why plant a false weapon when the murderer left a perfectly good one right at the scene?"

"I think I can answer that one for you, Nell. The one at the scene wasn't the murder weapon. There was no trace of blood on it, which isn't conclusive, but it was one of the rounded ones. Wouldn't have left the pattern that's on the neck. A straight one cut Jay Tuck's throat."

"And, of course, that is the kind that I just brought in. Beautiful. Wish I'd deep-sixed it."

"You know that's nearly all I'd normally need to hear to can your ass, Munro. Luckily, I know that isn't what you mean, or, at the very least, I can believe you are putting the force ahead of your own allegiances since you took it in."

"I still don't think Pashin has anything to do with it, sir. Whoever dropped the knife off didn't even know where Pashin was staying. I have a feeling that the crooked knife is more than a murder weapon."

"I'm not interested in your spiritual speculations at this point. I want you to follow up on any leads that you might have in respect to Pashin's movements on Saturday night. He's refusing to talk at all. Check with your posse of kids and see if you can figure out a timeline for him. And find out the source of that photo. If you're so hot to protect the kid, do some gumshoe work to make it so."

I sighed and took off my jacket. Renaud was right. Why bitch about it? Looked like I'd be stuck here for a while.

"Before you get comfortable, go over to Rebekah's with a kit and see what's there: footprints outside the window, prints on the sill." I did my best not to show my satisfaction. "You know the drill. And figure out that timeline. Oh, and tomorrow's your day off, isn't it?"

"Yes, but I can work it if you need me."

"No. You came in on Sunday. We can survive without you for a day."

"Sir, did Shirleen find out anything about the old photo of Jay Tuck?"

The sergeant looked up from his file. "Not that I've heard, but like I said, we haven't heard from her. She'll let you know when you're in next. Bring us back the kit after you've finished. Maybe she'll be in by then."

I didn't want to ruin my chances, but I had to shoot just straight enough. "Uh, Sergeant? Musgrave told me he was coming down to see about those prints. Sure it's okay if I do it?"

"Of course it is. Musgrave decided not to come down—some conference call he had booked."

✦

Rebekah was home when I got there, but no babies. "Don't worry," she said when I asked. "They're at daycare just for today. I had some things I needed to do, and I was worried about cops showing up."

"And here I am." I grinned to show her that I knew what she meant.

"And how can I help you, Nell? Tea?"

"No. I can't drink your tea, Rebekah. You might as well know it after all these years. I can't drink any tea I find in Sheshatshiu kitchens. You guys are trying to kill us." Then I realized what I'd said. "Sorry. You know I'm joking. I'm a big mouth. But your tea is just too strong for this paleface."

She laughed, so I knew it was all right. "Did you see Pashin?"

"No. I'm sorry, but they've arrested him. Don't worry. At least we know he's safe while he's there. I handed in the crooked knife. That's why I'm here. I want to dust for prints and see if I can find out how someone got it in the house without you hearing them."

Rebekah ran off a string of words in Innu-aimun that I knew

were exhortations to Jesus to help her. Her hands made a sweeping gesture over her body as if she were getting rid of cobwebs before speaking again. "They're determined to pin this on him, aren't they? You can do all you want to take prints and stuff, but what will that prove? Her prints are going to be all over that room."

"Yes, and where they aren't, we'll know someone was there, wiping up their own and his in the process."

"Oh. Smart."

"That's why they pay me the big bucks."

First, we went out back to check for tracks under Pashin's window. It had snowed Friday and again yesterday, so I wasn't sure what we'd see, but there were prints under Sunday's snow: frozen prints, a little mucked up by a dog or two, but still easy to see. It looked like running shoes with not too heavy a tread and about a size 11. Still, I measured them to confirm. I couldn't determine the brand. The tracks came from behind Rebekah's place where a copse of trees separated the houses from those higher up. I followed them back, but at a certain point they disappeared. The snow was too low under the trees, and the downhill incline meant that what snow had been there had melted and refrozen recently. But that's where the person had come from—that much was for sure. I headed back to the house to look more closely at the outside of the window.

There were some light scrapings along the jamb where someone had used a knife or a chisel to lever open the window. The window hadn't been locked, and it was a flimsy affair. The sill was nearly rotten anyway, so the effort would have been minimal. No point in dusting rotten wood, and the glass held no prints. Even a non-guilty person would have gloves or mitts on this time of year, except maybe macho kids. Inside, I dusted the whole room: any surface that looked like it might hold a print. I noticed something else: a nail about 2 inches above the jamb that the window would have hit had someone tried to open it enough to get in. It had a cobweb hanging from it, so no one had entered, just opened the window a crack and slid the knife in.

Curiouser and curiouser.

+++ Chapter 13

The crowd that had been outside the door was gone and the
detachment was empty when I returned: no Shirleen, no Pete, no
Renaud, just Constable Walker. Jordan had started working at the
Sheshatshiu detachment six months ago. Before that he was in
Sussex, New Brunswick. He appeared to be terrified of me, whether
it was because I was a woman or because the detachment had given
a defence course for women at the community centre during which
he realized that I could kick his butt, I didn't know.

I asked him where the others were and he just shrugged. I
checked my cellphone. I had forgotten to charge it. That wouldn't
make Renaud happy. I plugged it into the charger and sat down to
quickly write a report on what I'd observed at Rebekah's house.

When I finished, I decided to go up to the store in Sheshatshiu
and get the buzz around the reserve. I wanted to find out if anyone
besides Jay had been seen near the school Saturday night. I would
likely run into some of the kids there, as it was a popular hangout,
and ask who knew about Pashin's movements on Saturday night.

✦

I walked to the store—walking meant that I had more chances to
run into folks in the know. It took about a quarter of an hour to walk

from the detachment to the store, less if I boogied, more if I stopped to greet the kids, dogs, and adults that I encountered along the way. The place was quiet. Maybe there were kids up at the rink; lots of them played hockey. Or they could be at the school playground. Kids who didn't want to go to school liked hanging around the building because, I imagine, it felt safe. I did run into one kid, known as a badass, outside the store. I liked him. He was 16, living with his mother and grandmother, who were always wanting me to do something with him or for him, but we still managed, he and I, to have a good relationship. I asked him how he was doing.

"Not bad, Miss. What's with no car?"

"Felt like taking a walk while the weather still allowed it. Plus, I need the exercise."

He grinned. "What's up?"

"Oh, I was hoping to find someone who might have seen Mr. Tuck on Saturday night."

"He was home at 10:30. I went by there for my candies."

I laughed. "Oh ya, what were you dressed up as?"

"An Innu kid, Miss."

"Ha! So you saw him at his house at 10:30?"

"Ya. I had hoped to hang out with him a bit. My mother was having people in at home and it was shitty there. But when I was sitting with Mr. Tuck, he got a call and told me he had to go up to the school."

"No kidding!" This was helpful. "Do you know who it was that phoned?"

"Nah, I just heard him say something like, 'A meeting? I didn't know.'"

"Do you know what Pashin was up to for Halloween? Is he a friend of yours?"

"No. We're not friends. He used to be fun, but now all he talks about is race stuff. I don't know where he was. He wasn't at the parties I went to, and I never saw him round the rez."

We shot the breeze a little longer, then I made my way into the store: no kids there to question and the woman who sat on an old kitchen chair behind the counter didn't speak English, or didn't want to, so I moseyed outside and on up to the school.

I remember the first time I had come into Sheshatshiu like it was last week. I'd driven around with Nick when we first moved to town, but it was a while before we entered the reserve. It was a world away from the pleasant little houses and trim yards of North West River, but just on the other side of the water. The houses made me think of places I'd seen on the news: war-torn places like the Ukraine or Serbia. Most homes had at least one boarded-up window. The yards were composed of gravel, dirt, and garbage. Kids on rusty, broken, old bikes roamed around as loose and free as the packs of dogs. I realized how little I knew of how any of Canada's Indigenous peoples lived and how easy it was to apply our ideas of the "right way" to live to them. Without ever questioning myself, I had absorbed a subtle contempt for Indigenous ways. Now I was getting to know the people in the community and starting to understand what was important to them and what wasn't. I've been to their gatherings at Gull Island and seen their meticulous camping sites—how warm and inviting they were to me. I'd sat around inside their tents, close to their smoky stoves, drinking bitter tea and laughing at some story or another. The Innu were at their happiest out in *nutshimit*. They could let their guard down there; the days made sense. Kids loved those gatherings too. Lots of parties but no booze, no drugs. Just remembering a time when they lived off the land where they felt both competent and free.

Because I couldn't see any action at the school, I walked up the hill to Johnny's. His pickup wasn't in his driveway, but I knocked anyway and wasn't surprised when he came to the door—trucks, rooms in one's house, kids, dogs, or any property at all were a fairly fluid commodity in Sheshatshiu.

"Hey, Nell. How are you?"

"Didn't know if I'd catch you. Your pickup's not here."

"Nah. I lent it to Charlie Pokue. He had a mattress he wanted to take to the dump." Johnny rubbed his chin for a minute and then laughed. "Or one he wanted to pick up there. I don't remember which."

I followed him into the house and he sat down at a table where he was working on a piece of greenish black stone carved into what appeared to be Sedna, the Sea Woman of Inuit mythology. Beside it was a piece of bow-shaped bone, perhaps ivory, with characters partially carved into it. He showed me how it fit into the flat stone out of which she arose. In its final position, it would be a half-arc over her: a breaking wave.

"Sedna?"

He nodded. "Sedna, who represents all that is mysterious and interconnected in this world. Do you know the story?"

I gestured for him to go on. I knew several versions but I wanted to hear Johnny's.

"Her father tries to marry her off for some fish and she rebels. She runs off with a guy who says that he's a good hunter and lives in a palace on an island. Turns out he's an old sea bird that lives in a dump. Her father, maybe in a moment of remorse, comes to see her on the island and realizes that the sea bird is treating his daughter badly. He takes her in his boat to bring her home, but the sea bird and some of his pals stir up a wind storm with their flapping wings. Dad freaks and throws her into the sea and she comes up to cling to the side of his boat. He cuts off her fingers one by one, and each one becomes a sea creature: seals and fish and whales. Kinda hard to imagine, but there are similar stories in other cultures. Like Agamemnon, who kills his daughter Iphigenia so that his fleet will be safe from storms on the way to Troy. No wonder women are pissed off, eh? Used as bargaining chips."

I nodded slowly, enjoying the pace of conversation. "Same with the Catholic saints. Fathers and uncles trying to marry off daughters to hoary, old farts their fathers thought would be good bets. Maybe they didn't want any men, but who cared but them about that? Who was it? Saint Lucy? No, it was Saint Agatha who had her breasts cut off because she wouldn't consent to life in a brothel. Lucy took out her own eyes to give to a suitor who had admired them. Pretty ballsy. Still happens today—girls being bought and sold, killed for not behaving as property should."

We were quiet a while. I had gone somewhere black and Johnny gave me a moment before he pulled me back out.

"So, Nell. I bet you didn't come to talk about that stuff, did you?"

"No. I thought you might know about something that's bothering me. A detail." I looked him in the eye to make it clear why I was asking. "There's display cases at the school and ... well, something was taken out of one of them. Do you know anything about that?"

"I heard that a crooked knife was taken."

We were quiet for another moment.

"Can you tell me who told you that?" I was being careful to not say if it was true or not, but Johnny was no dummy.

He sat back, looking nonchalant all of a sudden. "Oh, I can't remember. Whoever it was thought I should know because I've made a few in my time. I didn't make any that Jay had, though. Some he'd collected, old ones, and then he started making them himself. He thought it was a good thing to do with the kids—teach them an old way that belongs to all the cultures. I stopped making them years ago. It takes too long, and I find the form boring. I do use them for carving wood though. They're no good for stone or bone."

"Do you know who *does* use one?"

He looked me in the eye then with a sharpness he rarely ever displayed. "Not so many Innu. Not many of them are carvers, as you know, and their uses for them don't apply anymore. They were called canoe knives at one time."

I sat and thought. If someone had told him about the crooked knife business, it meant that someone from the force had talked.

Revealing details about a murder investigation only days old was bad business. Silence was easy with Johnny. He never seemed agitated when there was no conversation. It was nice.

"Tell me more about Jay's interest in them. I don't quite get it."

"Jay believed that the crooked knife was important, that when everyone was getting all pissy about what cultural activity or object had been colonized or appropriated, the crooked knife stood separate from that. It was used by early settlers, the Inuit, and all tribes across Turtle Island. There have been many arguments about its origin but the truth is, no one knows. They're still used, unchanged, in Europe as a farrier tool. But we're circling the point. Whether correct in his assumption or not, Jay Tuck felt that a crooked knife represented the settlers' and First Peoples' interdependence. And many folks do not like that."

"Are you one of those folks?"

"No. I'm not." And he smiled at me. A warm and embracing smile that told me that I was supposed to figure something out. "Have you ever heard of the term *resource curse*, Nell?"

"No. Or I don't think so. What is it?"

"It refers to a paradox that occurs when a country or region is rich in natural resources, and yet its people get poorer. Corruption increases and all the money seems to flow one way: to the elite and the government, all but bypassing the citizens. The government soon starts dismantling the social safety nets, and, well, you know the rest."

"Right." I felt dense. "I think I can follow, but ..."

"I'm sure you will." And he gave me another enigmatic smile, one that said I'd have to put the pieces together myself.

I debated trying to winkle out what he meant by pressing him with more questions but I knew better. He'd told me what I needed to know right now. I trusted that he wasn't keeping dangerous secrets from me.

"Okay—a few more questions and then I'll leave you alone. Do you know anything about Pashin's movements on Saturday night?"

"Yes, I do. He was here with me for most of the night, and then around 10 or 10:30 he told me that he was going to meet someone. I figured that it was none of my business, so I didn't ask, and I don't know when he got in, except that I came out of my room sometime after midnight and saw the light on under his door. That's all I can tell you."

Okay. That answered a question I'd had as to why Johnny wasn't going into the detachment to speak up for Pashin. The kid had no alibi, or not one that I'd heard yet.

I nodded. "Last one, I promise. What do you know about Jay and the Catholic Church?"

Johnny paused long enough to suggest that I'd finally caught him off guard. When he spoke, he seemed to choose his words carefully.

"I know that he would've been seriously pissed at that question." Johnny smiled tightly at me. He put down his carving tool far too slowly. "Jay was a priest in Ireland. He only told a few people. He wouldn't talk about why he left except to say that he had been too young to know what he was doing. He said that he figured that anyone who'd divorced from an early marriage would get it."

"That's all he said?"

"Yep."

I nodded. I had run out of questions.

✦

I walked back to the detachment, filed my report, and went home, where I grabbed a bowl of soup and headed over to the Mary May Healing Centre for the play auditions. I hadn't had time to prepare my approach to this meeting, to think about how the kids who were closest to Mr. Tuck would be feeling, and who would even come. I left it to the students to self-organize, the way Tuck would've done it.

We had a group of 11 students and me. When I got there, Jeremiah, Kaitlyn, and Zann, who were the main force of the theatre group, were in the room we'd been given with copies of scenes to be read. The others came in slowly—some on time, most late. I knew them all, but they were slow to warm up. Before we started, I proposed that we sit in a circle and chat.

"It's okay that we take our time with this," I started. "Everyone, me included, probably feels awful about Mr. Tuck. So, let's be kind to ourselves and take it easy, okay?" The kids nodded. "Jeremiah was going to direct, and I'll be happy to help him with that."

"Miss? Miss, Pashin was supposed to do a ... I don't know ..." Zann looked at the other kids, but they didn't help her. "A version of the play, for us. I mean, for Sheshatshiu. Can we still do that?"

"I don't see why not."

Eddie spoke up, which was surprising, since I usually couldn't get two words out of him. "Mr. Tuck didn't want us to do that. He wanted us to do *Romeo and Juliet.*"

It figured. Eddie was a teacher-pleaser. It was understandable. He'd been taken into care when he was about three and had lived with several families locally and one in Roddickton. He knew that he had to go along with those in authority to survive at all.

"You guys should make up your mind about what you want to do among yourselves. I'll support whatever that is, and no one from the school will give you a hard time."

Was that true? I thought so, although this was clearly what Pashin and Tuck had been fighting about, and I was no closer to understanding why Tuck had changed his mind.

It took a few minutes for everyone but Eddie to say that they wanted to do *Hamlet*—they wanted to do Pashin's version. The fact that our playwright was in jail made things trickier, but the kids were cheered by the decision already. Since we were only casting right now, we would stick to the original script today and hope that Pashin had kept the main characters in his rewrite.

We'd take care of the lesser parts when we had Pashin's script. I gave a short summary of the play, and we had fun getting those who'd come to try out different roles. Apparently, Pashin had wanted no part in the production other than rewriting the script. I thought he would've made a wonderful Hamlet. As it turned out, not a single fellow present wanted to be the beleaguered Prince of Denmark. Fortunately, Zann spoke up.

"I want to be Hamlet, Miss. If men used to play women in Shakespeare's time, well, why can't I play Hamlet?"

"You can!" I responded so quickly that the kids looked at

one another, sharing a laugh. No problem, I was having fun and furthering the feminist agenda. Win-win. "Women have done it for over a hundred years. Sarah Bernhardt played Hamlet." Everyone looked at me with questions in their eyes. "How about Cush Jumbo? You know, from *The Good Wife*?" A few nodded. "She's been Hamlet. And you don't have to play Hamlet as a man if you don't want, but you'd have to work with Pashin on that. In fact, you could do a non-binary Hamlet."

Hamlet was hardly the epitome of conventional masculinity. And I thought that it might give Pashin something good to work on during all this. We could work on some of the more gender-sensitive parts of the play in a new way.

I sat there, listening to them laugh and make outrageous suggestions. I wondered what Shakespeare would have made of a group of young people with a heritage going back so much further than his own, adapting his play and fashioning it to their story. The Anglo-Saxons had invaded Britain in the seventh century CE, while archaeological evidence of the Innu peoples being in Labrador dates back thousands of years. It's easy to forget, since so few people are interested in acknowledging it in the first place. But when I thought about how these kids could stand on the land that their direct ancestors had walked thousands of years ago, well, to be truthful, it made me envious.

The rest of what we could do, we did. Esther, a quiet and efficient person, said she was born to be a producer. I got her number, as I knew she could start immediately with figuring out rehearsal times and all the rest. One of the younger boys had great presence, so we cast him as Horatio. Kaitlyn wanted to be Ophelia and one of the courtiers. Two of the other girls had a tiff over Gertrude, but when I suggested that one of them play Laertes, Ophelia's brother who has a sword fight scene with Hamlet, a deal was made. Eddie wanted the role of the Ghost of Hamlet's father; it seemed he wouldn't hold a grudge.

The meeting broke up, and everyone's spirits were lifted. Jeremiah was the only person on the production crew who could meet with me on Tuesday morning. I was secretly glad, as two organizers can get twice as much done as five. No matter what, we'd have the first rehearsal in whatever shape or form on Wednesday evening. I was more than happy to make my way back over the bridge to North West River for a nightcap with Nick and a well-deserved sleep.

The drum was in his hands when he heard the creep coming down the stairs. He was with someone else: a guy whose voice the boy didn't recognize. The boy was trapped, but he knew how to keep as still as a mouse under the snow while coyotes hunted. He heard the creep saying something about everything being kept quiet until the tenth. "Then we're in the clear."

"Yes, but—" the other man interrupted—a white voice, the boy thought. "I heard what happened to that Nighthawk woman. If you can't keep your goons in check, our little friend at the force won't stay in the game."

"Don't worry about Nighthawk. She'll keep quiet. As for our friend at the force, he's as hungry as we are. Besides, he's in too deep now. He doesn't know it yet, but I can make sure he does. Trust me."

"This is too much money to fuck with, my friend. I'm serious. Your little pharmaceutical business will become nothing but a side-hustle when this money starts rolling in." The white guy's laugh had a blade wrapped in it.

"Ya, ya. I got the message. You do your part, and I'll take care of mine. You just remember: no me, no contract."

Tuesday, November 3

✦✦✦ Chapter 14

At 7 a.m., I got a call from Ruth, one of the town's church ladies. Shirleen was supposed to have come over last night to work on a quilt that was being auctioned for the church, but she hadn't shown up. Ruth had gone to her house, but there was no one there. Shirleen's car was not there either. One of Shirleen's neighbours told Ruth that the light over the stove had been on all night. I called Pete's cell. He lived almost in Goose Bay, and he said that he was on his way to the detachment, just driving past the turnoff to Terrington Basin. *Terrington.* I remembered Shirleen's notes.

"Pete, detour down to the Basin. Check out the Labrador Hunting and Fishing Association's boat ramp. See if Shirleen's car is there. Call me back pronto, okay?"

Why hadn't I thought of that when I'd seen her note?

A few minutes later, minutes I spent asking Nick if he'd take me in our motorboat to Shirleen's cabin, I had Pete's response.

"Yes, it's here and it's unlocked, with the keys left on the seat."

I tried to stay optimistic. It wasn't like Shirleen not to lock up. "I'm going to head out to Shirleen's cabin with Nick. She probably went on a whim, but it's weird that she didn't tell anyone. If she's there, I'll let you know as soon as I get back."

Nick and I got everything we'd need for our quick trip and were ready to leave the house when Jeremiah showed up.

"Oh, Jeremiah, I have to go out on a quick call with Nick. I'm sorry, I forgot our arrangement. I owe you."

Jeremiah looked stricken. I'd forgotten what a big deal it was when an adult came through for these kids. Nick looked at me. "I wouldn't mind if we had an extra person on board. You guys could talk theatre, and I told Angie that I'd swing by her cabin and bring back that old generator the next time we went out that way. It's just past Shirleen's. I could use some help getting it on board and need one more person at the helm to keep the boat steady."

Maybe it was a dumb idea, maybe the whole thing was a dumb idea, but Jeremiah's face lit up at the thought of an adventure, and I hushed my inner voice.

There is nothing colder than a speedboat on Lake Melville in November. It was my day off, so at least I didn't have to wear my uniform, which was never warm enough. I was wearing the clothes I usually wait until December to don: silk long johns and a long-sleeved undershirt, lined jeans, wind-blocking rain pants, a down parka, plus a neck cowl which was surprisingly worth its ridiculous cost, my lined Tibetan wool hat, and lined gloves. The cowl came in handy almost immediately; Nick likes to go full throttle in the boat. No matter how often I begged him to slow down, he always pretended that he couldn't hear me.

A November sky can be a beautiful thing if you pay attention to it. The first look is grey, but the second reveals streaks of mauve and rose. The clouds are heavy with a gravitas not seen in summer's fly-by-day clouds.

The shore was starting to freeze up; small ice pans floated and knocked against each other. Soon the icy lace *ballycatter* would form a frilly banner along the edge of the land. The water out from the beach rose only to above your ankles for about 100 yards or so—then it might be up to your waist by 200 yards, meaning that the freeze-up happened around the shore much sooner. Of course, even though it was called a lake, it had salt and a tide, so it did take its time turning from wave to ice.

I could see our house from the boat as we whizzed by. A flagpole near our fence proudly flew a Labrador flag. We were headed north up the bay past the crescent beaches divided from one another by copses of trees and bog. The land swung out and formed a point that could be seen from the beach in front of our house. Nick and I had hiked to the point a few times—a four-hour hike, but on the water, less than 30 minutes. Past the point, outside of our view, the land curved back and held a protected area of coves and islands. The location of Butter and Snow. And Shirleen's cabin.

I loved being on the boat, even on the knife-edge of the brutal cold. The smell of the outboard fuel, the sound of the engine, and the freedom of moving so quickly to a part of the country that would have taken me hours to walk this time of year was exhilarating. The motorboat was a fat, beamy, little boat that had belonged to Nick's father. Rather ancient and not speedy enough for most, but it could easily carry us all (or just two with a Labrador tent and all the accoutrements) for a long weekend on the land. We always carried extra gas and we had a pile of food with us now, in case we needed it. We couldn't talk in the boat; the motor was too loud. Jeremiah and I would talk when we got to Shirleen's or stopped on the way back for a boil-up.

I had only been to Butter and Snow a few times. The name had always intrigued me. The settlers called it that because of the way the snow hung on after the yellow buttercups came in, I think. Whatever the reason, it seemed a whimsical name given by folks who weren't much given to whimsy. We made the farthest point that could be seen from the beach in front of our house, and 100 new points and bits of islands showed themselves. We went closer to the shoreline as we rounded that first point, and soon we saw the three cabins, nestled into a little nook. Shirleen's banner was hoisted, which meant that she was there, and I felt a rush of relief at the sight of it.

We drew the boat up to the shoreline; it was deep enough and a large boulder with a ring embedded in it was there to tie up. No other boats were in sight, but that made sense; Shirleen would've had to have cadged a lift. The guys jumped out as the motor turned off and pulled the boat up closer so that I wouldn't get too wet. Sometimes I didn't mind being a woman.

I called up to the cabin. "Shirleen, it's Nell, Nick, and Jeremiah— put the kettle on."

People really didn't worry about dropping in on cabins. As there was often no other way to tell anyone you were coming by, it was an accepted custom. A few folks had sat-phones or wireless radios, but they were few and far between. We trudged up the windy, rocky way to the cabin door. A skiff of snow lay over everything, just like in the village.

The cabin, like most in Labrador, was plain and serviceable, with a covered porch to stack enough wood for a while and a big caribou antler on the door. The door opened with a latch and I went on in, the others behind me. There was Shirleen, in her rocking chair beside the stove. Dead.

+++ Chapter 15

In the presence of death, our true natures arise. That sounds highfalutin but, at least for the generation that came of age in the 1950s and 1960s and those that followed, we don't know death like our ancestors did. We only know prepackaged death: death that's been gussied up, made to behave and look seemly. Death, for those who see it in its natural state, isn't like that. And I'm not talking about the gruesome aspects of murder like the blood pooling about Jay Tuck after his throat was slit. I mean the there-but-not-there quality of unvarnished death. Shirleen, who had liked to giggle, who flashed her eyes when anyone dared put her heroes down, who hummed while she filed, was gone. In her absence was a corpse that might have looked horrified, if you had learned from the movies that a mouth in an *O* and wide-open eyes signified horror. But as many people know, the signifiers aren't the real thing. Shirleen's eyes were wide open and her mouth was in an *O* shape, but I wouldn't say she was horrified. If anything, her expression mimicked the surprise that showed on one's face when met with an old friend you'd thought was long gone.

Now she is gone. Jeremiah swore in Innu-aimun, or at least that's what I think he did, and back-pedalled as if to get out of the cabin before good sense stopped him. Nick grabbed me and crushed me into his chest as if to protect me from the spectre before us. I untangled myself quickly and approached the body, telling Nick and Jeremiah to stay back.

"Nick, go down to the water and see if you can see any signs of the boat that brought her here. Jeremiah, go around the back—see if you can see tracks through the snow to the trail. I'll check the body. It's cold in here." I looked at the wood stove. "Why didn't I notice that there was no smoke coming out of her chimney?"

"Because you wanted Shirleen to be okay," Nick replied quickly. "We all did."

Nick and Jeremiah went outdoors and I examined Shirleen's body for signs of what had killed her. She was sitting fairly straight in her old padded rocker. There were no visible bruises around her face or neck, no open wounds. She didn't appear to show signs of being smothered—in fact, there were no signs of a struggle. Maybe this wasn't a crime scene.

I looked at her side table: a glass with a small amount of water, a basket with a sock needing mending, and a kit for self-administering insulin. I closed my eyes, swallowing against the unfairness. I knew that she carried the kit with her at all times, we all knew she did. Diabetes was rampant in Sheshatshiu, as it was on all Canadian reserves. The prescription label bore her name. The rubber tie-off was pushed to one side, like she'd just used it. Maybe she'd died of a heart attack.

A few minutes later, Nick and Jeremiah were back in the cabin. There were no footprints out back in the deeper snow and, although there had been a light snow in the early morning, something would have been visible. The only prints around the shore were ours, although the area looked scuffed up under the snow. That could be from the tide—so of no help. I didn't see a bag of her clothes or any containers with the food you'd bring out even if you were coming for the day. Nothing. Her coat was hung on a hook, but when I looked closely, I realized that it hadn't been hung up by Shirleen. She was meticulous with her clothing. Every day she tucked her scarf and hat in her sleeve and her gloves or mitts in her pockets. She always used the loop on the back of her jacket so as not to get a pooked-out mark from the hook. Her coat was flung on the hook carelessly, with nothing in the sleeves or pockets. Her regular boots that she wore to work were there. She would have worn rubber boots out here and a heavier jacket. Her slippers lay beside the bed in the corner. If there was no fire in the stove, I might have believed that she had simply sat down as soon as she entered, and then died, but she would have put her slippers on before doing any other task.

This was not a natural death. This was murder, and planned, at that. I was sure.

"Nick, I'd like you to take the boat and alert Sergeant Renaud. Jeremiah and I will stay here with the body."

Nick nodded. "Okay, but crime scene or not, I'm building up this fire. One corpse is enough."

I stopped him mid-chivalry. "We can do that. I'm anxious for this to be taken care of soon. There's lots of wood ready, and if I need more kindling, Jeremiah or I can split some. Now please go. I'll be nervous till I see you again."

Nick grabbed me and gave me a terrific hug. "Don't worry. You'll see or hear anyone coming."

"So what? I'm going to yell at them?"

"No. You're going to use the rifle I packed. You didn't think I was coming out to partridge country without my rifle, did you?" He kissed me quickly and went to get it. Then it was a flurry of him leaving. We were careful not to make extra tracks, although Nick brought the grub we'd hurriedly packed up to the cabin.

Nick set off, and Jeremiah and I tried to make ourselves as comfortable as possible, considering the company we kept. I got the fire going strongly without the need of an axe. We took water, a pot for the stove, some black tea, and tin cups from the grub kit. I found store-bought cookies in Shirleen's cupboard. I was careful not to touch any surfaces that might hold prints. We brought other chairs to put around the wood stove and tried to ignore the third person at the tea party.

It would likely take Nick an hour and a half to get back to North West River, find Renaud, and return with a posse. Jeremiah and I spent about half an hour futzing about; we had at least another hour to wait. I thought I'd better come up with conversational ploys—if only because Jeremiah was looking nervous. A scrawny kid about 17 or 18 in his last year at high school, he wore glasses that must have been of a strong prescription, since his eyes swam hugely behind them. He had acne, and he wore his hair below his ears. He would be handsome in a few years, but right now gawky was the best one could say of his appearance.

"Have you directed before, Jeremiah?"

"Nope. But I don't like acting, and I always have ideas of how the players could make it better, so Mr. T thought I should give it a try."

"*Hamlet* is a beautiful and powerful play, probably the most popular play of all time. We talked yesterday about Pashin's rewrite, but I imagine you'll work together to make something that can be staged."

"Pashin has good ideas, but I told her before Mr. T nixed it that we'd have to make it simple enough, or no one would do it."

"Have you read it?"

"Yes. I read it because Pashin wanted us to. He was bugging Mr. T for us to do it when Mr. T still wanted us to do *Romeo and Juliet*. Mr. T thought that we weren't ready for it, but Pashin said we couldn't be ready later because we'd all be out of school by then."

"Did you like it?"

"Yep."

"What was it you liked? I mean, it seems a far stretch from Sheshatshiu: a court in Denmark in the 1600s."

"I like Hamlet. He seems so sane and yet everyone thinks he is crazy. And his mother? That was some fucked-up shit. Uh ... sorry."

"No need to be, that's what I'd say too. It was fucked up. I always wondered why they thought it was okay for a wife to remarry so soon, but then I took a course in Women's Studies." I saw Jeremiah cringe. I ignored it. "It helped me understand that part of *Hamlet*. Women in Shakespeare's time had no power, not even the queen. She owned no land—no means of surviving without a husband, really." I looked up, but Jeremiah didn't respond. "I've seen lots of people here get married right after their partner dies, or they get divorced."

Jeremiah nodded. "Ya, well I kinda get why Pashin wanted to do this play. I mean, his family got really messed up. His father died, and his mother married her husband's cousin."

"What was Pashin's father like?"

"Gerard? He was great. He was the chief for a while before he got sick, and he was really good at it. He was always trying to get everyone organized about things going wrong in the community. Like health shit and Otter Falls and like that."

"And the cousin, Pashin's stepfather?" I smiled, leaning into the *Hamlet* analogy. "Did he have political aspirations?"

"Maybe, but nothing happened. Everyone knew he was a douche."

"How come Pashin lives with his sister, or his aunt? Why not his mother?"

"Because his mother killed himself."

Duh. I had known that. I'd heard Pashin's story, but I'd forgotten it. His mother had hanged herself.

"Right. I forgot. Sorry. I can't remember what happened to the guy she married. Is he still around?"

"Ya, he has a house in Shesh and an apartment in Goose. He's got money, always wheeling and dealing. He only comes to Shesh to lord it about."

I thought I'd better get back to the conversation about *Hamlet* before Jeremiah guessed that I was grilling him.

"Since we have some time on our hands, why don't we look at the script. Even if Pashin's script is radically altered, he'll need to have the bones of it in there somewhere."

I had the script and the notes on roles from the audition the night before, so we looked at which roles were left to be filled and who might fill them, and which parts could be doubled or eliminated. We had worked for 20 minutes or so, when we both heard a motor. It was way too early for anyone Nick had alerted to get here. We both scurried to the door, Jeremiah grabbing the rifle on the way, but holding it so that it couldn't be seen by anyone looking up from the water.

I didn't recognize the guy on the boat at first, but then I saw his face and realized that it was Bobby Saunders, a North West River fellow who did odd jobs for folks. He'd turned the motor off but made no move to get out of the boat.

"Hi." His brow was creased in confusion. "Isn't Shirleen here?"

I had to think fast, and I preferred taking my time. Did I want to tell him that Shirleen was inside the cabin, dead? I did not, because then he would have the opportunity to act all surprised (or actually be all surprised). I wanted to see if he was expecting to be surprised. I caught Jeremiah's eye and gave him a steely glance that said I was sure he'd understand. "No. Nick and I came by because Sergeant Renaud needed her to sign something time-sensitive, and he drove her back to North West. He's bringing her right back. I'm surprised you didn't see them on your way here."

"Shit! No, I didn't see them. I came out earlier to pick up something at my cabin farther on in the Islands. Her niece left a message for me on the phone. Guess I wasted all this time coming out for her." He looked ready to turn the ignition and head out. "She'll still be on the hook for it."

The Islands were the North West Islands. An appealing enclave of cabins was there with a gorgeous view of Mokami Mountain. I believed that Bobby didn't know. Which niece had phoned? Shirleen had a pack of them. Maybe whoever killed her planned on using Bobby, so they'd have someone "discover" the body without too much bother. Someone who wouldn't know that she hadn't just keeled over. Made perfect sense. And the niece? Have to look into that story.

"You didn't bring her out here?"

"No. Apparently someone was bringing her on the way to their own cabin. I didn't ask who and her niece didn't say. Not my business. Why?"

I realized that I should limit my questions because he'd wonder why I just didn't ask her. Plus, it wasn't my business, or it wouldn't have been if she wasn't dead. Subterfuge was tricky.

"Uh ... just that she was in a hurry to do what the sergeant wanted that she didn't say, and I'm curious. Doesn't seem like anyone else is out here." I looked out across the bay. This was too weird. "Do you want to wait?"

"No. I got other things to do back in North West. As long as you can take her home. Just tell her that I have to charge her regardless."

"I will. By the way, I'm so confused. Which niece called you?"

He laughed. "Beats me. It was a message left about noon yesterday. I've done it before, no big deal."

With that, he started up the motor again and headed toward North West. I wondered if he'd meet the police boat.

+++ Chapter 16

Forty minutes later, I had my answer. Nick returned with a doctor from the clinic. The police boat was right behind, with Renaud and Constables McLean and Hind. Renaud jumped ashore as I asked if he'd seen Bobby going back out.

"I sent one of the constables back with him. They are taking him into Goose to talk to Musgrave."

"Oh, Musgrave isn't coming out here?"

"No." Renaud grimaced. "No. I let him know, because of the possible connection to the Tuck case, but he said that till an obvious link was made, he'd prefer that it be handled locally—like any accidental death. And he had a teleconference with Ottawa that he didn't want to miss. Show me to the body, please, Constable Munro."

The respect and reverence in his tone caused my own sadness to rise, my breath caught in my throat. I quieted it by paying attention to the details of the examination. There'd be time for mourning later.

Where I had been tentative, the doctor was confident. With Renaud's help, he checked the body for signs of foul play. He noted her injection site and took a close look at the insulin kit.

"We'll have to get the body back to the hospital in Happy Valley so that we can do an autopsy. It might be connected to her diabetes, but I can't be sure without further investigation. I can't tell if she was too late with the injection or if she inadvertently overdosed, causing a diabetic coma and death. Whatever it was, there are no signs of struggle. We'll have to check her blood, organs, especially her lungs and stomach, to find out the amount of insulin in her system, before drawing any conclusions."

"Before you take the body, we'll dust for fingerprints on the glass, on the kit, on everything." Renaud's tone implied that he was not about to accept that this was accidental. "Of course, the cabin will be full of her fingerprints, but we should be able to tell if she drank willingly from this glass or was forced."

Everything was dusted and gone over while we stood around outside, shivering. Once all the prints had been taken and the glass and diabetes kit bagged, it was time to move the body. Renaud and I wrapped her up using the quilts we found stored in plastic bins and put her in the police boat. Constable Hind would stay and keep the scene secure until a full team came out.

✦

We were all back at the detachment in less than an hour—all but the doctor and the body, which were met by the ambulance at the dock. News had gotten out, and if we thought there would be an uproar about an Innu boy being fingered for the first murder, a good Innu woman being found dead in unusual circumstances caused all hell to break loose. Renaud left us to fill out endless paperwork, to drive to Goose, a look of terrible resignation etched on his face.

The boy waited until he heard the men leave. They'd only stayed a short time, the creep telling the other one that he had to get back to the hotel. He knew that what he'd heard was important, and so he whispered it in the rhythm he'd been given by the dream. He felt the words being pounded into his memory by the caribou, the grouse. Who should he tell about what he'd overheard? He could only think of one person. He slipped out the same window he'd come in through, closing it carefully behind him. He made sure not to leave any tracks, using brush to sweep the snow clean like his father had taught him when they were hunting. He had his grandfather's drum, the very drum his grandfather had used to bring him here. He was sure that the creep wouldn't realize that it was gone. The creep wouldn't even have known it was there. He'd had his dreams. He was called—simple as that. Now it was time to drum.

Wednesday, November 4

+++ Chapter 17

When I walked into the Goose Bay detachment, I saw the receptionist, Tina, tighten her lips. I knew that she'd been friends with Shirleen, or at least chatty with her, fellow colleagues who conferred often on the phone. But why the pursing? I'd known her ever so casually since I'd started with the force. Might as well approach her, since she was willing to show her emotions so freely.

"Hi, Tina. I wondered if Sergeant Musgrave was in?"

"He's not a sergeant anymore. He's been made staff sergeant."

If Musgrave had achieved staff sergeant, he wasn't going to be here much longer. He'd likely be getting the transfer he wanted. I wondered if he'd stay long enough to see this investigation through.

"That's wonderful news. I'm sure you were a big help to him, Tina. Can I go in and congratulate him?"

Tina bobbed her head with the pleasure my remarks gave her, before she remembered something—probably that she was to keep pesky CCs away. "Actually, he's in a meeting right now."

I was about to slink over to the plastic chairs and wait it out, when my luck changed. Musgrave and two men came out from the back offices. They were laughing: out came Chesley McMaster and Murph Lee, two of the Big Eat four I'd hitched my lunch hour to yesterday.

Now it was Musgrave's turn to pinch his mouth at the sight of me. Why was I, a simple community constable, the source of so much obvious irritation? I might as well leap in—who knew what my blundering might uncover?

"I understand congratulations are in order, Staff Sergeant Musgrave. You must be so pleased. And to get it before this case is even wrapped up!"

McMaster and Lee looked at me with unconcealed surprise, taking stock. Looking at their faces, veils were dropping from my innocent eyes. Why was Musgrave in bed with these slime buckets if it wasn't to feather their nest, along with his own?

"Do you have something to report, Community Constable Munro, or are you merely playing tourist in our midst?"

"Nothing to report, sir. I was just inquiring, as the youth liaison, about the conditions of Pashin's release so that I can make sure he stays out of jail, sir." For that was, indeed, why I had come, or at least why Renaud had given me permission to come. Musgrave had let Pashin go last night.

"Why don't you come back to my office?"

His tone implied that it wasn't a request. Musgrave waved his civilian visitors away in a curt but friendly manner (was he warning them not to say more, although they'd said nothing?) and turned on his heel. I followed like the good woof-woof that I was. He closed the door as I took a seat. "Would you care to explain your overt disrespect toward me out there, Constable? And in front of two of the leading citizens of this town? I have heard of your maverick tendencies, and

I'm afraid it's not a trend I can support."

"I'm not sure what you mean, sir? I congratulated you on your promotion."

"Do you think that I'm stupid, Constable? I heard your tone and some implication regarding this investigation, and I don't like it."

"I'm sorry if I had a tone, sir. I wasn't aware of it. I'm wondering why you care what those two think, Staff Sergeant Musgrave."

It was like flashing a red rag to a bull and, although I knew it would bring trouble, I enjoyed it.

He smiled, tightly and quickly. "I'm not sure where this disrespect is coming from. I'd like to remind you that insubordination is a serious charge." He seemed to execute some calculation in his mind before he spoke again. "I'm going to accept that you are saddened by the death of your colleague Shirleen and that you have yet to master managing such grief within a professional setting." He watched me, daring me to make an irrevocable move.

The feeling that had come over me was not helpful for what I wanted to accomplish. I wanted to rein myself in. After all, Musgrave had done nothing wrong. It was just a feeling that had been festering for a while, and the sight of him smirking with those two jerks had annoyed the hell out of me. I had to remember that people needed me to keep it together—like Pashin. I mustered my best look of gratitude. "I'm sorry, sir. Not sure what came over me. Of course, I'm concerned about Shirleen's murder, and I considered Jay Tuck a friend—"

Musgrave interrupted me, his voice icy. "Constable, the only information we have to date is that the death of Shirleen Gregoire is undoubtedly an accident. And we have nothing at all linking it to the death of Jay Tuck."

My anger spiked again. I took a deep breath. I didn't need this job. I could work as a counsellor on the reserve whenever I wished, but it did afford me certain power to make changes that my former job did not. I tried a different tack. "I wonder if you could let me know about the status of the crooked knife I brought in, sir?" Waiting for his response, I felt complete futility.

He leaned forward, made an easy gesture, as if to confide in me. "You know, Nell, I think, but unfortunately can't prove that you brought that crooked knife in to obstruct this investigation. There were no prints on it. And the blood was a different type than Tuck's."

I strove to retain composure. "I wouldn't do that, sir." But the drug of speaking truth to power was irresistible. "I don't think the Band Council will be happy with how this investigation is being managed. I was put in place because they trust the work I do. In the last few days, you've gravely endangered any trust the Innu have in the police department with the unconventional choices you've made. They're already furious that you hauled in Pashin on such skimpy evidence. If you ignore the murder of Shirleen Gregoire, you'll have a protest on your hands—to begin with."

Musgrave's hands pressed white against his desk and the heat rose in his face. "I think you have mistaken who I answer to, Constable. It isn't the Band Council of Sheshatshiu." He smiled as if this were the quaintest suggestion he'd ever heard. "I'll be talking to Sergeant Renaud shortly to discuss your conduct and what might be done about it. Tread carefully. I'm confident that, despite your inflated view of what the Innu think of you, it will take no time at all to erase your presence in the community."

✦

I drove back home slowly, lost in thought. Sergeant Renaud was waiting at the detachment and didn't look happy. I immediately felt repentant.

"Well, you've done it now, Constable. You're in Staff Sergeant Musgrave's bad books with your big mouth, and there's nothing I can do about it."

Why hadn't I buttoned my lip? Being defiant hadn't helped anyone. Better that I had put that energy into solving these murders, one way or the other. "What's going to happen to me?"

"The sergeant would like you to be put on suspension, but that involves too much paperwork and administrative hassles for everyone, so I convinced him that you'd be taking a stress leave. We left it open-ended. Musgrave has more important things to do right now, so if you lay low for a while, we can see you through this. And don't think for a minute that the Innu Band Council will help. They have bigger fish to fry, which you should have damn well thought about before you went rogue."

"What do I do now?"

"First of all, consider why you think the death of Shirleen is not an accident. I happen to agree with you, but I know better than to march into an office without having documented evidence to prove my feelings. If you believe that it was not an accident, back it up with further work to convince me first, and Musgrave second, that the deaths of Jay Tuck and Shirleen are connected."

Oh fuck! Of course, the reason I'd connected the two was because of the fact that I knew Shirleen had been at the sweat and was committed to finding out how Jay had been killed, but I'd given my word to Johnny not to reveal the gathering to anyone. And even if I could tell Renaud about the meeting, I didn't think he'd accept it as a reason to connect the two deaths. All right, challenge accepted. I'd figure this out if it killed me.

"Hand in your gun and go home. Get into your civvies. Then get out in the community and talk to anyone who doesn't care that you don't have a badge or a uniform anymore. And phone any updates in to me on a landline. Got it?"

I handed in my gun, which didn't tear me up like it does the police you see on television. I didn't like my gun. I'd rather use my mouth or, if pressed, my feet and hands. I thought about who I wanted to see. This might be a blessing in disguise.

+

Nick was surprised to see me home mid-afternoon and even more surprised when I told him I was on a stress leave and why.

"I knew that mouth of yours would get you into hot water." At least he accompanied it with a grin.

"Luckily, I love hot water. It's my favourite place to be. Besides, I might find out more without my uniform than with it."

"True!" He watched me as I started to change, following me into the bedroom. When I pulled my head out of my vest, I saw that he was stripping too.

"Whoa! What do you think you're up to?"

"I'm up to no good. The only possible way you can assuage my terrible anxiety about the trouble you're in is to take me in your arms for a little afternoon—"

"No! Don't say it. I'll do anything you want but don't say those words!"

"Okay, I won't. As long as you jump into that bed, I'll not say the words *afternoon delight*. Whoops!"

"Gah," was the last word I spoke for a while.

✦

After a pleasant interlude, I made a list of who I wanted to see, and hit the road. The first were Jenny Black, the doctor that Shirleen once worked for; Lucy Goodeye; and Lonesome Johnny.

Jenny Black was at her house in North West River. She was an expansive woman, in nature and in physicality. Tall and firmly built, she wore her grey hair in a long braid down her back. She embodied warmth and individuality. Colourful Guatemalan weavings hung on her walls alongside children's drawings, matted and framed in bright colours. In front of a massive fireplace stood a reclining chair with furs piled on it.

Jenny, a come-from-away who has worked in Labrador since she graduated from medical school, was passionate about the Innu and the land, often too passionate. She'd fought a tough fight trying to get the community to embrace more healthy practices, but that was hard to do without being seen as another colonizing know-it-all. She'd pushed for breast-feeding (complicated when babies were being snatched at the hospital by Family Services), nutrition, and educating the population on the likelihood of having babies born on the fetal alcohol disorder spectrum if mothers wouldn't, or couldn't, stop drinking.

It was an exhausting and heart-breaking job, but what had completely burnt her out was when the Lower Labrador Project was proposed. Jenny campaigned heavily against the project, as any right-minded individual would do. The idiocy and greed of the government and companies involved was staggering. Jenny focused on how the project could, and likely would, affect food security for Labradorians; the methylmercury contamination would poison the water table, the rivers, and Melville Lake itself and taint traditional foods such as salmon and seal. Nobody knows for certain, but after years of writing letters to the editors, being interviewed for her opinion on CBC, and talking at any round table she could get herself on, Jenny shut up. Her silence lasted about six months, after which she stopped doctoring. Now she runs a catering company, which she says she loves.

"Sit down." She pointed to the chair. "I'm going to treat you."

It was pointless to protest. She was a heady mixture of enthusiasm and withdrawal. Like the tide, like the blood in our veins, she was all diastole and systole. Now she was riding the expansive wave of her personality: welcoming, nurturing, warming, and including. Another day, like Bob Dylan, she might be in hiding, being sulky, withdrawn, and cool. I was glad I'd caught this side of her today.

Jenny wore a long skirt with a man's shirt. Silver rings adorned her fingers and her hands were big and square. She wore hide moccasins, heavily beaded, and her braid was gathered up with a large heron-like beaded clasp. It would be easy to assume that she had Indigenous heritage, but she was quick to tell folks that she was mostly of Irish and French stock. Despite her agenda, the Innu community accepted her because they knew that she was authentic in everything that she did.

The living room and kitchen were all one. She was busy cooking up something, or *somethings*, in the kitchen area. I saw trays of yummy bits—must be a cocktail party in the works. She insisted that since I'd arrived so close to dinner (as they call lunch, hereabouts) that I must be her guinea pig and try some of the food she was preparing for an event in Goose Bay. I moved from the lounge chair to the big wooden table. I was too much of a slob to try her delicacies while reclining. She made up a plate for me with several appetizers: pigs in a blanket, spinach fritters, and lovely stuff wrapped in thin rice paper with a peanutty hot sauce. It was scrumptious, and it did calm my fevered brain.

"What's up? I take it you didn't know I was cooking today, or maybe you did by the way your eyes lit up."

"Just a lucky perk of today. I need to understand more about Shirleen. I knew that she had diabetes but not what her care of it entailed."

Jenny eased her weight into a kitchen chair. "Fairly common in the community. Taking away a people's ability to eat natural foods— caribou, salmon, and so forth—and keep them poor and uneducated is a surefire way to end up with three times the likelihood of contracting diabetes. Shirleen was smart about it. She hardly ever ate her own doughnuts."

"Knowing Shirleen as well as, or maybe even better than, anyone in this community ..." I caught Jenny's eye before I finished my question, "do you think she would have taken an overdose of insulin on purpose or by accident?"

Jenny's face hardened. "Neither. She wasn't remotely suicidal and she was, as you well know, extremely particular, as she would say, OCD to the rest of us, which makes an accidental overdose highly unlikely."

"Okay. I understand your reasoning, but why would anyone murder Shirleen?" I looked deeply into her eyes when I asked this one, and she flinched in obvious pain.

"My fault, I think."

"What!"

"I don't mean I murdered her. I mean that I got her all fired up about Otter Falls and the Lower Labrador Project." She put her head in her hands. She looked tired. "She was happy being a good member of her community and living a healthy life, but I got her going. I politicized her, and when she took to activism, it endangered her. Why do you think I gave up doctoring? I was threatened at every step once they realized how serious I was. When I quit it all—the doctoring, protests at the falls, looking into methylmercury poisoning—it broke Shirleen's heart. She fought with me about it, but I was done. I felt I'd caused more people harm than good with all my fighting. And the kids, they were the ones that were most at risk. Shirleen said I was full of shit. She said I hadn't caused the problems, and I wouldn't fix them on my own, but to quit was a terrible thing. It showed I'd lost faith in what was important. I was over my magical thinking. We agreed to disagree."

I gathered that what Jenny meant was that she may have quit, but Shirleen hadn't. "How far in was she?"

"Very far." Jenny became quiet. "I'm not going to talk about this any further. There's more at stake, and I feel responsible enough. I'm sorry, Nell, but you're on your own."

What could I think? She was frightened. Was this what happened to Jay Tuck? Had he given up the fight but left it too late? What were these people scared of that they hadn't already battled?

"Jenny, I'm not sure what's going on, but two people have died and they were both friends of yours and mine. You might not wish to talk to me or anyone right now, but you *will* talk sooner or later. I'm going to leave now and do more investigating, but the time for withdrawing is over. If you know something, it's time to let it out."

Shortly after, I was out on the porch going over what just happened. I knew that I couldn't push her any further, but perhaps the sergeant could. I'd have to point him in this direction. Meanwhile, I was off to see Lucy.

✦

Lucy Goodeye lived in Sheshatshiu. I hadn't seen her since the night of the sweat. She worked part-time for the Band Council—in the Social Welfare Department, I believed. I went to her home first, but she wasn't there, so I headed over to the Council offices. They were open but deserted.

"Anyone here?" I called from the empty reception area.

A woman's voice called out from the back, so I went on through. It was Lucy. She was on the phone in her small but neat office. She gestured for me to sit down, so I grabbed the only available chair: a folding one made for camping. I lowered myself gingerly onto it, waiting to see if it was going to break and send me to the floor.

"Hey, Nell, what's up?"

"Lucy, why did you folks have me come to the sweat?"

Lucy looked at me with a stony expression. "Shirleen pushed for you to come to the sweat. She'd been after that for ages. Johnny took a chance, hoping that the last time would be good. I don't know what she expected. She just thought you might help. Me, I don't get why we depend on white people at all."

"I get that." I gave her the same straightforward look she was giving me. "Was Tuck part of your ... ah ... group? Like, those of you who meet at sweats?"

"Do you mean the Crooked Knife Society?"

Crooked Knife Society? How stupid I'd been. They'd brought me to their meeting and let me know what they wanted and I still hadn't realized how organized they were. Hell, I hadn't even realized they had a name. I managed a nod, and Lucy went on.

"Yes. But we have a split in the group. Some of them, including Tuck, want to go slow. Fine for him. He was white. Some of us are tired of being patient while we get screwed by both our own people and settlers." Lucy kept her eyes steady on mine, her mouth a grim line.

"Okay, I get it. So why should you trust me, right? Only Shirleen did, and I'd like to find out what happened to her. I mean, who'd kill her? I can't see it for the life of me, but I know it wasn't an accident or suicide."

"Oh ya, how do you know that?"

"Because of evidence taken at the crime scene, which I'm not at leave to disclose."

"Right. Oh well."

This was going nowhere, but if nowhere was where we had to go, I was willing. I noticed Lucy's fancy nails and took a chance. "You and Shirleen both went to Brenda's Beauty Spot to get your hair and nails done, right?"

"Why?"

"Because I see Brenda too. She's a bigmouth that likes to keep in the know. I want to know what she's been talking about—if she mentioned Shirleen to you."

Lucy softened a little—if begrudgingly. "Even if she has to stand on a stool to cut hair, Brenda is a good hairdresser. And she's great with gels and shellacs, too." Lucy's nails were done in what looked like chrome. It was gorgeous against her dark skin and silver jewellery.

Brenda Petrie was about 4.5 feet tall and as opinionated as a person could get. Nick called her a "gossipy banty hen" and couldn't figure out why I went to her. Maybe because in North West River, as far as a beauty technician went, she was it.

"I'd like to know what people were saying about Shirleen. Or what she'd been saying to others."

"Shirleen didn't gossip."

"Yes, I know that. But I also know that Brenda can get details out of even diehard anti-gossips like Shirleen. I know that because I've been had by her a few times. I'm trying anything I can to find out what the hell is going on in Sheshatshiu that's causing some to go all quiet and others to go dead."

"Okay."

I could tell that Lucy was working through some shit. She must have decided to let me in a smidge, because she kept going.

"Brenda said that she was worried about Shirleen. I told her that if she was truly worried, she should bake her a pie or charge less on her next appointment. I only said that cause I'm sick and tired of people saying they are, quote, 'worried' about people and then never doing anything about it. What does that mean? Usually, it's that they want to give their opinion on what someone else has been up to.

"After I said the pie thing, Brenda got all snippy and said that I didn't know squat about shit, that Shirleen was in big trouble, and that she should quit hanging out with those—and I quote—'shit-disturbers that don't like Otter Falls.' There was nothing wrong with the Lower Labrador Project and 'you people' hadn't been so all-fired concerned when BECorp was handing out big cheques, so what right did we have all of a sudden to be all precious with our land and our water?"

"Really? Looks like I'll be cutting my own damn hair from now on." My joke landed and Lucy cracked a smile.

"You do on occasion, don't you?" she shot back. I laughed, and she joined me. "I think I'm done going there too, honestly. It just costs so much to get my nails done in Goose."

"I'm sorry that she made that stupid 'you people' comment." And I was. I was sick to death of the utter predictability of people.

"Oh, forget about it. If I got mad at every narrow, racist remark that one of *you people* said ..." Her grin told me she was kidding. "Truthfully, many people on both sides of the river don't understand why we Innu took the deal. Brenda has no inner regulator; she says whatever shit floats to the top of her head. Besides, her new boyfriend works at Otter Falls, so she hates anything said against it. And there are sleaze-balls here in Sheshatshiu who do take advantage of the lefties to further their own goals."

"Was Shirleen in danger—I mean, did you or others think she was in danger?"

"I don't know. I guess not, or I would've done something about it. I know that she brought up some issues she felt strongly about at an open Band Council meeting—stuff about Otter Falls, and in particular, the methylmercury. She was shut down very quickly."

"Who shut her down?"

"Oh, there's a whole crowd that doesn't want anyone ruining the money tree for them, and half of them don't even live on the reserve. Some of them have their noses so far up BECorp's ass you could mushroom farm on them. I mean people like Frank Andrews: he acts like he's some big-deal Innu businessman when everyone knows he's just a low-life drug dealer. He's one of a few people who will sit on any board that needs a token Innu so that they can make money for doing nothing. Fucking traitors."

I'd heard about Innu who didn't want change, but would they

hurt their own? "Did it work? Did she stop talking at meetings?"

"Shirleen said she knew that the Band Council had worked hard to overcome the early days of graft and corruption. She told them that she thought they'd done fairly well, but till they were willing to clean house, she was wasting her time. Said she was going to try other avenues—that's what she said: 'Other avenues.'"

"She must have been some fed up to say that."

Lucy looked at me with resignation on her face. Then her face changed—the skin around her eyes tightened, and her eyes glittered like mica. She sighed heavily before she spoke again with a force that felt like weight.

"Shirleen was sick and tired of what was going on. She was sick of mega-dams going onto land our ancestors had walked upon and a government that goes back on every promise. She was sick of the Innu getting a bad deal and sick of the government thinking that it could throw money at a reserve and forget about its every other honest need. She was sick of the pipeline and big oil and big power and tiny brains run by even tinier penises. She'd had the friggin' biscuit. And then the real trouble started."

I nodded for her to go on.

"Every time the Crooked Knife Society made any advancement, something horrible would happen to the kids or those who took care of them. There was a sexual assault: a young Innu woman—hell, she's a kid. They left a crooked knife beside her once they'd finished raping her. There's an old lady here who ran a little store—not even cigarettes, just candies and such. Someone found out that she let her store be used for a CK meeting and they destroyed it. People say it was kids—vandals—but a crooked knife was left there, too. It's a taunt, or maybe whoever left it is trying to shift the blame to the Innu. Hard to say. So far there's four of these instances that we know about. Who knows who might have been threatened but didn't tell. As well, some of us think that there's been an increase in kids being taken out of their homes by Family Services. The rumour is that someone is making false allegations. It's a sure way to keep the community messed up. What we know is the tip of the iceberg."

"Can you tell me the name of the Innu girl who was assaulted?"

"Crystal Berry. She's 15."

"I know Crystal. She dropped out of school this year. Was it because of this?"

"Yes. She was an easy mark, and I think they just wanted to show what they were capable of. The poor kid was devastated. Frightened and without support. Her parents are both drunks. I heard a rumour that she might be on opioids. Opioids! What the hell is happening here? It's always been a hell realm, but now it's much worse. Do you know what happens to these kids on opioids—OxyContin, white drum, whatever they call it? They mix these depressants with booze and then they stop breathing. West of here—Nova Scotia, Ontario, the Prairies, and the west coast—it's a living nightmare. Zombies for real. Whole reserves are dealing with it; they're in a state of emergency. Those drugs have been around for a while, obviously, but not with the kids. Just recently, kids have been showing up with them. We thought maybe it was a random few, but as you know there's cancer in the community, so there can be access to drugs like hydromorphone and OxyContin, or maybe they picked them up in the city, but this is much bigger and darker than that. There's plenty of altered street drugs, even Fentanyl, being sold *here*. It's lethal. The parents are getting it too, and soon enough they're either dead or too stoned to care about anything anymore. They won't care about Otter Falls or their own children."

Lucy was preaching to the choir on that issue. I'd done plenty of training in the last few years on the horrors of opioids. "But what does this have to do with Shirleen's death, or Jay's for that matter?"

"Who knows. Some of the CK want to go public, and some want to go slow. Political groups get broken up by outside forces all the time. Like in a union, for example, management will poach members to defect with the promise of lifting them into management positions—turning like against like. Some of us have asked if maybe it's been happening with our group, like it is the Band Council, since whoever's committing these attacks knows about CK. We Innu are easy to tempt; we're hungrier than most and get tired trying to do things the 'correct' way. You only came to the first part of the meeting Sunday night. We wanted to sound you out before we told you more. Shirleen said that she needed to figure out something before acting on information she'd received. We asked if it had to do with Tuck's murder, and she said she wasn't sure. She told us that it could be dangerous to make assumptions right now, and that was all she'd share. She wanted us to be careful, as no one was free of suspicion."

Lucy vibrated with emotion. She pushed her arms out to the sides as if pushing against a strong wind. "Some people want Sheshatshiu

JAN MORRISON

to be in a constant state of chaos. Many are making money off misery and ignorance. They run the elections and protect the drug dealers." She looked me in the eye. "We think Shirleen must have discovered something in her work at the detachment."

This was the third time I'd caught a whiff of something corrupt about the force. I nodded. "Okay. I'm going to find Crystal and talk to her. Thanks for this. I know you've gone out on a limb here, and I'll protect you as much as I can. Can you tell me the name of the woman who owned the little store?"

"Elizabeth Nighthawk. Don't bother protecting me. They'll find out what I'm doing. I refuse to stop. Killing Shirleen was a turning point for me. I'd rather be dead than put up with this shit."

My heart broke. I could feel tears like cement, wanting to loosen and flow, but anger made them hard, and that hardness hurt my chest. I felt like exploding or breaking apart. What could I do? What could any of us do?

But despair wouldn't help. "Your group brought me into this when you had me attend the sweat. It's not like I can bust anyone or shoot the bad guys. Why me? I'm just a dumb white chick who loses her temper when she needs to keep it most. I am so close to Vesuvius-ing here."

Lucy grimaced. "It's only because of Shirleen that I'm trusting you. Neither I nor any other Crooked Knife member holds any hope with the other police officers. You say Renaud is good, but I don't know it. The police haven't protected our kids. Do your best, but I don't hold any hope."

I believed that my best wouldn't change a thing. I went off to see Johnny and added Crystal and Mrs. Nighthawk to my list of those to visit this afternoon.

✦

Johnny answered my shout from the front door, telling me to come into his workroom off the kitchen. He was working on another carving. Sedna sat on a large, low shelf that ran along the window. This carving, of three people of indeterminate gender holding the body of a fourth, was being carved out of serpentine, a dark green rock. The three standing figures had bowed heads and defeated postures. The fourth was definitely a woman's, a young woman, vulnerable in death. I stood there looking at the piece, overwhelmed with sadness.

Johnny smiled at me. "The body is the Innu people, and the forms around it are hope, love, and compassion. They're bowed but not broken, and if you notice this detail," he touched the young woman's hand where it rested on the arm of another, "you'll see that she's still alive."

I hadn't noticed the hand, so cleverly had Johnny placed it. "I'm speechless, Johnny. It's so beautiful and tragic. Is it being shown somewhere?"

"It's part of a large group show that will be at The Rooms in St. John's. It's for their permanent collection."

"I had no idea that your art was so popular. Is that the right word? The Rooms—that's the big time, isn't it?"

"Yes, well, I'm riding a wave right now. Who knows where it will deposit me. I've fought against the corporate art scene for years, but I've decided to see if working within the system will make a difference. Probably be called a sellout, eh? We Aboriginals are the in thing right now. I'm not complaining, but I'm suspicious of my own rise to fame. Is it me or my DNA?"

He said it with a sly look. I knew he was mostly kidding, but I didn't doubt that his new identity would be tricky. Getting used to being wanted after being Lonesome Johnny was a leap.

As Johnny put away his carving tools, he wrapped each one in a piece of stroud to keep its sharpness, I imagined. My memory twigged on something, but then I lost the thought. "I'm thinking you didn't come to talk art with me, Nell. What's up? I'm not harbouring any criminals today—I wouldn't do that to you twice."

"You didn't do anything but trust me, and they took him anyway. I heard that he was given back into your care."

"Uh, technically correct, but he's over at one of his sisters' or aunt's."

"I'm not looking for him. I'm on a mandated stress leave due to being obnoxiously mouthy, so I'm doing a little quiet talking with folks. I wanted to know if you could tell me why a woman like Shirleen would be killed? And what was your hope for my involvement in the sweat? I think the time for hidden agendas is over."

Johnny grinned. "Oh, you're going rogue, huh? We were trying to send you a message so that you'd know that there was a group watching out for you. I'm sorry you're on leave ... unless?" He looked up from his carving table after placing all his tools meticulously in a small, tabletop cabinet. He stroked the sculpture, which was about 3 feet long and 2 or so feet high and then gestured toward the living room.

"It's just for a few weeks and it might be a good thing." We both settled into comfortable chairs. "So why not tell me right out? Why all the smoke and mirrors?"

"Because we had to be sure of you and your intentions. It's too dangerous for those who aren't fully in. Look at what happened to Jay Tuck."

"What *did* happen to Jay? Seriously, I'd like to know. All I know so far is that he was killed. Nothing else. How important a role did he play in the Crooked Knife Society?"

"He was one of the major players. He started the society with Shirleen. A few weeks ago, he asked to be released. We told him that that was fine. He knew that if he told anything we were capable of taking action. I think that something caused him to pull back but he hadn't lost hope like Pashin said. Maybe he just thought that his interest was a little dangerous."

"Dangerous to him?"

"Oh, I wouldn't think that would stop him. He seemed to have a bottomless supply of personal courage."

"Is it possible that someone in your group felt that Jay needed to go because he wasn't ... 'fully in'?"

Johnny nodded as though he'd been expecting this question. "I don't know. Truly, I don't think so, but, like any groups that centres around social action, we have divisions, and those divisions are played on by external forces."

Complicated and complicated. I needed to get back to basics. "What is the point of the Crooked Knife Society? I mean, there's already the Land Protectors and the River Keepers."

"Yes, but they're purely environmental activists, and they are public—aboveground. We wanted to go deeper—to find out what we could do to stop the group that's trying to keep us in chaos, those harming our kids and stopping those who would help. It arose after the decision to dam Otter Falls. One of the issues we've been fighting for is that the Aurora Agreement might not be legally binding, since information was withheld from the community on its likelihood of contaminating our fishing and hunting areas. Not as many Innu as you might imagine think that their leaders made the right decision. That led to conversations around the methylmercury contamination, health, youth, drugs, and suicide. Indivisible issues. Do you think we'd have invited you if we were taking the law into our own hands?"

"No. I had to ask. I trust you. I trust Pashin. I trust Lucy and I trusted both Shirleen and Jay. So I guess I'm fully in."

Johnny looked at me. "You *guess*?"

"I'm in."

+++ Chapter 18

Crystal Berry was home, such as it was. She belonged to the lower classes in Sheshatshiu. A reserve has a strict class system. The main families held positions of power on the Band Council, as well as all the other arms of the reserve government. They obtained the good houses and if their kids needed to go to treatment somewhere, those kids moved to the front of a very long line. If they wanted a job or a job for one of their extended family, they got it. Everyone, including any whites attached to the reserve through work or otherwise, sided with the hierarchy. The Berrys had either come on the scene late or had done something to make them untouchables.

The yard was paved in garbage and two Ski-Doo carcasses had been stripped to their bones for parts. The one window that wasn't boarded up had a crack in it. I knocked with some trepidation, steeling myself.

Crystal came to the door. Once a beautiful girl, she now looked ravaged. Her skin had a greenish pallor and her clothes, although clean, hung on her thin frame. It looked like she had dressed in the dark: buttons didn't match up with their holes, mismatched socks, a blinding green and pink shirt, and faded plaid pyjama bottoms.

"Hi, Crystal. Do you remember me? We've met a few times. I

used to work at the school, but now I'm a community constable. My name is Nell. Can I come in?"

She looked behind her, as if someone would tell her what to do. No one there. "I don't know." She looked at her hand as if it were an unusual animal that she had never seen before. Then her eyes flicked up and she blushed. "Oh. Sorry, Miss. Yes, come in." All of this was said in tortuous tones with much blinking and nodding. Stoned as hell.

She went into the living room. It had an old, kid's bed in the corner and nowhere else to sit, so I grabbed a kitchen chair and brought it in. Other than the bed there was the requisite enormous television. It was on, with a reality show about four girls and a tattoo parlour. I didn't catch the drift, although it was plenty loud enough. And I was wrong about her being alone. On the floor was a toddler, about two years old I figured, with his fingers in his mouth and tears sliding down his cheeks.

"What's the matter, little buddy?"

"Nothing! He always looks like that. He's so stupid."

"Is he your brother?"

"Ya. Well, he's my half-brother, sort of. I take care of him because my mother is in the hospital. She's got cancer. She's supposed to come home tomorrow or the next day, I guess."

"Is anyone else living here?"

"My stepfather, only he works at Voisey's Bay, so he isn't here. And my other brother, who's my full brother, but he hardly ever comes home. He's mostly at his girlfriend's house."

"So you're taking care of this child all on your own?" And I thought, *fuck this world.*

"Well, yes. Who else?" And she started a long languorous scratch of her legs and her stomach. Sitting there on the ripped seat of a vinyl kitchen chair, I wanted to sleep. I felt like I could die of tiredness. Perhaps I would. I was infected by the despair that always threatened to consume these people. Why didn't the older ones do something? What could they do?

"Thanks for agreeing to talk to me, Crystal. I guess you know that Pashin was in jail, eh? We're worried about him. Don't you know Pashin?"

"Of course I know him. He always was kind to me. Even after it happened."

"What happened, Crystal?"

"Well ..." She stopped and stared at me, her face all soft and slightly stupid looking. She began another long lazy scratch of her legs and belly. Scratch, scratch, scratch. It drove me mad, but what could I do? I waited patiently. She started talking again, in slow motion.

"What happened? I was kind of drunk and out with some friends. We were looking for a draw—you know, dope—so we went up to this house where a friend lives who usually has some, but he didn't have anything and told us to fuck off. Not like him at all. So we kept going, even though it was getting late and all. We really wanted a draw. Then I saw a guy I knew over by the playground in front of the school, so I went over there and that's where it happened."

"Who's the guy that you knew?"

Crystal was a little quicker in her response to this question. Like she'd answered it a few times. "Uh ... I don't remember. Just a guy."

That door was closed. I guess I couldn't blame her. "What happened?"

"Uh ... the guy called some other guys I didn't know. They showed up in an old truck. When they came, the guy I knew just left, like that's what he was there for: to catch dumb-ass girls like me."

I nodded encouragingly.

"Ya, well my friend that I was hanging with just took off, but I didn't know why. I guess she did. They just did me right there. They didn't talk. It wasn't like, you know, a date rape or nothing. They didn't even seem like they liked it. It was like it was just a job. Then they hurt me. They did it up my ass and they kneed me in the belly and then they started kicking me till I passed out."

"How many guys?"

"Fuck, I don't know. I was stoned and drunk. Three or four, I guess. I was going to go to court, but my mother told me not to. That it would be better if I just shut up. I did get the morning-after pill though."

"You must have felt pretty bad. I think I'd have been sad and mad if that happened to me." I looked at her for a response, but no, just more of the vacant stare and the scratching. "Did you know who any of them were?"

"Nah. They were disguised, sort of. It was the end of last winter, like, May. Still plenty cold and lots of snow. They had those things that go over your face—those knitted things. I didn't recognize their voices or nothing, but I was so drunk and out of it. It was all my fault. That's what my mother said. That's what my brother said."

Breathe.

"Tell me about the crooked knife, Crystal."

She looked up from her hands, like she didn't know what I was talking about.

"Wasn't there a crooked knife left near where they assaulted you?"

"Ya, I forgot. They never used it on me, though."

"I know you didn't go to the police, because here I am not knowing about this attack, but who did you tell?"

"My mother had to tell my homeroom teacher, because I was out of school for a while. So she told him, I guess."

"Who's that?" Crystal looked confused. "Who was your homeroom teacher?"

"Mr. Tuck was. I don't go anymore anyway. No point. I'm useless."

"Look at me, Crystal."

And she did, like a deer or a dog when it's been run over and knows it's dying and wants you to make it better but isn't holding out much hope.

"This wasn't your fault. It wasn't okay for those guys to assault you. They were trying to scare the community, and they used you."

"That was stupid. No one cares about us Berrys anyway."

I suppose it was a response of sorts. I tried not to give in to my apathy or my rage. They were born from the same despair, and neither would be helpful right now. It wasn't as if I hadn't heard it before.

Heard it? I lived it when I was a dumb cluck of a kid. How did Nick see the good in me? It was hard for me to see the good in Crystal, and I'd been her in another life. Maybe that was the issue. I sat quietly and focused on compassion. When the toddler started crying, I realized that here was something I could do. No one would like it but this girl was seriously stoned and no one was watching this baby. I picked up the little guy. He had soaked through his diaper, and I was sure that he was hungry.

"I'm going to call Family Services now, Crystal. You shouldn't have been left with this baby. While I call, can you find some diapers? Did anyone leave anything for him to eat?"

I think, due to the major stone she was on, that she couldn't quite rouse a fighting response. She looked at me dimly, then at her little brother, and went to get the diapers in a room down the hall. She wasn't long but perhaps long enough to have another hit of whatever she was smoking. I had already reached Family Services, and someone would arrive in a few minutes. Sometimes you didn't want the shipping company and sometimes you did. I was relieved to have someone take over here.

"Uh ... when are they coming? I might go out. You know, just because."

"They'll be here soon. I'd wait for them. This isn't your fault. You're too young to be left with a baby, with no money or food or anything. No one's going to be mad at you, I promise."

Could I keep that promise? I wasn't sure, but she settled back down and nodded out.

"Crystal? Before they get here, just so I know how to protect you best, what are you on?"

She opened her eyes a slit, smiled, and scratched for a while. Then she nodded out again for a few minutes. When she awoke, I asked again.

"Crystal, what did you take? I need to know so I can get help. You seem very out of it."

"No big deal. Just weed. Honest. I don't feel so good though."

"Was it from someone you've gotten it from before or someone new? They might've laced it."

It occurred to me that a laced drug could have been accidental, or maybe someone was worried that Crystal would remember something.

"I don't remember. I'm going to sleep now." And she did. Just like that.

Moments later I had my naloxone kit out of my jacket pocket and administered the opioid antidote. Naloxone doesn't affect you if you don't have opioids in your system. Crystal woke swinging, which meant it was a good call. I managed to subdue her and called for the ambulance.

Just as they were taking Crystal out to the ambulance, Shania showed up. Thank goodness it was her. She scooped up the little guy, whose name I never did get. Shania would take the baby to her office to round up someone who would take on yet another child. She grabbed my arm before she left.

"You got to this situation at the right time, Nell. There could have easily been two corpses for what's left of this family to deal with. Honestly, I don't know how you knew to come here, but thank goddess you did."

✦

Mrs. Nighthawk was in her tiny home not far from the police station. With a face like an old wallet, she looked about 90. She was little, wizened, bent over like a candy cane, and full of fury. I could see it in her walnut eyes. She didn't care to let me in but I asked in a way that could not be refused by any old-timer in Labrador.

"May I come in?"

Sounds innocuous enough, but not if you know the history of Labrador. The settlers were, for the most part, trappers who spent months and months on their trapline and who, if they came to your door, you were completely obligated to host. They came bearing gifts like a little meat when times were lean or a story that might include a relative of yours on a trapline farther up. Your job was to give them a bed and a meal in whichever order they wished. You were also obligated to catch them up on any news you might have. The same was true for the Innu and the Inuit—both nomadic tribes—who depended on the kindness of those not in their own kinship pattern. You have to let folks in around here; it is profoundly rude not to. It took some getting used to when I first moved here. I was used to friends and family phoning first. You might be watching your favourite trashy TV show after a hectic day at work, settled in for a long evening's nap as it were, but come hell or high water you'd better put down your remote and fire up your kettle if someone came knocking. You are at your visitor's mercy.

Mrs. Nighthawk let me in and led me to her kitchen table. Her house was tiny, but compared to Crystal's family home it was the model of clean living. Every surface gleamed. The bright yellow and red check linoleum was buffed to a high polish that matched the shine on every table. The kettle was put on before I even had my shoes off. A brightly crocheted cozy with a fancy fluorescent orange and green flower on top sat next to the tiny teapot. I sat down on a bright red chair, and Mrs. Nighthawk fussed with the kettle and the teapot until everything was ready. I hadn't even told her my name at this point.

"Thanks so much, Mrs. Nighthawk. You might not remember me, but I met you a few years ago at the grand opening for Place to Be."

"I know who you are. You're Nell Munro and your man is Nick Wheeler. I knew his grandmother. Bella and I were as close as bandits back in the day."

"That's right. I never had the pleasure of meeting Bella. She was quite a force, I've heard."

"Sure she was. She was a fighter, that one. What can I do for you?"

"I'm trying to figure out what happened to Shirleen and to Mr. Tuck. I thought you might know something. I heard that you were attacked a while back?"

"Yes. Attacked. My little store was trashed and I was threatened."

"Are you okay to talk about it?"

"I don't know. The last time I talked I lost my store. What is it you want to know?"

"When you were attacked, did you recognize the assailants?"

Mrs. Nighthawk took her time answering. She checked the teapot and poured us both a cup, gesturing to the milk and sugar on the table. I kept my eyes on her while I took a sip. Freshly brewed and not boiled for ages—finally, a good cup of tea.

"I don't know. They wore orange coveralls and those knitted toques that cover your face. Balaclavas, I think they call them. They tied me to a chair using my own duct tape. They spoke in deep, forced voices that I didn't recognize. They told me that they were going to destroy my business and that I knew why. Then they did *that* in front of me. They shit on my floor when they were done knifing open the flour bags, tossing molasses all over everything, laughing and snorting, and carrying on. A third guy outside stopped people from coming in just by looking at them—or so I was told. People were too scared to ask what was happening. These guys took my tin of money and shot out anything they could be bothered with, including all my glass bottles. They said that kids who used to come to see me could now come to see them and get something better than candy. I didn't open again. Why would I? They said that they'd kill me next time, and I believe them."

"Did you go to the police? I don't remember."

"No. You can't clean off shit with more shit."

"I guess I belong to the more-shit club, but I'm trying. I'm trying to find out why a great kid like Pashin ends up being questioned over a friend's death. I keep trying to figure out why someone would kill a diamond of a woman like Shirleen, and I keep wondering why half the people most affected won't talk, while the other half won't shut up. It's a quandary but not your quandary." I got up and made my way to the door. "Oh, one more question. I heard they left a crooked knife. What did you do with it?"

"I took it to the sweat lodge. We burned it up and used the steel for other knives. Do you understand?"

"I think I do." Purifying and transforming the object of threat seemed a righteous move. "Thank you, Mrs. Nighthawk. You are a powerful woman. I'm honoured to meet you."

On that note, I left.

+++ Chapter 19

I regretted that we'd set up the first rehearsal for tonight, the night before Jay Tuck's funeral. I needed to process the information I'd gathered throughout the day, and I was unsure how the kids would be feeling so soon after the latest two deaths. The school was opened that morning for business as usual, but I'd already made arrangements with the Mary May Healing Centre.

When I got there, several of the students were waiting for me—including Pashin. He was deep in conversation with Jeremiah, Zann, and Kaitlyn. There were more kids present but not as many as I'd hoped. Before I got a chance to talk, Pashin approached me.

"Miss? Me and the others were just talking, and we wondered if we could put off a proper rehearsal till next week. A few of us would like to work on something for Mr. T's funeral tomorrow—a sort of tribute. We'd kinda like to do it on our own, if you don't mind, Miss?"

"Pashin, that's good. I've plenty to do, believe me. Michele is on the desk so he can let you out when you're done. He'll lock up. I'll let him know on my way out."

I made my way home, wondering what tribute the kids had in mind.

+

When I got home, it wasn't late but already dark. I remembered that Nick was going to be gone for the evening to see someone about his book, or maybe he was going to the *Them Days* office to access their archives. The quarterly *Them Days* has documented the oral, written, and visual history of Labrador since the early 1970s, a revered institution and a huge resource for those who write about the region. I made myself my favourite single-girl dinner: popcorn with Parmesan and cayenne liberally sprinkled on top and a dark and stormy. After that delightful repast, I took Beany for a walk on the beach. We had access to the beach through our yard: a chain-link fence separated our wooded lot from the sand and seagrass. A skiff of snow covered everything. Probably the Innu or the Inuit had a word that conjured that amount of snow, but I didn't know it.

The beach was dark, the sky clear with a sliver of a moon. Because it was supper hour, there were no other dog walkers in sight. Beany was off leash. One of the true treasures of living in a small village right on the beach was that we hardly ever had to have him on a lead.

It was always good to be on the beach. No matter the time of year or day, it was a beautiful sanctuary. Scanning the horizon, I was rewarded by a strange glimmer to the north. I either imagined northern lights when there are none in sight, or they are right there and I'm busily turning them into something else. This was the latter. My first thought, although I'd seen the crescent moon already, was that a full moon was rising. It appeared like a swirling cloud of smoke, except that a person knows that you can't see smoke against a night sky. Then I realized what it was. The cloud started undulating and the colour changed from white to a luminous green. The colours hung like organza curtains in the breeze and changed again, to a deep rosy hue like a not-quite-ripe plum. I'm not one of those people who thinks seeing the northern lights is ho-hum. Each time I see the northern lights, and it's been over a dozen times so far, I'm grateful for the sight. Gossamer silk fireworks without the bang but plenty of awe.

Beany was off on a chase. I found a log, brushed off the snow, and sat down to watch the show. Some like to whoop and holler and dance back at the lights, but that is not my way. I let my mind go blessedly blank and my senses come to the fore.

I smelled the wood smoke that swirled from houses in the village, felt the soft driftwood log beneath me, heard huskies howling a ways down the beach, tasted the metallic air of a November night, and watched nature's greatest light show. It isn't quite meditation as I understand it, but it has the same effect. It makes me feel renewed and delighted at the world. After the stories I'd heard today, this was the best medicine.

After the lights had pulsed and danced and dimmed, and my butt was nearly frozen, I looked for Beany. I could hear him way down the beach and I headed in that direction. He was barking at something toward the woods and the trail. Maybe he was responding to the crazy-ass howling contest conducted by the huskies in the yard of one of the last houses on the beach, or maybe he had found some creature that had flown or jumped up at the wrong moment.

I loved walking on the lonely beach. I hadn't brought a flashlight.

Maybe it was foolish, but flashlights always made me more scared of the dark. If I simply stayed in the dark long enough, my eyes adapted and I could see well enough. But not in the woods. No reference points and too many places a person could trip and fall. I could still hear Beany barking his head off, but the huskies had quieted. They knew he was barking at air.

Just then I saw Beany, near the entrance to the woods. As I moved forward to grab his collar, someone grabbed mine. They had me held from behind, a gloved hand over my mouth. I bit down hard, but they kept hold of me.

"Quit struggling. I'm not going to hurt you. I have a message for you: leave this alone. It isn't any of your concern. If you don't, you might find those dumb-ass kids you care so much about in worse trouble than they're already in."

With that, the attacker pushed me hard enough that I landed on my hands and knees and I slid across the snow's skittery surface. By the time I got up, the person, or *persons*, was gone, disappeared back into the woods, leaving me licking my wounds and holding on to my silly dog who'd come just in time to miss the show.

✦

I lay in bed for hours stewing over the attack and the events that had happened in the course of a few days: the deaths of two good people, rumours of corruption within the RCMP, and the ongoing problems like the bizarre lives of so many kids in Sheshatshiu who thought it was normal to be passed around among neighbours like pesky cats at the whims of social workers. The underlying hopelessness threatened to overwhelm everything. I tried to remember how it felt to walk around Sheshatshiu when optimism was high, everyone feeling that change could happen. I couldn't conjure it now.

Plus, there was still the whole ongoing mess of the Lower Labrador Project. In a short time, the reservoir would be flooded and BECorp had not met a single obligation. There had been no fair and reasonable discourse on sacred grounds, no efforts to prevent the poisoning of waterways, no nod to the right of Aboriginal folk at large to have a say about what happened to the land they'd been forced to leave. BECorp wanted the power, and they had it. They wanted the trees, the water, the mines, the roads, the air. Who cared if it technically belonged to someone else? Money trumps all.

Now the Crooked Knife Society had entered the arena, full-on warriors. Now—when it was too late. Now they spoke up about the injustices, the suicides, violence, drugs, and environmental crimes. Were they being killed for it? In a conversation with Innu elder Gilbert Achini about why the community had decided to receive the payout from BECorp rather than wait and see if a more equitable deal could be made, he said, "We feast when the hunt is good. When the caribou are plentiful, we kill as many as possible and feast for days. We can't save food. When the hunting is bad, we starve."

Somewhere in the midst of my fitful attempt to sleep, I heard Nick come in. I don't keep much from him, but I decided that I wouldn't tell him about the attack. At least not until I knew what to do about it. I feigned sleep and made a grumpy noise when I felt him slip into bed so that he wouldn't talk to me. I heard his breath steady as he fell asleep.

I couldn't sleep. Too many ideas floated around in my head, too much adrenaline from the attack, too many questions. I decided that I could use my own therapy: *accounting,* to simply think about those things you knew were true instead of spinning stories about things you didn't know were certain. Thinking only about the murders and not my concerns about the community as a whole, I mentally listed what I knew and what I had definite questions about.

Two people had been murdered, both of whom had been involved with the Crooked Knife Society—although Jay Tuck had seemingly left the group for unknown reasons. Why had he left? While I thought about Jay, I remembered that Crystal Berry's mother had told Jay about the assault of her daughter. Had Jay told the Crooked Knife Society? And further to that—was the reluctance that victims like Crystal and Mrs. Nighthawk had toward the RCMP part of the distrust that had grown over many years, or something more specific—corruption in the force? I knew that lots went on in the community that the RCMP didn't know about or deal with. Was that because the force lacked the capacity, or were we, as an institution, inured to the crime that was happening? Then there was the crooked knife itself. A crooked knife was left at Jay Tuck's murder scene, but not at Shirleen's. Was that significant? If Tuck's death was a warning to those who were fighting against crime on the reserve, what did that make the death of Shirleen? Then, the photo found at the first murder scene. Was Pashin being framed, or was I not seeing that he had reason to kill Tuck? I now knew that a rift existed within CK. Maybe it was more serious than I'd imagined. I knew that Pashin couldn't have killed Shirleen. That was an indisputable fact. I also knew that some of those involved in criminal activities, the goon who'd attacked me for instance, were willing to weaponize the youth in Sheshatshiu. I believed what Lucy had said about chaos being something the criminal element furthered for their own gains. Heck, that was true everywhere and certainly on plenty of reserves. But why did the thug who'd threatened me, or his boss, think that it was worthwhile assaulting a cop?

Before I fell asleep, I thought of one more fact: today I had visited several people on the reserve to get questions answered about the murders, and today I'd been attacked.

The boy had done the right thing—at least he thought he had. He'd gone to see a grown-up that he trusted and told the grown-up what he'd heard. Then things really went to shit.

Thursday, November 5

+++ Chapter 20

The funeral for Jay Tuck was at 3 p.m., so I headed in to work beforehand to see what was up. I was also avoiding being alone with Nick. He was working at home and as I hadn't decided what I was going to do about the attack on the beach, I thought it best to avoid him. I do have a lousy poker face.

The atmosphere at the detachment was gloomy. Pete was sitting at his desk, and some young woman from Goose Bay was at the dispatcher's desk, Shirleen's spot. She looked about 12 years old, as thin as a blade, with a bland expression on her highly made-up face. Renaud was in his office with his door closed—a bad sign.

"What's going on, Pete?" I asked while the young one looked at me wide-eyed over her Tim Horton's cup.

"They want to bring Pashin back in for more questioning."

"But he was in *their* jail when Shirleen was killed. What could they be thinking of?"

Renaud came out of his office looking grimmer than I'd seen him in years.

"Sir—"

Renaud silenced me with one hand. "Listen up, Munro, because I don't want to have to tell you again. Musgrave is in charge of the

Tuck investigation and the investigation, such as it is, for Shirleen. He insists that they have evidence that puts Pashin at the centre of the crime and Pashin isn't helping by staying mum. Pashin has never made a secret of the fact that he's homosexual, and the photo paints a peculiar picture. Musgrave, quite reasonably, also doesn't necessarily think that the two deaths are connected. Just because you've connected them is no reason for him to. Further to that, he has a warrant, so the courts agree. He also said that it isn't his habit to worry about what people think regarding investigations, and neither should we. And that's all she wrote."

"And by 'people' he means the Innu, I'm guessing?"

"I'm not sure, but I'm wondering why you are here."

Right. I was on stress leave through Renaud's kindness, and I realized that he could just as easily make it probation, paperwork, or nothing at all. He'd allowed me to keep detecting, but coming here made it obvious. Would that stop my mouth? Apparently not. So much for following Renaud's orders. "If they try and bring him in before this funeral, they'll have a riot on their hands."

"You know that isn't true, Constable. Just let's do the best we can and hope for a reasonable outcome."

The phone rang in his office, and he left me standing there thinking about everything he had said. He was right about one thing: the Innu were given to having protests, but they were always peaceful, even the ones years ago about the flight testing that had gone on over their land. I wished they would make a slightly more aggressive protest, but the fact was, that just wasn't their style.

Renaud came out of his office again, looking even darker and grimmer. "Come on, Constable," he said, motioning to Pete. "We've got to go pick him up."

"Do you know where he is?" Pete asked.

"Yes, he's at Johnny Tuglavina's. I've made sure to know where he can be located at every minute for his protection." He looked over at me. "I don't know why you don't trust me, Constable Munro, but it is pissing me off. Perhaps you'd like to decide who and what you work for. I realize you have an allegiance to the Innu youth, but you took an oath to make the laws of this land your first loyalty, so when one of your loyalties conflicts with another, you should be aware of which you are obligated—by your own word and choice—to uphold."

I nodded, speechless that he should have turned on me so harshly.

"I'm going to get Pashin now and hope that I can have a reasonable discussion with Musgrave about this. I've informed Penny at Legal Aid to be ready for us. She, like you, is steaming mad, but has the wisdom to know what she can do about it. Shirleen, get Goose on the blower and—" Renaud stopped. His composure wavered a second. "I'm sorry, Miss. Just call the Goose Bay Detachment and tell them we're bringing Pashin in."

I left for home, where I stayed until it was time for the funeral. I told Nick that I had to write a report about the interviews that I'd conducted the day before, and he let me be.

✦

The funeral, as was common for large events, was held at the school. The space seemed at once familiar and strange, transformed by the fact that we were all gathering to mourn a man who had been killed right here by the good deeds for which he was known. It was like coming home after a long trip; everything was familiar but coloured with the surreal light of the unfolding events.

In the gym, the dividing wall had been collapsed into its nest and chairs set out. The platform held a podium and a row of chairs for the speakers. People didn't dress in black for funerals here. Do they anywhere but on silly television shows or for the deaths of princesses and kings? Everyone was dressed casually, the high number of deaths in the community probably having something to do with that. Still, there was a formal air: the quiet that death brings.

I'd come with Nick and Shania; we'd driven over in silence, lost in our own thoughts. I was thinking of the attack the night before, of the threat in the voice and the physical touch of the repulsive person who'd delivered it. I knew that he was probably a hired hand, not the perpetrator of everything that had happened, but still I had a terrible feeling. I was also worried about Pashin. I wondered if Sergeant Renaud would get back from Goose in time for the funeral.

We sat near the front. I wanted whoever had threatened me, if they were there, to see me walking unafraid. My mind wandered to the sergeant. Renaud usually held himself at a distance from the community, which I understood, although I didn't like it. Jay had not been like that. He had jumped in with both feet—said that he didn't care what was considered appropriate, that "love was never appropriate and always correct." Not to confer sainthood upon him, so easy to do after death, but he lived according to the dictates of his own conscience. That's why I did not understand what Pashin had told me about Tuck's cautioning him to take it slow with his activism. It simply didn't fit with the man I knew, the man who was not afraid to be himself or to meet the true selves of others.

People were sitting based on where they understood themselves within the community hierarchy. The Innu Elders sat at the front, and I saw what I thought were the students most affected by Jay's death sitting together without that made-for-television grief you see on nighttime-news shows. Innu funerals had taken much getting used to. They were long. People walked in and out at any point. It usually was to have a smoke but it might be to phone the babysitter or because they saw someone at the door that they needed to talk with. But now I appreciated their casual familiarity with death. This, however, was not an Innu funeral, and if the Innu were still to be casual, it was unlikely that it would be as long. I noticed Jay's colleagues sitting together sombrely. If this could happen to him, could it happen to them?

Maybe that's why I actually liked funerals. They seemed, unlike weddings, to which I could not but help compare them, to strip away false tones and the frippery of society, and lay it bare for anyone with a slightly jaded eye to see. Like weddings, you may go to a funeral due to a sense of duty. That's why some of the Elders were here, and perhaps also their peers in North West: the mayor in all her finery, the principal and a few teachers from the North West River school, and the person who owned the gas station—the principal players in any village. It was an odd thing: a white man's death being honoured on an Innu reserve.

On Saturday, the funeral of Shirleen, an Innu woman, would be held at the church in North West River. She had embraced much of the white culture in a quiet but decisive way, having given up the religion of her parents—Catholicism—to join the United Church. She had volunteered with the church groups, the volunteer library, and craft circles in North West. Shirleen had been a cheerful enthusiast, but she hadn't given up her own heritage to do so. She had made her quiet mark on both sides of the river.

The funeral was about to start when Zann came up to me. She was carrying a red book, with her finger in it. She leaned down, gave it to me, and opened to a page with the play within the play. I looked at her, surprised.

"This is the reworked playbook, the one Pashin worked on. Lonesome Johnny said that you are to read this part at the funeral. You're to come up and join the rest of us who'll be talking on the platform. You'll take the spot that Pashin was supposed to do. Hamlet, just one line. We need you to look out as we're reading and see how people react. Watch for whoever looks shady, okay?"

What could I say? The brilliance of my young thespians, their bravery—shining in their faces. They had loved Mr. T, not with blind allegiance but with an intelligent, burning regard. I was in. I squeezed Nick's knee, and followed Zann, clutching the red book. What would I find?

I'd barely sat in my seat when the priest stood and started the ceremony. I wanted to read ahead, but I couldn't. I had to look at who was there, at their faces. I had to watch. At the last possible moment, I saw a uniformed Renaud take his place beside Nick in my abandoned seat. He looked grim.

I couldn't concentrate on what was happening. The priest bade us join him in several prayers. We stood up. We sat down. We had already been informed that this would not be a full funeral Mass due to the wishes of the deceased. I'd been surprised that it was even a Catholic funeral. The priest started talking about death in general, but then his homily took an unusual detour.

"The deceased, James Tully, known as Jay Tuck, began his young life safely in the sacrament of baptism, was confirmed at eight, and then, as a young man, took vows to become ordained as a priest. He spent some years as a priest in Blackwater College, a Catholic boys' college in Ireland. That is where he became separated from the love of Jesus. We don't know why he forsook his vows and left the Church, but we have the results. If we understand that heaven is communion with God, then all our life in this world should be a witness to what the communion of humankind means: the believer in Jesus Christ must be one who is alongside all those who are trapped in loneliness and isolation, through sinfulness and narcissism, through being excluded from society, through doubt and anxiety and fear. We pray for all our priests today, especially for those who are ill and for those who suffer and are troubled in their ministry. Through our prayers, we enter into communion with their ministry. We pray for those priests who have become lax and disheartened and where the spark of ministry has become dimmed. We pray for those who have fallen from the love of Jesus."

Did leaving the Church mean that Jesus didn't love you anymore?

I swallowed my fury to watch the faces in the crowd. The Innu didn't seem surprised; perhaps they were used to priests saying bizarre things at funerals. Several members of the white community, including the teachers, looked shocked. I looked hard at the priest. He wasn't familiar. I would ask about him later. He sat down and gestured to the next speaker.

The principal talked about Jay's long service to the school. Then a teacher told a funny story about Jay and his antics. The teacher introduced Johnny, who wore a tie, which he straightened as he stood to speak.

"I'm here to help the students through a reading. It was their idea to do a part from a play that was a favourite of Mr. T's—*Hamlet*. The drama society will be putting on a version of *Hamlet* they've titled *A Northern Hamlet* in December. Some of you who know your *Hamlet* will see that there's been some changes. These have been made by one of the students. We think you'll see why. Esther, the producer, will take you through the scene."

And we began, just sitting in our chairs, facing the crowd. Esther cleared her throat and then, giving Zann a grim smile, began.

"We're doing our reading from "The Play within the Play," act 2, scene 2. It's a play in which Hamlet has commissioned a group of travelling players in order to 'catch the conscience of the king.' Hamlet is trying to see if the ghost was right and that his uncle has killed Hamlet's father."

Esther made a flourish with her arm in true Elizabethan courtier style. "And now we shall hear from the two players normally called King and Queen, but in our version are the King Labrador Falls, played by Jeremiah, and Queen Mokami, played by Zann. Constable Munro, who has agreed to help with our production, will read the part of Hamlet.

Jeremiah spoke as KING LABRADOR FALLS:

Fifty times has the earth hauled it self 'round the sun,

with fifty-dozen full moons shining

since we, most honoured white bosses,

married you and

took dominion of this land and water

only thinking of your betterment.

What was done then with the Upper

shall we do now with the Lower?

Zann held forth as QUEEN MOKAMI:

You speak as if I had chosen

the first marriage when all know it

was but a simple rape.

And now you grow greedy again

and would marry me off to your younger

brother, Prince Otter Falls.

Should I trust you now, when I recall

those early days?

And as my word is given, my fear is so:

Where promises have been great, the littlest doubts are fear;

Where little fears grow great, great distrust grows there.

KING LABRADOR FALLS:

But think carefully on this,

Your memory does not serve you.

If it ruins this sweet deal for you and your people,

Your dreams will be nightmares soon enough.

I looked around to see how these words were being received by the crowd. The teens in the room looked excited—as if something forbidden was happening. For their classmates to take on such an action during a funeral was likely surprising. But what was particularly interesting was the look on the faces of three white men, looking paler than usual, scattered near the back of the congregation: Mr. Big Eat himself, Fred Goudge, sat centre; to his immediate left was Dick Freemantle; and nearby sat Chesley McMaster, the lawyer, with other bigwigs from the town. McMaster was the one I watched most closely because I knew that he had gone to college and therefore might catch some of the drift. When he heard the names of the king and queen, he flinched. His lips parted and his face flushed.

QUEEN MOKAMI:

The instances that second agreement move

Are base respects of thrift, but none of trust:

A second time I kill my trust dead

When a second contract finds me in its stead.

It was time for me to deliver my few lines. I stood and spoke as if I were a commentator, my hand to the side of my mouth.

HAMLET:

The Queen is harsh with her contracted husband. She seems loath to be twice-tricked.

QUEEN MOKAMI:

And shall I, knowing my innocence and your smooth tongue led me to the first malcontent partnership, fall again? I shall not.

KING LABRADOR FALLS:

'Tis deeply sworn, but poorly defended.

As the king spoke the final words, the audience was hushed. Esther held their gaze in hers for a few moments and then said the words that made sense of all that we'd heard.

"For those of you who haven't read Shakespeare, King Labrador Falls represents BECorp in this reading, and Queen Mokami, Labrador's Indigenous people. The queen knows that she has been duped. She married the Upper Labrador Project first, against her will, and now it looks like she'll marry again to the Lower Labrador Project. Both appear to be contracts made under duress. We think that Mr. Tuck would have agreed. We think that he'd rather be dead than see what is about to happen to our land. We know that he didn't kill himself, and so we wonder, who did?"

Whispers and mumbles broke out among the attendants, but Johnny called order so that Esther could repeat the explanation in what I later learned was flawless Innu-aimun. I looked once more to check reactions. When Esther made her brave and bold assertions, I noticed that Chesley looked grim indeed. Fred's and Dick's heads remained bowed together for much of the reading and the song that followed; a small choir sang Leonard Cohen's "Bird on the Wire."

I walked past sobbing and sober-faced teens. I passed the men in business dress here with their own agendas, agendas that I no longer had any desire to plumb. Past the women wearing headscarves, past the other teachers who, come to think of it, must have been scared themselves. Then I passed my own sweet man, who looked up from talking to an Elder, noticed my expression, and let me be.

+++ Chapter 21

The rest of the day passed without my full attention. Without work to go to, I felt a strange restlessness, and the events of Jay's funeral had me rattled. I was glad to have something social to do tonight. I phoned Legal Aid just to double-check that Pashin had been seen to. He had. I napped—I'm no good without my full eight hours and I hadn't slept well for days. I looked at the notes that I'd taken the day before and studied the script I'd been handed at the funeral.

This was as good as any other time to check in with the priest who had officiated at Jay's funeral. I called the church in Sheshatshiu, and a quiet woman who sounded Innu told me that I could talk to him right now if I liked. So off I went, anxious about what I might find out.

When I arrived at the office within the church, the priest was at his desk. A mild looking man, seemingly in his 50s, he looked up at me, somewhat befuddled.

"Hello Father Ryan. I'm Constable Nell Munro. May I talk to you about Jay Tuck?"

After an odd pause, with the priest looking down at the paperwork on his desk, he answered. "Of course, my dear. Have a seat. Can I get Mary-Margaret to bring you a cup of tea?"

I declined, looking around at the austere room with nothing that seemed personal or warm at all.

"You haven't been here very long, have you, Father?"

He busied himself putting away some writing he had been doing before looking up at me, his eyes a milky blue behind the strong distorting lenses of his glasses. "That is true. I'm only here for a few months while Father Karr recovers from a recent hip replacement. I came last summer to visit the northern coast as part of my ministry. I was asked then to fill in for the Father while he was away."

"You don't have a regular parish then?"

"No. I'm a tumbleweed." He smiled self-effacingly. "I go where I'm needed, but you came in regards to Jay Tuck, didn't you? I'm happy to help if I can, although I really didn't know him. He didn't attend any Masses during the time that I've been here."

Yet you seemed to have quite a bit of information about him— information most of us didn't know. I decided to keep those thoughts to myself. I would let discretion lead me for a change.

"I suppose people in the parish told you about Jay's past then?"

"Yes, such as they knew. He seemed an unhappy and angry man."

"Oh?" That I could not let slide. "I knew Jay very well, Father, and those words do not describe him. Perhaps whoever was telling you about him had an agenda, although that in itself is hard to imagine. May I ask who said that about him?"

"I talked to several parishioners." His eyes remained on mine, his voice vaguely dismissive. "I'm not sure if those were the words I heard, but it was definitely the impression. A man who lived alone, who had turned away from the Church, without a significant relationship—what would you think?"

I took a breath. This was his bias, not anyone's in the community. "I think he was a man passionate about his work who gave the kids the benefit of his intelligence and kindness. But I digress. I was wondering if you had any information about his family members back in Ireland? We would, of course, like to inform his family of his passing, but we've had no way to find them."

"No. Sorry."

"Father?" I had one more question. "If you don't know about his connections, how did you know that he had been a Father, or what his original name was?"

That grabbed his attention and his milky-eyed, humble look shifted to something more contrived. His voice was tighter when he answered my question.

"I was given that information when I contacted the Bishop's Office in St. John's. Since he had given testament in his will to be desirous of a Catholic funeral, I looked the matter up and found the record."

"Well, in that case, I won't waste any more of your time. It was good to meet you, Father Ryan."

"Thank you, child."

✦

As I reached the bridge to North West River, I saw the sign outside the community hall, reminding people that this was Bonfire Night on Sunday Hill Road. Each year people make *Guys* and bring them to the bonfire; with their the floppy bodies dressed in old hats and plaid shirts, they look more like dead trappers than historical figures.

I had come to like the festivity. I liked a bonfire, but there was something, as Shania had pointed out, so gruesome and weirdly ritualistic about burning fake bodies that I hadn't gotten into the fun of it until I'd been around a few years. Now I was a full-on enthusiast. Bring on the Guy. Burn him up, the rotten revolutionary! I liked it for its pagan qualities. It offered a means of celebrating what has been sanitized in modern times: rebellion, explosives, violence, life, and death in its odd complexity.

Nick had volunteered to help set up the fire and, as far as I knew, had gone to the brush dump early in the afternoon to gather wood. Later, after the large communal bonfire, everyone moved to smaller less inclusive ones in their own yards or on the beach—although the latter was not encouraged.

I headed to Sunday Hill Road about 5:30 with provisions: a large stainless-steel thermos full of hot coffee, a flask of Saint James rum, and leftover Halloween candy. Stew simmered in the slow cooker at home, but we might not make it back there for hours. I knew that the main gathering would be over by 7:30 or so, but we planned to go to our friend's home in Upalong. She'd have a bonfire in her big backyard that looked out over Little Lake. Perfect spot for it. Sunset was 4:30 this time of year, so it was already dark when I set out. I thought about the fact that we would have seven and a half hour days by the winter solstice at the latest. I would be going to and coming home from work in the dark.

I was more curious than fearful about the threat I'd received on the beach, but even so, I usually harboured a little fear walking at night in Labrador. I didn't have to worry about bears; they were all safely and fatly in their dens. It had been a berry-rich summer and they wouldn't be stirring for months. But a wolf had been sighted a few days ago in town—in Upalong, actually. There were more wildlife at that end of town, due to the lake or less traffic. At any rate, I was happy to see others, as I had hoped, making their way up Sunday Hill Road.

The Sheshatshiu crowd usually didn't partake in events on this side of the bridge. There had been too many years of bad feelings, on both sides, for it to be completely forgotten. Some events transcended that feeling: the Beach Festival was happily attended by all, and in fact, the Aboriginal presence was a draw for those who came from other parts of the country and world.

As I drew closer, I saw a gang from the school—the Theatre Steering Committee, no less. I was happy to see Jeremiah laughing with Zann, Kaitlyn, and Esther. Small groups converged, many carrying Guys representing global leaders and local schmucks. Some were wrapped in garbage bags, waiting to surprise watchers at the unveiling, where they would be paraded in front of the judges before being tossed onto the bonfire to the screams and yells of onlookers. I greeted the kids but didn't linger. They were with their peers, and I was a keen reminder of all that had gone wrong in the past few days.

I looked about to see if Nick was there and was a little unnerved at being unable to locate him. What had he told me? I'd been distracted the last few days and perhaps had failed to listen to something important. It happens to the best of couples—a slow taking each other for granted—and when all else was so unstable, I had perhaps unwittingly ignored the one person who consistently had my back. I realized even as I gave these thoughts room that I was exercising the opposite of reason. I should pay Nick the most attention. Without him, I was alone in the world. Yes, I had family and friends, but there's nothing like moving to the edge of civilization with someone to make that someone crucial to one's well-being. And Nick has always been that important to me.

I thought back to the first time I'd met him. I was living in a crack house in downtown Halifax. I'd left my parents because I thought I could handle life on my own and moved into the city. I'd been okay for a short time. I was barely 17 and yet I was more naive than any 12-year-old I'd met in Sheshatshiu. It didn't take long for me to fall under the sway of a persuasive man. I thought that he was older and wiser (he was older, 28 to my 17) and smarter, too. He knew how to make lost and lonely ones feel special and beautiful. And I did feel that way with him, until I was being pimped out to feed his crack habit. Luckily, I'd had a bad reaction to the drug—never, I realize now, was I more blessed than to have an overly sensitive system— but I remained enthralled with the asshole. Then along came Nick. He was working for a small, independent newspaper and was doing a story on street life. I met him in front of the library, where I panhandled for easy money. Nick started asking me questions about how I was living. I felt comfortable with him, like I still do today. I told him everything.

I didn't know what I was doing and was extremely lucky how it turned out. He told me later that he'd immediately wanted to go to the cops and get the crack house busted but thought that might not work out so well. So he was patient, like "feeding a squirrel by hand," he'd teased later. Takes a long time to gain their trust. He met me every day for about two weeks. Said he'd pay for my time, enough to keep the pimp off my back, and he fed me. He didn't take me to restaurants or to his apartment; that would have been a mistake, for many reasons. He brought picnics of homemade meals to where I sat in front of the library. At that time, my pimp had five girls working for him, and he couldn't keep tabs on all of us all the time. Nick quietly made me understand the choices I'd been making without ever being judgmental about them.

After two weeks, I agreed that it would be a good idea for me to go home. Once I was safely home, the place was raided. I don't think my pimp ever knew that it was me. He was back in biz in a few weeks anyway, and I was living back out in the country, finishing high school. Nick never rushed me; he treated me like a younger sister until I turned 23, then he asked me out. My parents liked him, of course. He'd saved them the bother of figuring out what the hell had happened to me. My parents aren't bad people, just indifferent parents. Too caught up in their own lives to notice that their kids weren't exactly doing well.

Sometimes I wake at night and images of the crack house fill my mind. The funk of sex and booze and smoke, the constant bass beat with voices raised in anger, and the shitty miserableness of everything.

A three-bedroom apartment in a North End high-rise, harbouring low-lifes like us, with holes bashed in the walls, festering piles of takeout containers lying around, and a TV that was always blaring. The living room curtains were constantly closed against a decent view of the harbour. Endless shouting. It didn't matter the time of day or night, someone was pissed off about nothing. I'd toke or drink until I passed out and then be woken up after too few hours of sleep to be offered to some guy for a poke. But I'd learned how to numb myself. When those memories assail me in the night, I remind myself of what I have now. I move close to a sleeping Nick and wrap my arms around him.

Right now, though, I was annoyed. Where was he? I wanted to surprise him with the coffee and the booze, but how could I surprise him if he wasn't here? I approached some of the men who were standing closest to the fire, the regular fellows that would have set up the fire.

"Have you seen Nick? Thought he was coming to help you?"

"He said so, but he never showed. Must have changed his mind."

Unlikely. "If you see him, tell him I'm looking for him."

If Nick had changed his mind, he'd have been at home. He would have made sure to tell me where he'd gone at any rate. No point getting into that. I checked my cell. No service. I wandered over to another group of people, a crowd that included Jenny Black. I had seen her at Mr. T's funeral but she'd ducked out quickly, not sticking around for the post-funeral conversation. Maybe my eyes didn't work so good in the dim light of the bonfire, but I'm sure I saw a look of distress cross Jenny's features. I bulldozed on, despite the warning look. Sometimes one has to move into territory they have no business being in; that was police work most of the time. I ignored my inner voice saying that's the sentiment all colonizers hold.

"Hi Jenny. How did the catering gig go? Keeping busy?"

"I'm plenty busy." Jenny's look held worlds. I waited. "Christmas is coming up fast and I'll be flat out for that."

"I've been meaning to ask you. Do you find it satisfying? After doctoring I mean."

"Yes." Jenny looked directly into my eyes. "What you really want to know is how could someone who was a valued member of the community stand such lightweight work? Is that right?"

"Busted. Only I do understand for the most part. I often feel like I've had enough—that I'm no further ahead than I was when I started out. And I know Nick feels the same from time to time."

"Yes. That's about right. I do like how when I'm finished a catering job, I'm truly finished. Nobody second guessing why I chose cheese puffs over crab dip for an appetizer or caring to bring it up. Nobody asking me to do more and more and more."

I laughed. I did get it. "Is that in reference to the doctoring or to the environmental activism?"

Jenny became serious. "I'm done with all that. The activism was worse than the doctoring. No one would budge on anything. I don't care to talk about it."

"Right, gotcha. You're doing the clam thing again. Well, before you completely close up, what nieces of Shirleen's would she likely contact if she needed something?"

"She has a pack of them. She was closest to Charity. Pammy is too busy with her job at Otter Falls, and Marilyn, you've heard about her, I know. She's trouble. She relied on Shirleen, not the other way around. There's more, but I can't remember their names right now. I've got to go. Sorry."

Clearly, I wasn't going to get any more from Jenny. Time to move on. I'd get her to open up eventually.

In the meantime, I needed to find Nick.

+++ Chapter 22

The burning of the Guys didn't take long. The usual jokes were made, and the Guy that garnered the most attention was dressed as a BECorp scientist—a joke, as BECorp was always going on about how they had "their scientists" looking into quick clay or mercury poisoning, and they never found any downside to what they were doing. The "scientist" was not only outfitted in a lab coat, but sported a makeshift white cane and sunglasses—no wonder they could never find anything wrong with the project. As the Guys were torched, I slipped away from the crowd, wanting to get to Upalong for the next part of the fun. I didn't see Nick, but figured he'd probably gone home to walk Beany and would find me at the party. There was no Shania either. I was used to her being called away on some emergency, so I didn't fret it. I'd call Nick from Eleanor's house and solve that mystery. Eleanor was a retired archaeologist who had worked for years on digs in and around the community. Smart, independent, and knew how to host a convivial gathering. Nick adored her for her quirky mind, and I knew that he wouldn't have missed a chance to spend an evening in her company. Once again, I pondered the richness of female presence in this community.

Some hung around the remnants of the fire; others slowly moved homeward or to one of the post-Guy parties. I walked up the hill, making my way in a rambling fashion to the river. Once I got there, I'd get on the road that led to Little Lake and Eleanor's house.

The road to Upalong had no streetlights. Some who lived in North West River were against the light pollution, and I was among them. We had one blazing light at our end of town—near our house— and I often thought I'd like to shoot it out some night when no one was watching. It was especially annoying when Nick and I took a thermos and our folding chairs down to the beach on nights when the northern lights might be likely. You'd think that here at the end of civilization we could have less light.

I took the shortcut through the cemetery, chockablock full of glowing angels and battery-powered tea lights—because everyone knows that dead people like light. Modern mourners had turned a beautiful, ancient cemetery into a ridiculous display of kitsch: bouquets of plastic flowers, angels with solar backpacks and lambs in their laps, their plastic hearts glowing eerily in the gloom. I stepped carefully so as not to disturb the many white stone demarcations or tip over any ugly displays. I made my way to the other side of the graveyard, to the dark path beyond. That's what I hated about the lights: you were blinded after you made your way past them, your eyes closed to the subtleties of the starlight because of their feeble shine.

Passing through the darkest corner of the graveyard and up the path to the road that led along the lake, my arm was grabbed. I shouted, or I think I did, but a hand quickly covered my mouth. A large masculine hand that smelled like the tar soap used for eczema.

Two men. They were silent as they dragged me into the woods, as was I, having no breath left to scream. In addition to the smell of the soap, I smelled fear. From them or me or all of us, who knew, but it was there: tangy and metallic and engendering even more fear in me. I wondered, in those elastic moments that seem to descend in accidents or near-death experiences, if this is how the hunted feel. Did the caribou experience this loss of boundaries, this feeling like you are the hunter and the hunted in the same terrifying moment?

Where were they taking me? Were these the same people who had kidnapped and killed Shirleen? Would it hurt? Were they going to hurt me? I couldn't find any fight in me. It was as if the brutality of the attack, the primal coming out of the dark and grabbing me like a hundred childhood terrors, dispelled any hope I might normally have had.

In that moment, I remembered what one instructor had told us during RCMP defence training: "It isn't lack of skill that's the problem. I can teach anyone how to adequately defend themselves from an attack, but I can't make you be willing to use those skills. Most people will not attack another human being, even if their life depends on it. Sometimes it's easier if you're defending someone else." I thought of Nick, how he would suffer if I were killed or hurt, but even that did not call up the fight in me. I thought of the Sheshatshiu kids' vulnerability: Pashin, Kaitlyn, Jeremiah, and Zann, and how they depended on a few sane adults; that whoever was behind these deaths was preying on those kids to manipulate the whole community. I thought of their faces at the funeral this morning, their emotions so ready. These criminals were using the kids to get their way—filling them with drugs, assaulting their bodies, and keeping the chaos fresh so that they could continue getting away with anything they wanted. Energy rose within me.

I made myself stumble in such a way that the man who was holding me had to let go. I lay there on the ground for a moment and whined. "I twisted my ankle."

The man closest to me bent down to reach me, but I cried out in pain, rubbing my leg and moaning in pantomime. The men kept their distance, assessing. I got myself up slowly. They were standing there looking at me when I gathered my energy into the centre of my body and kicked out with my right leg, catching one of the guys square in the goolies. At nearly the same time, I chopped the other guy in the throat as hard as I could, and leapt into the dark and away before they could regain their wits. I didn't go far, thrashing around in the woods would only bring them to me, but I found a little dip near a large spruce and crawled in, settling my breath. I listened carefully; they were a few hundred feet away, mumbling and stumbling and casting blame on each other.

It seemed to last forever, but I knew it was probably only about 10 minutes when one of them said in a strained voice, "This is stupid. The dumb bitch is gone, and I don't care what you say. The longer we're out here the more likely it is that we're going to be found. I ain't spending any more time on it. She's scared plenty, that's all that counts. Fuck, my throat hurts."

The other guy mumbled an answer, and they seemed to wander off. Just in case, I waited another half an hour before I gingerly started moving down the hill toward town. I was cold and tired and generally messed up, but I walked over the bridge to the detachment in Sheshatshiu.

✦

Jordan was manning the detachment. He looked, surprised to see me. I know that I looked a mess, covered in bracken, my face scratched. I told Jordan what had happened; I wanted a report filed on this one. I'd kept my mouth shut about the first threat. A part of me had thought that if I kept quiet, they wouldn't hurt any of the kids. But their desire to eliminate me was a direct result of their intention to keep harming them—I saw that now. And I wanted it on the record that an RCMP officer had been threatened with bodily harm.

Jordan took down all the information, and when he was finished, I cleaned myself up in the bathroom. While I was in there, I heard someone come into the detachment. It was Pete. It was obvious that Jordan hadn't had time to fill him in. He didn't look surprised to see me.

"Good. I wanted to talk to you. We've got information back about those photos you found at Tuck's apartment. Want to hear about them?"

"Of course. What did you find out?"

Pete grabbed a file from his desk and flipped through it until he found a copy of the photo of Jay and three other men.

"Ya, kinda weird. I guess the sergeant gave the photo to Shirleen on Monday morning and she sent out queries. A fax came from the seminary saying who was in the photo. Here's the weird thing: one of them is the priest."

"What are you talking about? What priest?"

"Father Ryan."

"Father Ryan who led the funeral? He knew Jay Tuck?"

"Well enough to have their photo taken together. They were at seminary together."

This omission constitutes major lying for a priest. "I went to see him this afternoon. He told me that he didn't really know Jay Tuck. Guess we should have another visit with him, eh?"

Pete looked away, tugging at his shirt collar.

"Come on, Pete. I don't care if he's a man of the cloth, he flat out *lied* to me during a murder investigation, and he as much as accused Jay of suicide, at his own funeral."

Pete's face took on the obdurate look of a man at odds with his principles. "It's too late tonight to visit him."

"It's only 8:30. We'll swing by, and I'll pop in and tell him I have a few questions to ask him that I forgot earlier (like, why did you lie to me?). Then you can take me home. I didn't drive here." Jordan looked like he was bursting to blurt out the reason I'd come, but I cut him off before he could talk. "Constable Walker, show that report to the sergeant when he comes in, okay?" I raised both my eyebrows, daring him to speak.

✦

A few minutes later I was at the presbytery, a small, pleasant-looking house next to the church. The same woman as before showed Pete and me into a small front room. Father Ryan entered, looking ruffled. He was obviously not used to being disturbed. Too bad. My sympathy was at an all-time low.

"I'll cut to the chase, Father Ryan. I just found out that you did know the deceased. In fact, you went to seminary with Jay Tuck. Isn't that true?"

"Yes." His eyes narrowed.

"Why did you lie?"

"Because it has nothing to do with James's death, and I was fairly certain that he didn't want anyone asking me questions about his time as a priest."

"And why would that be?" I looked across at Pete, who was writhing in an agony of discomfort. I wondered at some people's deference to authority, to the cloth in particular.

Father Ryan drew himself up, haughtily. "Because I heard that he had left the priesthood under a cloud of suspicion in the 1990s. I'm not sure what the situation was, but it was clear when I took this temporary post that James was not interested in renewing our friendship. And now, if you'll excuse me, I have to see to one of my parishioners who is sick. The woman will let you out."

It took me a moment to regain my equanimity, and then I let him have it. "I'm not sure you understand the severity of what you have done. You lied to an RCMP officer during a murder investigation. You don't get to choose which facts are pertinent to a case or not. I hope your background is squeaky clean, because you've just become a person of interest in this investigation."

I don't know which of the two men, Father Ryan or Pete, looked more shaken, but I gave neither a chance to say anything more.

✦

Pete was quiet, driving me home. Finally, he mustered up his courage. "I told you it was nothing, but you had to drag me into it. My mother will kill me if she finds out."

"Nothing? Really, that's what you took from the conversation? He had no need to lie. He could've just told me that they'd been to seminary together without my thinking anything of it. My curiosity isn't satisfied." Furthermore, I thought, but didn't say aloud, I don't trust someone who calls another human being "the woman."

Pete groaned. "The sergeant is right. You're like a dog with a bone once you get an idea in your head."

"Thanks."

And then we were at my house. I thanked him for the ride and made for the door.

I wasn't home but five minutes—time enough to see that Nick was still AWOL, make a fire, pour myself a hot rum, and convince Beany that it was safe for him to come out from under the bed (his refuge during fireworks)—when a knock sounded on the door. Sergeant Renaud came into the room like his ass was on fire.

"What the hell is going on?"

Before I had a chance to answer, he waved the report I'd just filed in my face. "Constable Munro, is this true? Were you attacked last night and *again* tonight?"

"I wasn't really attacked last night. Some idiot shook me and told me to watch my step, or else, and to stop looking into things."

"*Or else?*" Renaud looked crazy. "That's an attack, Munro. That's threatening a police officer. And tonight, they carried out their threat."

"Well, when you put it that way—"

"Did you get hit on the head? What other way is there to consider it? I should take you into the hospital so that they can check you out for concussion—or lobotomy."

I looked at him, willing myself not to laugh. I couldn't remember ever seeing him so wrought up. "Sergeant, sit down. I know you won't have a drink, but take a chair. And let me sit down again, I'm exhausted." I wondered if this woozy feeling was just tiredness or an aftereffect of being attacked.

He sat and heaved a huge sigh. "This isn't even why I was coming over here. I tried phoning you earlier but—"

I grimaced. "My cell isn't charged. Sorry. But it hardly ever works this side of the bridge, you know that—"

"Shut up a minute. Nick's been arrested. He was with the protesters at Otter Falls."

"What? But he's a journalist. It must be a mistake."

"Yes, well, as you know, we were given the word last week that we were to arrest anyone who violated the injunction to go on the property. I'm not sure how he got put in with the protesters, but there's nothing to be done about it this evening. Twelve people were arrested late this afternoon, Nick among them. They're all being held till they can be processed tomorrow."

I looked out the window. The falling snow would make the kids happy. The adults too. My mind refused to process Renaud's words. I must have moaned because Renaud put his hand on my shoulder and gave a little squeeze.

"He tried phoning you but you must have been out or ..."

"The cell. Right."

It was a few minutes before I spoke. "I'm trying not to get pissed off, Sergeant, but I'm failing. I don't understand why the officers in Goose would arrest Nick. They know he's a journalist. What about the freedom of the press?"

"Ya, well, he was named in the injunction. Musgrave told me that they told him that it would be sorted later, but right now he's to be treated the same as the protesters."

"Musgrave. I shoulda known."

"I don't think you can blame Musgrave for this, Nell. He's under the same pressures as our detachment. It's simply a matter of procedure."

"Oh, come on! Why do corporate entities get protection that ordinary citizens don't? It's all politics and you know it." I put my head in my hands. I felt like tearing out my hair. "I don't know how much longer I can play this game. It doesn't seem to be doing anyone much good anyway."

He stared at me for a moment and then spoke in a voice I'd rarely heard him use. "Nell, I won't argue with you about the politics of the police force. You knew that it existed before you signed up, and yet you signed. You begged for this job. You sent emissaries from the community to vouch for you, which, I might add, anyone would consider a political move. If you're rethinking your commitment, resign."

On that note, he left.

+++ Chapter 23

It felt lonely in the house after Sergeant Renaud left, which was crazy, because I was often in the house alone with Nick and I working as we did. Beany came over while I sat by the fire and rested his funny, square head on my knee. I refused to be scared. The doors, front and back, had strong locks, which we rarely used, but tonight they were secure. Besides, I doubted even the stupidest thug would come after me in my own home.

I thought about what Renaud had said. Of course, it was true: I was happy to use political means for my own sake, for what I determined was the greater good, and hated it when it went against what I believed in. But what I'd expressed was also true. It was becoming more difficult to work for an organization that appeared to be manipulated by corporate agendas. It was futile to try and reach Nick. His arrest would be sorted out in the morning, and I knew more than most the red tape involved in any arrest, but I could at least go online and find out what social media was posting about the protest.

It was all over Facebook, and I was happy to see that there was a unanimous outcry against the fact that a journalist had been taken into custody. Apparently, the Goose Bay detachment had issued a statement saying that Nick had acted in defiance of the injunction and that other journalists did not go onto the work site as he had. One of these journalists, who worked for the CBC, said, "They are considering laying criminal charges for reporting on a matter of public interest. I didn't go in because I was directed not to by a higher-up. I'm sorry I didn't ignore that direction. Mr. Wheeler did the right thing and this is a travesty."

I was thinking about what Johnny had said about "resource curse." How he'd inferred that in a resource-rich environment, corporations and government collaborated to destabilize a community so that the resources could be taken with little argument. Dismantling the free press would go a long way to ensuring such destabilization.

All of this was going through my mind when I heard another knock at the door. Since Beany was wagging his tail, I knew that he recognized whoever was standing there. I peered through the kitchen window.

Jenny Black came in, full of purpose, shaking the snow from her parka and soft boots. "I know it's getting late but I was walking by and noticed Nick's truck wasn't in the driveway. I thought you might like company."

I was about to tell her that I was just going to bed, when I realized the effort that it must have taken for her to come to the door. She knew I was miffed, or at the very least disappointed with her, and she obviously hadn't wanted to talk either, but here she was seeking me out.

She looked at my rum toddy and the bottle on the counter. "Why don't you mix me one of those? Drinking alone is a silly exercise."

I wondered why she hadn't asked me where Nick was, but I wasn't long in the wondering.

"One of my old compatriots called me this evening. I heard that your man was arrested with the Land Protectors. Have you talked to him?"

"No, I missed my chance." An understatement, but I didn't want to get into the attack with Jenny. Too complicated. "What do you know about it? I was just checking Facebook, but as always it's sketchy."

"I was talking to Roberta."

"Roberta with the Land Protectors? But she must have been with them—she's their leader. Why wasn't she arrested?"

"They knew that there was a chance that the cops would come in, and they wanted an organizer on the outside. Besides, her knee is bad." That is one of the amazing things about many activists in this part of the world: their ranks are full of the silver haired. They've been at this game a long time. They stay the course.

"Why did they think the cops would come in tonight? I mean, BECorp has had that injunction for a while but didn't seem too hysterical about its being enforced."

"Tonight was different because of the deadline."

I had quietly been adding more honey and lemon to the warming pot. I took another mug from the cupboard while my mind fixated on the word *deadline*. Deadline. Deadline. Deadline. What the hell had I been blithely ignoring all this time?

"Deadline?"

"Where have you been? On the tenth of this month, BECorp will begin flooding the reservoir. After that, any protest will be a moot point. All the groups interested—River Keepers, Land Protectors, any Metis, Inuit, or Innu who aren't involved in those groups—decided to ensure a continuous presence at the dam site till then. The last chance to get this turned around will be this Monday."

I wordlessly held out a steaming mug to Jenny and we headed into the living room to sit by the wood stove, my mind clicking away. I had heard about the date the reservoir was to be flooded; the whole thing had been background noise to our life for what seemed like years. I suppose I had despaired of anyone effecting the kind of change required. My mind caught on a memory from childhood: watching *The Empire Strikes Back*, when the AT-AT Walkers moved in against the rebels. I remember feeling hopeless: how could a band of puny humans fight ginormous machines? I don't even know how they ultimately prevailed, and that was only fiction. In real life, it seemed all the more impossible that David could beat Goliath. I thought about the mess at Otter Falls. Too big to fight. Might as well give up now—was my response to the news. I'd become so used to giving up. I was so far out of that particular fight that I didn't think about it anymore. Instead, I focused on the kids in Sheshatshiu: the biggest-sized problem I felt that I could stand to look at. What I'd failed to see was that both issues, like so many others in this community, boiled down to the same problem: commerce was more important than human life.

Jenny watched me. I had heard the word *deadline* recently. When was it? When I'd been eavesdropping at the Big Eat, on the Monday after Jay's death. What had been said? One guy had asked if the murder changed anything for the deadline. I wondered why the death of a schoolteacher in Sheshatshiu would have any bearing on a deadline concerning a bunch of Goose Bay business types, but that was when I'd been caught listening in, so I hadn't heard the response.

I fought to keep this thread in my grasp. "Jenny, here's a weird question. Have you heard of any business venture that Chesley McMaster, Dick Freemantle, Fred Goudge, and Murph Lee are in on together?"

Jenny sat back, holding her mug in both hands, quiet for a minute. "I've heard something, only it's ridiculous, so I figured that it was like all the other rumours that run rampant around here."

"What did you hear?"

"That McMaster and Freemantle were going into business together—an adventure tourist company called Mokami Trekking Adventures. I didn't hear about Goudge, but apparently Murph Lee's consulting business, Big Land Solutions, is involved in setting it up. The only reason I heard of it was because a Sheshatshiu woman helps me with the bigger catering jobs. She was all fired up because she thought that she might get to run the food portion of their business. I didn't pay it much mind. Most of the businesses Lee works on seem like they're organized only for the grant money, and then they dissolve like snow in June."

"What does Big Land Solutions do?"

"Supposedly they're a consulting firm. They bridge the gap between folks with money to burn and the various logistics of doing any sort of business in Labrador. They started up a few years back, in the early days of the Lower Labrador Project. The Aurora Agreement between the Innu and the government makes it easy to get investment money for Innu businesses or organizations. Murph is one of many who thought he'd take advantage. Big Land Solutions makes it easy for him to see who is bringing money into the province. Sort of like a union of rats, you know: for any deal to go through, you need a certain percentage of Innu board members, and you need to figure out the various land agreements. In principle, it makes sense, but I've never heard good things about it. I'll tell you one guy who's on many of their boards: Pashin's stepfather, Frank Andrews."

"Frank Andrews? The slippery shit everyone knows is involved with drugs but can't pin anything on. That Frank Andrews? He's Pashin's stepfather?"

"The very one."

That gave me pause. I'd been hearing about Andrews ever since I started working in Sheshatshiu. Hell, Lucy had mentioned him when I'd talked to her. Everyone knew that he was involved with illegal stuff, but he managed to keep going. I'd talked to Renaud about him once, and he had said that he was definitely a person of interest, but until there was reliable intel on him, the RCMP wouldn't move. I got it. It's sometimes better to let cocky bastards like him think that they are invincible. Then they are likely to make mistakes, but so far nothing.

"And you think that Mokami Trekking, or whatever it's called, is ridiculous because ...?"

"Come on! Have you ever seen a group less outdoorsy than that gang? Unless you call staying home and watching *Duck Dynasty* outdoorsy. It's just too wholesome sounding. It stinks to high heaven! But there's something else fishy." Jenny took a long slow sip of her toddy.

"And that is?"

"They aren't applying for any government start-up money. Or not that I've heard. Susie, the woman from Shesh, said that they were pretty much set. Just getting staff in place, apparently, so that they can start next summer."

"Do you think it's true?"

"Check the internet. Businesses have to register with the municipal government as well as the province. Or at least, I did."

I nodded, my mind already out the door. "Okay. Drink up, maid, I have some work to do."

Jenny laughed and did as she was told. At the door, she stopped. "I'm sorry I was abrupt with you earlier, Nell. We believe in the same things. You're just being braver than I'm able to be right now."

I hugged her and she was gone.

He curled up on the hard, narrow bed. His cellmate's snoring was laboured, and it was cold, but he wasn't going to ask for another blanket. He hoped that the reading at the funeral had gone well. He remembered what Tuck had told the class once, when someone had said there was no point in anything—that they'd never get anywhere beyond this shitty reserve and end up drunks like everyone else: "Could be true, could not be true. But what if it's not true and you give up? Sometimes I don't want to do what I do— don't want to come in and talk to you lot of misery guts. But what if today is the day that one of you listens? What if your life is the life that makes a difference? Quit worrying about the big things. Think about the little things you can do. Be kind to your grandmother. Learn a trade that gets you some kind of life. Fall in love. Be in a shitty, little play that causes someone to wake up. Your choice."

That's why he'd insisted that they do the play.

He wanted Tuck to know that he wasn't giving up, even if Tuck had.

Friday, November 6

+++ Chapter 24

It was hard to leave my bed, but I had to get to the plan I'd cooked up. Nick called me from the jail as I was making my lonely cup of coffee to say that he'd be a while getting processed and not to do anything foolish.

"Like quit the force, you mean? I might."

"Just wait till we can talk. This might work in the Land Protectors' favour. It's certainly got the attention of the press, nationwide."

"Okay, but I do have some things to take care of today, so if I'm not here when you get home, don't sweat it."

He knew better than to ask.

My plan was to visit each of the guys I'd overheard at the Big Eat. I was going in with my hunch like it was a real lead, but at this point I was willing to kick up dust. I wanted to see if they looked surprised when I showed up all bright and cheery instead of dead or damaged. Plus, I wanted to find out what kind of soap they had in their offices. Just like Perry Mason, I was. My grandmother watched reruns of that show endlessly, and I, her trusty sidekick, did too. That's it—I was his sidekick, the detective! What was his name? I went through the alphabet in my mind: Paul Drake. Come to think of it, we sported the same hairstyle. First, I'd visit Chesley McMaster, the lawyer. Nick and I needed a will. We'd been putting it off for years, and since he was presently in jail and someone was out to kill me, I figured now was as good a time as any.

✦

The reception area in the lawyers' office was quiet and bland. Boring canvases of meadows purchased from cheap art warehouses hung on beige walls. Here we were in one of the most striking and beautiful parts of the world, and these cheeseballs couldn't find anything more aesthetically pleasing to decorate their walls. I despaired of this sterile corporate world. Everything ugly and hateful. Nobody cared. For more money, or in-trade, Chesley could have beautiful Indigenous art on the walls or photos of Labrador's stunning wilderness. An array of magazines meant to soothe us about Big Oil and Big Hydro lay fanned in front of two leather couches and mentioned nothing of the communities and people who lived here. I waited for the receptionist to notice that I'd come in. She finally looked up from her computer quizzically.

"Is Chesley in? I need to talk to him about a will."

I'd heard the scuttlebutt around town that most folks got their lawyering done in St. John's. Everything was more expensive in Labrador, so people generally visited specialists when they were in Newfoundland. It might have kept the local lawyers a little hungry. Hard to say.

"He just had a cancellation, so he might be able to see you."

Right. A cancellation. Such a busy guy.

"I have to use the bathroom. I'll be back in a shake."

She pointed to the bathroom door. No tar soap. Just that stuff that comes in a bottle and smells like pumpkin spice.

But that didn't mean that Chesley didn't hire the goons. Just because they didn't use his lavatory doesn't mean squat. I went back to the reception area and was motioned through to Chesley's office, which was more of the same: bland by the yard and the gallon. He looked like a deer in the headlights, but I pretended not to notice.

"Hi, Chesley. Thought it was about time I acted like a grown-up and made a will. Do you have time to start on that?"

Chesley smiled and gestured to one of two chairs drawn up to his desk. "I think that's a good idea."

"Why? Know something I don't? Have you been talking to my doctor?" My tone was joshing and overly loud, like I was one of his good old boys. Chesley gave out a noise somewhere between a squawk and a laugh.

"No, I just meant that everyone should have a will. I'm always surprised by those that don't. Have you ever had one?"

"No. I don't have any money, so I never thought that it was necessary, but then someone pointed out that since Nick and I aren't married under the eyes of the law, it might be a mess should one predecease the other."

"Will Nick want a will too, then?"

"I have no idea. He'll have to figure that out for himself. We aren't a salt and pepper set. Not sure who he'd even like as a lawyer." I stared into Chesley's pale blue, twitchy eyes.

"I only meant ... well, usually couples do their wills together so that they can figure out all the bits and pieces in one process."

I nodded, seeming to give it some thought. "We've never been conventional. Also," I gave him a penetrating stare, "I have reason to believe that I might die before him."

Chesley blanched, coughed, squeaked out a snicker, a medley of nervous hits. For a lawyer, this man had no poker face. I was having fun. Nervous people make mistakes.

"Nell! Are you joking?"

Why not shake the tree for all I had and see what fell out. "I've been threatened twice this week by goons in the woods. And as I don't mean to stop what I'm doing, I suppose they'll keep on."

Maybe Chesley knew about the hoods in the woods. Maybe he didn't. But I was willing to bet either way that he knew that his chummy group had something to do with it, and he was smart enough to realize that I was on to them. I sat quietly: a Russian negotiator's trick. Because people can't bear silence, they'll produce all kinds of talk to avoid the embarrassment of sitting quietly. Weird, but true.

"That's terrible." Chesley's eyes were glued to mine, a technique he'd probably perfected in the courts. Look them right in the eye and don't waver. I knew it too and gave it right back.

"I guess you went to the police?" He asked before coming to his senses.

"Good one. Yes, I reported the assaults. Right away. And we have some leads, though they might find me before we find them. They weren't very smart, you know, said a few things. But I can't say more about that."

I had my hand on my cell in my pocket. I pressed a button so that it would vibrate.

"Sorry. Have to take this. Might be in reference to what we're talking about." I winked at him, then looked at my screen and texted nothing to no one. "Oh jeez, I'll have to cut this short. We've got an issue back in North West. I'll call to reschedule. Sorry about this."

I got up and left in not too big of a hurry, just enough to make Chesley unsure of whether I was yanking his chain or responding to a crisis. No. 1 crossed off my list. Now for No. 2. Dick Freemantle over at the lumberyard. I was there in minutes, but even so, when I went into the office Dick was just getting off the phone with someone.

Dick looked at me in surprise and lowered his voice, gesturing to me to sit down. "Thanks, uh ... Miss McDonald. I'll get back to you about that matter and we'll make sure that it's taken care of."

I smiled at that. "Sorry to bother you, Dick. I know you're a busy man, hands in many pies and all. New buildings going up all the time with this Otter Falls project, eh?"

Dick isn't slick like a lawyer. But he was stronger in other ways, hardened by making it in a rough community, I'd guess. He'd built this business up through his ability to be ruthless and conniving; that was no secret.

Dick looked at me disdainfully. "How can I help you, Ms. Munro? Are you building a shed?" He disliked me enough not to hide it, then.

"No. Nick and I *were* thinking of building a cabin, but now we might buy Shirleen's from the estate. Apparently, her family isn't interested in keeping it after what happened there. So sad about her passing, isn't it?"

"Terrible. Just terrible news. Shirleen was well liked in this community. I remember her father. He was well liked too, on both sides of the river."

"Yes. I've heard that. I never met him; he had died before I came to North West River, but Nick spoke highly of him. He was known for not giving up once he got his teeth into something—isn't that right? Well, the apple doesn't fall far from the tree, they say. I guess Shirleen left letters and papers about whatever she was working on. Real juicy, apparently."

I saw a mild flinch disturb his fixed expression. "Oh? I hadn't heard that. So, if you aren't building, what can I help you with?"

"I understand you install alarm systems. Nick and I are thinking of getting our home fully alarmed. We can't be there all the time and, well, we have reason to believe that we aren't always as safe as you'd think someone in a small community like North West River would be."

He leaned back in his chair. "Have there been break-ins around North West lately? I haven't heard of any."

"Oh, I'm sure you and your cronies would be the first to know of any gossip like that." I twinkled at him like a real charmer. "Don't think I haven't noticed you at the Big Eat with your gang of old boys." I chortled in a warm and phony way. "No, it's just that I've been threatened lately. Comes with the job, I guess. You know I work for the RCMP in Sheshatshiu, right? I'm a community constable. Well, someone's decided I'm being too nosy. Tried to scare me. Nick and I thought that an alarm system might be one thing that could help."

JAN MORRISON

At this, Dick became very official. He stood up, motioned me toward the door, and started walking me out to the store proper. "Come on through and talk to Barry. He takes care of all the security systems and he'll be sure to help you." He patted me lightly on the shoulder, feigning concern but looking like he thought I might bite him. "So sorry to hear you've had a spot of trouble. Terrible times. My oh my, terrible times."

Before he could pull away, I grabbed his hand and gave it a lingering shake. Unfortunately, there was no residue that my nose could discern when I surreptitiously gave my hand a sniff.

Two down, two to go.

✝

After being completely noncommittal with Barry, I headed off to the Big Eat. I figured that even if the others hadn't begun to gather yet, and I bet they had, I could talk to Fred Goudge, since he was usually somewhere on the premises.

Fred was sitting alone. Perfect. I went up to the counter as if I were there for the food and ordered a burger, onion rings, and a large root beer. Once my order was up, I took the tray over to the booth where Fred sat glumly, looking at his cup of coffee.

"Hey, Fred. Can I join you? Don't usually see you here alone. What's up? Everyone too busy with their actual jobs to come and hang out here? Ha ha!"

Fred pooked out his bottom lip like a sulky Cabbage Patch Doll. In fact, he resembled one, come to think of it, and didn't say a word. I made like he was welcoming me anyway, sat down happily, and dug into my meal.

"You know, a councillor has a lot of duties," he said sulkily, looking up at me with his puffy, big eyes. "And running this restaurant isn't a piece of cake, no matter what you might think. I have a lot of weight and responsibility here."

"Sure, Fred. I know that. I was just teasing." I took a big onion ring and slowly crunched it. Then I looked up at Fred, who appeared to be in shock that I would sit with him. I sighed. "I suppose you heard about poor old Shirleen, eh? We're sure going to miss her at the detachment."

Fred opened and closed his mouth a few times before daring to respond. "Yes, I heard. I didn't know her, but I understand that she was a good worker."

I was perhaps feeling overly sensitive, but that struck me as the sort of thing people say around here when they mean *for an Innu.* I wasn't going to get sidetracked, however.

"Yep, she was a hard worker, and very community minded. I understand that both her and Jay Tuck were against the Otter Falls hydro project. Did you know that?"

"I have no idea. I don't listen to those naysayers. They're against progress, and I don't like it."

"Oh? I guess you could call a dam that won't provide one megawatt of energy that we haven't already paid for *progress.* I guess you could call dumping methylmercury into the waters that supply food for so many of the Indigenous peoples of Lower Lake Melville *progress.* I guess you could say that a dam built on quick clay is *progress.* I guess Shirleen and Jay being gone could be called *progress,* eh?" Although my words were aggressive, I spoke them in a calm and gentle voice. He took it in the manner in which it was intended, however.

The heat rose crimson in his face. "What! How dare you." He paused, obviously trying to regain some composure, his hands gripping the edge of the table and a vein throbbing on his forehead. His eyes narrowed and he turned spiteful looking. "Look here, little Miss. I don't know what you're up to, coming around to all of us and casting exasperations, but you won't do it in my restaurant. Apologize, or get out!" The man was purple and spluttering. This was way too easy. I had known not to bother with subtlety when it came to this asshole.

I chomped a few more rings. "Sorry, Fred. I thought I heard you say that you didn't like naysayers so I guess I just surmised ... I certainly didn't mean to cast exasperations or anything." I smiled up at him with my best angel face. He still looked like he wanted to throw me out by the scruff of my neck. "Really, I am sorry. And what did you mean saying I've been coming around to all of you? All of you who? Do you mean to say that my meeting with my lawyer wasn't confidential?" I shook my head in mock disbelief. "That won't sit well with the ethics board. I suppose looking at security systems isn't the same, but still."

I stopped for a minute and itched my nose. "Ooh! I just smelled something strong. Are you wearing cologne?" Before he could reply, I grabbed his right hand and smelled it. Bingo! It was definitely tar soap. Not that it would hold any water in a court, but at least I'd satisfied my own curiosity. I had thought that one of the thugs was

Fred. He was the sort that would rather do things himself than pay out dough to goons that might blab. Plus, he was a sucker. He did what he was told in that four-way circle jerk. So, who was the second goon? Before he could make anything more of my weird behaviour, I grabbed my lunch and stood up.

"Sorry, have to dash. Allergic to that soap you use. Gives me a rash. Nice talking to you. Hope to catch up on all the news later. I guess you heard about the protesters at the falls last night. Hell of a thing, isn't it?"

✦

I ate the rest of my lunch in my car in peace, pondering the whole scenario. I wished I could think of a reasonable purpose to see the fourth member of the happy gang: Murph Lee. He was the only one with definite ties to the Lower Labrador Project, but I couldn't fathom a reason for visiting his office. I figured Nick might be home by now, maybe he could give me a clue. He had the journalistic knack of knowing where everyone in town could be found. I called him and gave him the rundown. I had to tell him about the attacks, but he was pretty cool with it—maybe a little too cool—for my liking. I thought he was probably saving what he wanted to say until we were together.

"Do you have any idea where I might run into Murph Lee and what excuse I could have for talking to him?"

"Murph's office is upstairs in the Labrador River Hotel, headquarters for Big Land Solutions. He spends a lot of time in the hotel restaurant. You might be lucky. I know you'll think of a reason to talk to him easy enough. It's Labrador—what reason do you need to be friendly?"

JAN MORRISON

So off I went to the Labrador River Hotel. Built in the 1960s, it still had that oh-so-modern look of those years. It boasted three floors of serviceable rooms and a large, open dining room with windows onto the Labrador River, which ran wide and slow. There were patches of ice across its surface but freeze-up didn't usually happen until later in November. I walked into the dining room to have a look. Maybe I was turning into a true Labradorian, always searching the view for minute changes. I liked the room, the big windows with their view of the river and the trees along it.

When I turned from the window to look over the dining room, I saw two people seated at a table in the far corner. This was my lucky day. One was Murph Lee; the other Frank Andrews, stepfather to Pashin. Now I had my reason to chat.

They looked surprised to see me walk over to their table. I guess Murph hadn't been on the same phone chain as the others.

"Hello." I smiled. "It's Frank Andrews, isn't it? I need to speak to you for a minute about your son."

He looked up with a frown. "I don't have a son. I have three daughters, no son."

"Oh. Sorry. I thought you were the Frank Andrews who was Pashin's father."

He frowned. "He's not my son. I was married to his mother. I don't have nothing to do with him."

"Oh. My mistake. I thought that since his mother died when he was 13, you must've raised him after that." I waited with a blank face for him to fill up the space. While I waited, I turned, expressionless, to Murph Lee who was displaying an interesting study in conflicted emotions. I plastered on a smile. "Murphy Lee, isn't it? I met you at the fundraiser for the new library. Nice to see you again. You must be one busy fellow. I hear your name all over town." Lee scowled, and I turned back to Andrews, who gave me a stony gaze.

"Pashin split after his mother died. No problem. We never got along, and as I understand it, he's in all sorts of trouble now." His gesture denoted *good riddance*.

"Yes. That's what I wanted to speak to you about. If he winds up in court over the murder of Jay Tuck, he's going to need some character references, and you seem to be a big name in the Innu community. I know you've had your differences, but I'm sure you'd agree that Pashin's not a violent kid. I'm thinking that we'll probably tie the two murders together. You know, Shirleen's death is looking suspicious despite what you might have heard, and of course Pashin was in jail when Shirleen was killed."

There, that's all I'd needed Murph Lee to hear. My job here was done. It was a bonus to observe Frank Andrews's response. He'd coloured at my comment about his being a big name but quickly detected the thorn in the rose. As I kept my eyes on him, he realized that it was his turn to speak.

"I can't say anything about Pashin's character. I've had nothing to do with him for the past four years. Nothing."

"Sorry to have bothered you then. It's difficult being a youth liaison officer. I don't always know who to turn to." I shrugged, keeping his eye. "Thanks for the information, though. Have a nice lunch."

+++ Chapter 25

I headed back to the detachment to check on the investigation into Shirleen's death and catch Renaud up on my shenanigans. He might be pissed that I'd spoken about the investigation to Frank Andrews and Murph Lee, but he'd intimated that I should use my leave to do a little probing into the case. I'd try to clear my mind on the 40-minute trip back to Sheshatshiu.

When I got to the detachment, it was empty but for Pete and the woman who'd replaced Shirleen. I'd forgotten her name already. Did I ever know it? Pete waved at me in an uncustomarily brisk way, as if he was deep at work. Maybe he was. I decided not to be brushed off by his efficiency.

"How's it going, Pete? Any leads on the curious death of Shirleen?"

"Uh, no. I mean ... curious?"

"I mean has anything come through that would lead us to believe that this was either a crime or just your everyday oh-I-forgot-everything-and-rushed-off-to-die-at-my-cabin occurrence?"

He frowned in disapproval. "No. There's a report from the medical officer, but no autopsy yet. Sergeant Renaud took the report and went off somewhere. Well, he said where and I wrote it down, but I can't locate it. Just a minute, I'll ask Shirl ... crap. Sorry. I'll ask the new girl."

"The new girl"—yikes! But then, I couldn't remember her name either. Pete called her over and I asked about the sergeant.

"Sergeant Renaud has gone into the Goose detachment. He said he'd be back by 4 p.m. and it's nearly that now so ..." she said quietly.

"Okay, thanks. I'm not really here anyway, being on leave and all, so I'll just go. But before I go—what's your name? Mine's Nell Munro."

"Yes, I know your name, Constable Munro. I'm Shelley Castle."

"Good to meet you, Shelley. I'm sure we'll get along just swell. Don't let Renaud scare you. He's a pussycat."

She smiled like I'd given her the keys to the city, and I left the detachment. I wanted to talk to Melissa, Pashin's half-sister, again, and now was as good a time as any.

✦

Melissa was even quieter this time around, but she invited me in and even offered tea. I accepted the invitation to come in but refused the tea. I thought I might ask her about Frank Andrews.

"That asshole? Forget it. I left home after my father died, before my stepmother took up with that shithead. The reason I put up with Pashin sleeping here at all is because I felt like I'd abandoned him to that creep."

"Okay, so I'm taking it you never see the guy?"

"Only if he takes me by surprise. The last time I saw him was when he thought I might help him get on some board. He thought I had an in with the Antoine family who control some of the business ventures around here. The Antoines have an electrical contract with the Band Council. I told him I couldn't help him, and if he ever bothered me again, I'd make sure that they'd never consider him for one of their enterprises."

I was starting to appreciate Melissa and her brother more and more. The fact that they made it out of such a crummy past with any compassion or a moral compass was astounding. I was about to leave when I thought of something. "Melissa, who in your family would've kept photos? Ones of you all when you were children?"

"My stepmother took photos all the time. Don't remember anyone else taking them. So I guess they'd be with her things."

I looked at her with my eyebrows raised.

"Far as I know, all her stuff is still at Frank's. I don't remember Pashin getting any of it."

✦

Back at the station, Renaud came into the detachment just as I'd gotten comfortable with Shirleen's day-timers. He looked unhappy to see me and I immediately felt guilty for some of the things I'd said on my rounds to the good old boys this morning. I pushed that aside.

"Sir? Any word on the investigation into Shirleen's death, sir? Has there been an autopsy report, sir?" At the third *sir*, Sergeant Renaud looked at me hard, but he found no irony or mischief. Just humility and hope that I wasn't about to be sacked.

"Nell, I had a call from Musgrave. He seems to be under some impression that you've been terrifying the good citizens of Goose Bay. Is that true?"

I started to answer him, but he held up his hand to stop me. "No, wait. Think hard before you answer me. Do not tell me anything that I don't want or *need* to have down on record right now. Do you understand? Just nod if you do."

I nodded.

"I only want you to tell me if you have done anything that could be considered using your badge to gain something personally."

I went over everyone that I had seen and what I had said. I didn't think I had. Actually, I was not in possession of my badge. With McMaster and Freemantle, I had gone in as a citizen and asked for their professional help based on something that had occurred. With Fred Goudge, I might have been imprudent, but I hadn't said anything that could be used against me in court. To Frank Andrews, I had said that I was the youth liaison for his stepson. Again, all true. I hadn't *had* my badge, let alone flashed it, or even insinuated my rank in any way. Nonetheless, I was a police officer and they knew it.

Renaud was looking at me with an odd look on his face, as if I were a kid who might disappoint or delight him. I answered him with the most confident tone I could muster. "No, sir, I did not."

The slightest smile lit the corners of his mouth. "Okay then. I'm going to assume that you've gotten over your fit of pique from last night and that there's a method to your madness. In other words, I'm going to trust you. Now, did you come in here as a citizen making a complaint or are you after some information? Why, oh why, when you're supposed to be on a leave, are you here?"

"I needed to find out something about Shirleen. Did Pete tell you about our trip to see Father Ryan?" Renaud nodded. "So, I want to know if Shirleen ever contacted the priest. I've checked out her planner but I can't find a relevant note. Also, is there an autopsy report?"

"'No,' is the short answer. The medical officer has not made a complete report yet. It's still too early. Musgrave's taken over that investigation. Right now, we're to proceed on the information that the initial medical examination gave us. She died of an insulin overdose, which will, in all likelihood, be deemed accidental."

This was confusing. "But they'll still do a full autopsy?"

"Yes. As you know, even in the event of suicide or accidental death, they have to complete a full autopsy. Once they do, the Chief Medical Officer of Newfoundland and Labrador will sign off on it. If they find something fishy, which so far they haven't, they'll run lab tests on tissue, blood, and stomach contents, which can take up to two weeks to complete."

Renaud looked up at me to make sure that I was getting it. His tone, matter of fact and gentler than some of our previous transactions, caused the knot in my belly—a knot I hadn't even known was there—to slowly unwind. He went on.

"The preliminary report says that, based on Goose Bay's investigation so far, it was perfectly ordinary for Shirleen to be at her cabin. They're saying that she made arrangements to be picked up, that there were no signs of struggle, and how would anyone have made her overdose on insulin without a struggle? They're saying that our looking around and reporting that she didn't have the stuff she'd normally bring is just idle conjecture, and they won't even listen to anything about Shirleen's typical care of her belongings. Right now, we'll have to be satisfied with that, till we have something more irrefutable than her sartorial habits."

"Meaning no disrespect, sir, but is that okay with you?"

"I detect no contempt in your question, Constable, so I'll tell you what I've said all along: this is not a war. If we want to find out what happened, we can't do it by calling out our own force. There are means. Employ them." I took that in. Did I agree that we should stop wondering about the slow-up on the investigation? No. But I did see that it didn't get us anywhere. Trying to find the killer would.

"Okay. I'd really like to know everything that Shirleen found out about Father Ryan and his relationship with Tuck, and whether she contacted the Father before she disappeared."

"What did you find out already regarding this? Pete was rather reticent."

"Father Ryan lied to me when I first visited him, and I'd like to know if he's hiding something. He told me that he didn't know Tuck, when really the two were close pals at seminary. He also told me that Tuck had left the Church under a cloud. I thought I'd check into that. Just a hunch that it might be important."

"That seems like it could be a good use of your time, Constable. Why not go in the back office with Shirleen's laptop and see what you can figure out? And, by the way, that's one benefit of Shirleen's death being considered accidental. None of her things were seized. You can find a record of incoming and outgoing calls during the hours before Shirleen left the office. If you want to follow up some of the questions unanswered from your foray today, feel free."

"Great! Will you get in trouble if Musgrave finds out that I'm here?"

"Oh, don't worry about Musgrave." I realized that he seemed more relaxed than I'd seen him since this whole thing began. I looked at him, puzzled, and he scoffed in a friendly way. "I forget you don't really understand the ways of the RCMP, having only one posting to your credit. The rumour train says he's likely to be posted to Montreal, to replace someone who just died of a stroke. He's busy trying to make sure of a smooth transition. Just don't get in his eyesight, and all will be fine."

"What about Pashin, sir? Any word on his arrest?"

"Just be patient. Frankly, I'm glad that Pashin is under lock and key. The kid likely knows something that could get him harmed. In fact, I think he made it all too easy to find him. I suspect Lonesome Johnny had something to do with that. He's a genius, that fellow. Now get to work."

He didn't have to tell me twice.

+++ Chapter 26

"Hello. This is Community Constable Nell Munro calling from Sheshatshiu, in the province of Newfoundland and Labrador, in Canada. I was wondering if I could talk to someone at the college who has worked there since at least the late 1980s?"

I felt a tingle as the call went through, as if my body was telling me that I was finally on the right track. The receptionist at Blackwater College for Boys was polite, if cool. She asked me to hold for a moment while she found Father O'Toole. She said that he'd been there since 1971, but I'd need to speak up because he was becoming deaf and, priest or not, refused to get a hearing aid.

Seven minutes later, a gruff voice with a thick Irish brogue came on the line. "Constable Nell Munro, is it?"

"Yes. Just call me Nell, Father." I spoke loudly and deliberately. "I'm looking into what might have happened to a priest who worked at the college in the late 1980s. He left the college, I believe, in 1992. His name was James Tully, though we knew him as Jay Tuck."

The line crackled. "Yes. Yes. I said to the young lady who called a few days ago from this same number: I was here when he was teaching. He was a grand teacher, just grand, and the boys loved him. It's a terrible thing, a terrible, terrible thing."

JAN MORRISON

Well, this was confusing. "Father, do you know why James left the priesthood?"

I heard his sigh rumble over the lines. "Yes. Yes, I do. One of the other priests was accused of sexual misconduct by a boy here at the college. James didn't like how the college, and indeed the Holy See, handled the situation. He felt that the students had been betrayed by those who were supposed to protect them. I agreed that some mistakes had been made, but I felt that it was better to be on the inside making reform possible rather than leave in an outrage. James wouldn't listen to me. Perhaps he was right not to."

I thanked Father O'Toole for his time and told him I'd be in touch if I thought of anything else I needed to know. As I hung up, a ping sounded on the laptop, an answer to an email I'd sent an administrator at the municipality office asking what businesses had created start-ups in the last five months.

The email listed seven businesses: Feed the Need, a caterer; three construction companies, all probably after the inflated Otter Falls house market; a tax accountant; Atik Enterprises, designers of specialized engineering tools; and Mokami Trekking Adventures, the company that Jenny had told me about. The last two belonged under the umbrella of Big Land Solutions and had been filed within a few days of each other.

By the time I'd done some research on all of these, I was tired, and I wanted to see Nick. I printed off a copy of the email, grabbed my notes from the Blackwater College call, and left the detachment for home.

Nick had a fire going, drinks ready, and a pot of slumgullion on the stove. He met me at the door wearing an apron and holding a scotch. Well, not *just* an apron—that isn't our sort of kink. He gave me the drink and an uncommonly brief peck on the cheek. For the second time that day, I wondered at his odd coolness. I chalked it up to the fact that he'd been arrested and hadn't been around to console me after the attack I'd suffered. Typical male ego.

I turned my attention to the dish on the stove. Slumgullion is one of my favourites. It's also a dish we love to argue about. Not the dish. The name. In my family, a pot of macaroni, fried-up beef burger, and onion with a can of stewed tomatoes was called *slumgullion*. Because my mother was originally a prairie chicken, it might have been local to her. Out east they call it goulash. According to those on the coast, millions of Hungarians are wrong.

"Perfect." I took the glass of scotch from him and curled up on the warm, padded bench in the kitchen. Our wee house is great, but the kitchen is so pokey that only one of us can cook at a time. Tonight, I'd occupy the lounging position.

"You made a big impression in town today. They were talking about it when I went into the Them Days office after they let me out of jail."

"Talk about burying the lede. I'll be wanting a full account of what happened last night, please. Till then, who was talking?"

"The woman who volunteers there. I don't know her name, and she obviously didn't know who I was or she wouldn't have said what she did right in front of me."

"What did she say? Why are you torturing me? Spill!"

"She was talking on the phone. She had one of those voices that carries, even when she's trying to be whispery. She should be on the stage." He grinned at me, clearly enjoying keeping me in suspense. "She said that she'd been into the Midtown Cafe at lunch, and one of the women who works at the hotel said that Frank Andrews tore into Murph Lee right after you left. Andrews said that he was tired of dealing with white assholes who didn't know how to keep their partners in order and that if Murph thought that Andrews would continue to do business with these idiots, he had another thing coming. Some of it was in Innu-aimun apparently, Andrews was so pissed off."

"Was the word he used really *partners*?"

"According to a gossipy volunteer, it was. I noticed it as well."

"Well, I think I've made myself safe, at least for now. No wandering on the beach tonight though."

"Good. We'll just drink scotch and eat slum food." That was Nick's way of dissing my name for the stew, but I refused to bite. He made both of us big bowls of the stuff with healthy-sized pieces of homemade bread. We ate and talked about normal stuff for a while, and then I couldn't help myself.

"Why aren't you telling me about what happened yesterday? Why were you arrested?"

Nick mumbled something into his drink.

"I can't hear you. Why aren't you talking about this?"

Nick must have realized that I wasn't going to let it go. We'd had to make a concerted effort, over the past few years, not to let each other's jobs too far into our relationship, but it was tough. He had to realize that I felt terrible that he'd been arrested, that I could've, conceivably, been ordered to arrest him. I got that, but I still needed to know. He sat there, looking at his hands, as if they might hold an answer that would satisfy me. Finally, he spoke.

"Nell, I don't want to discuss this because you'll react badly." I started to protest, but he put his hand up. "Sweetheart, please listen. I don't know why I was put on the list of those who breached the injunction. I don't know how far they're prepared to carry this. They were shockingly quiet about it today when I was being processed for release. I'm still charged. They've lifted nothing. I've contacted all the bodies that I need to: the Canadian Civil Liberties Union, Canadian Journalists for Free Expression, the CAJ, and a lawyer they've set me up with, from St. John's. I'll be talking to her tomorrow. There's nothing else I can do."

"They haven't dropped the charge? That's just plain crazy. I'm calling Renaud and getting this straightened out."

"Nell. You aren't. You don't get it, do you?"

I looked at him. I was sure that he wasn't being even remotely condescending. What was it?

"I'm not sure of the connection between my arrest and the attacks made on you, but I *am* sure that there *is* one. Both of us, in a span of 24 hours, have been told to shut up. Till I can figure out why or by whom, we need to step very carefully."

"Is that why you went all quiet this afternoon when I told you about the attacks?"

He looked at me grimly, rose, and started putting the dishes in the sink. The lovely, homey evening with my pal ran cold. How precarious life sometimes feels. I had wanted to run my ideas by Nick—keeping my counsel, of course—but having a partner who was smart and savvy and so much more cool-headed than I was had become a great assistance in my work. Now I felt like it was my fecklessness that had endangered us both—not just my own skin, but my man's and his livelihood. The feeling creeping up on me was familiar.

Shame. I felt shame that I'd been careless with my own life, and by extension, with his. He would never say that. I'd spent the day feeling like some sort of Nancy Drew, winkling out the bad guys with my clever schemes, while he'd been carrying on, quietly, trying to report on a story that no one wanted told. I knew that if he was tried and the defence failed, he could be put in jail, get slapped with a whopping fine, and, on top of that, lose the job he cared so much about.

I so wanted to make it better, to reel back the days and find where I'd gone off the rail. After all, as Renaud had ever so impatiently asked me: *why didn't I trust the system?* Why did I go all rogue instead of quietly doing the work and trusting the team that was in place? I didn't know the answer to that question, then or now. Who else besides myself had I put in jeopardy with my dog-with-a-bone approach? I know that I had hurt Pete with my business with the priest. If I hadn't pushed so hard against the idea of Pashin being responsible for Jay Tuck's death, maybe Musgrave wouldn't have held on so steadfastly to his theory. How many people were, in fact, out there covering or protecting me while I acted like some sort of adolescent Rambo?

I sat there, sipping my scotch, watching as Nick cleaned up the kitchen.

When I had calmed down, I realized that neither Nick nor Renaud was telling me that I was useless, and it wasn't helpful for me to think this way. If Nick wouldn't make himself available for my brainstorming, I would have to do it by myself. I gave him a squeeze, took my notes into the office we shared, and set to work. Hoping that by focusing on the job at hand, I could quiet the demon's voices in my head.

He felt paralyzed. He hadn't made one right step. Okay, maybe getting the drum had been right, but ever since then, he'd made mistake after mistake. He should never have told Shirleen, but she'd been his dependable adult since his mother died. She was always planning shit with Mr. T. She probably told him. A few days after he'd told Shirleen what he'd heard, guys wearing ski masks ambushed him. They held a knife to his throat and told him that they were going to kill him. They called him a bum boy and other unoriginal names, and they cut his arm. Then they said that they'd let him go, but only because he had friends in high places. He should stay away from those Knife assholes or they'd finish the job. A few days later, Mr. Tuck was dead. Before he could even talk to Shirleen again, she was gone too. He was scared to tell anyone else what he'd heard when he was finding the drum—and he was scared not to.

Saturday, November 7

+++ Chapter 27

Two hours after I'd gone to bed, I woke up thinking about that priest in Ireland. I hadn't finished with him and I knew the question I needed to ask. What time was it there if it was nearly 1 a.m. in Labrador? 5 a.m. Too early, even for priests.

I slept. I dreamt.

I dreamt that Jay and Shirleen came to me at the house. Jay looked cheerful and Shirleen was quiet. But then, she was usually quiet. As a counsellor, I'd learned to pay attention to my dreams; sometimes my subconscious was quicker at coming up with a solution than my awake brain. Years ago, I'd made it a habit to write down my dreams first thing every morning. Maybe there would be a small sign or a clue or maybe nothing, but it cost me not a penny to pay attention. So if it only worked now and then, that was okay.

Last night I looked up the businesses on my list as best I could. I'd found information on Mokami Trekking Adventures without too much difficulty. The board of directors was a curious mix: Chesley McMaster was the chairman, and the other directors were Murph Lee, Dick Freemantle, Fred Goudge, Frank Andrews, and a woman, Belinda Gardner, whose name rang the tiniest of bells. I'd check that out later. The ones I knew certainly didn't appear to have an interest

---

in the great outdoors, but perhaps it was only a money-making idea for them.

The other business that registered at about the same time, also under the umbrella of Big Land Solutions, was Atik Enterprises. Apparently, the company had developed a prototype of a connector for hydro-transmission lines. The chairman of that board was Frank Andrews, and the board, judging by the names, was made up of Innu residents of Sheshatshiu. They were in the process of trying to get a grant from the Aurora Agreement.

Before examining my dream further, I phoned Father O'Toole to ask the question that had begun to burn in my mind. Again, I went through the rigmarole with the office staff, waiting for the priest to come to the phone. Then I heard his now familiar, gruff voice on the other end of the phone.

"Father, it's Nell Munro calling again, from Canada. I do have another question. What was the name of the priest who was under suspicion of sexual misconduct?"

A long pause. I understood, but I thought that O'Toole was one of the good guys, so I waited him out.

"I shouldn't be telling you this. He has, I understand, been reformed."

"But you know how unlikely that is, don't you, Father?"

"Yes, I'm afraid I do. His name is Adrian Ryan."

"When Shirleen Gregoire called you from the detachment a few days ago, did she ask you that question?"

"No. No, she didn't. Sure and I'd remember that."

I phoned the detachment. This new information and the fact that Father Ryan had been shifty about his previous association with Jay Tuck put him squarely on the suspect list. He needed another visit, and this time it had to be by someone in uniform. It made sense that it be Pete, since he'd been at the second interview.

I told him what I had just found out. He groaned. "You think I should go over and talk to him again?"

"You know I do. Check it out with the sergeant if you like, but maybe it's time you took the initiative. You can ask to talk to his 'woman' as well."

I knew that that would bug him, but I wasn't above using a little manipulation.

"I'll go over this morning. Tell me the name of the Father you talked to again?"

I did, and we went over what was important to find out. I could hear in Pete's voice that he was nervous about this, but I also heard a strength that was usually missing. Good then. I'd let Pete take over.

Nick had gone out while I was on the phone. He'd left a note saying that he didn't want to interrupt me and that he was going into Goose to talk to a few other journalists. He mentioned that he'd see me later at the service for Shirleen, if he could. I was grateful for the reminder; in all the action, I'd forgotten. It was to be held at the church in North West River at 11 a.m. Just enough time to get a few things done.

I made myself a coffee and sat thinking about my dream. Jay had been looking at me, with his usual wry look. Shirleen had been quiet, but I sensed agitation. Before I could tell them how glad I was to see them, Jay held up one of his hands, a single strand of pink, fake hair caught in it.

Bubble-gum slut.

The Halloween party. One of those four had been gussied up in a pink wig and huge tits the night of Jay's murder: Fred Goudge. I remembered because the thought of his physique on the dance floor, laden with fake tits and sleazing on girls, was an image that I hadn't been able to shake. That strand of hair would put him at the scene of the crime.

I had time to make some inquiries.

✦

There are only two ways a person could purchase a costume in Happy Valley-Goose Bay: order online or buy something at the Cheapo Store. A woman named Karen answered the phone and said that they did sell a costume that included a bright pink wig called Princess Bubble Gum.

"Ya, we sold one of them the other day, maybe two. No idea who to. Busiest time of the year. Let me go ask Trish if she remembers. She's the Halloween freak around here."

I could hear Karen call out to Trish and then some low voices. I heard someone pick up the receiver and a young voice said, "Hi, it's Trish here. Ya, one guy bought two of those costumes. I only remember because I thought it was, like, weird. But whatever. They called first asking what costumes I had doubles of. It was that one or two Batman costumes, but they weren't large enough."

"Do you remember who it was?"

"Uh, I think it was one of the councillors. The guy who runs the Big Eat maybe?"

"Thanks—you've been a big help."

Next up was a visit to Shania's. She loves live music and I knew that she'd gone to the dance at the community hall.

"Come on. I'll treat you to some coffee," Shania said after I knocked on her door. Once she settled a mug in my hands, I asked her about the dance.

She chuckled. "Way fun—danced for hours."

"Did you see any guys dressed as women?"

"Only about 12 of them." She rolled her eyes. "Makes you wonder, doesn't it?"

Sure did.

"Were there any men dressed as princesses, wearing a bright pink wig?"

Shania didn't miss a beat. "Yes. Fred Goudge."

"Are you sure? I mean, could you make out his features?"

Shania looked at me with her eyebrows raised. "What's this about? Does this have something to do with the murder investigation? I thought that it was a done deal with Pashin. I heard that Tuck had some nude photo of him. Is that true?"

"I can't talk about anything found at the murder site, but there have been two murders and one of them took place when Pashin was under lock and key. I know I'm asking a lot, but can you just trust me on this?" But could I trust my own conclusions about Tuck?

Knowing that he'd been a priest and had gone into teaching caused me to question my own certitude about Pashin and his innocence. I thought of the kids I'd known that had protected people who had sexually assaulted them. How far many of them would go to preserve an unwarranted loyalty. I shook my head to clear the thoughts and looked at Shania.

She nodded.

"How did you know it was Fred?"

"I couldn't see his face, because he had a stupid mask on, an animé thing, but he asked me to dance and I recognized his voice."

"Did you dance with him?"

"Yes, and I wish I hadn't. Dances like a fat robot. I got tired of his stepping on my feet, so halfway through I told him that I needed to get some air, and went outside."

"How long was he there for?"

"Right to the bitter end. He stopped dancing at some point and was sitting by himself. Made me wonder why he was still there. Maybe he was pissed by then. I only noticed because he wouldn't go up for the costume parade."

"What time was that?"

"I don't know—I guess it started around 12:30."

"And Fred Goudge was definitely still there?"

"Uh, Nell, I don't drink remember. He was there till the room emptied."

I sipped my coffee. It was almost as bitter as the stuff we brewed at the detachment. I tried to remember who else had spoken of going to the dance in the conversation I'd overheard at the Big Eat. One of them had mentioned having a cousin in the band The Grand River Stompers. I couldn't keep the myriad of family connections in my mind, but I bet Shania could.

"Bear with me Shania. I wouldn't be asking if it wasn't important. Was Murph Lee at the dance?"

"Oh yes. Saw him at the beginning. I go out of my way to avoid him. He's always got some twisted little deal in the works. He left early though."

I sat there, feeling like I'd spent much of my life sipping coffee, thinking, and trying to put it all together.

"Uh, Nell? Did I hear a rumour that you were on leave?"

"Yep. I got uppity at Musgrave. Sergeant Renaud saved me from suspension by putting me on stress leave."

"You know, Nell, you'd do a lot better if you'd just not fight every single battle. Some hills are for walking *around*, you know. The Innu think you're one of the good ones—no, I don't mean whites, I mean cops. It'd be a shame to ruin that because you can't keep your temper in check."

"Preaching to the over-preached to, Shania. I'll work on it, okay? That Musgrave wouldn't even consider the oddness of Shirleen's death. It just ... fried me."

Shania looked at me with a look I hadn't seen in a long time. "Spill, Nell. The whole thing. If you like, I'll sign a document saying we have client-social worker privilege. You need to get this out— you're like a simmering pot of stew gone bad."

And so I did. Truth be told I was grateful. I needed to let it out.

I told her about Pashin, about the sweat, about what I knew about the Crooked Knife Society. I told her about being threatened and the ambush after the bonfire. I told her that I didn't trust Musgrave and about what happened to Nick at the protest. I told her about the priest and the lies, about the good old boys, and Frank Andrews. And when I had finished, she sat back and regarded me with her steady brown eyes.

"I know you won't like what I'm about to say, but I'm going to say it anyway, because that's what friends do." Shania leaned way back in her chair, as if to gain some space from me. She closed her eyes and then blew air out forcefully before continuing. "What if you are wrong, Nell? What if your boss, who's been working as an officer for many years, has a handle on the investigation? What if you just don't like the idea of one of 'your' kids being up on a murder charge? Why don't you trust the system that you signed up for? If Pashin's being railroaded, why don't you trust the courts to sort it out? And why don't you see that maybe what's happened to Nick is just part of the regular way that BECorp handles protests. If they were wrong to have him arrested, and I agree that they were, then he'll see it through. Why do you have to mix it up with oily sergeants, priests, and conspiracies among dunces?"

I took it in. It hurt, but I could see the truth in it.

"I have nothing to say to that, Shania. And I want to thank you for being so honest. I have some thinking to do. Are you going to Shirleen's service?"

Shania's eyes flashed with a hint of joy. "Unlikely. I have to meet with some parents who are working hard to get their children back. I hardly ever have good news, but when I do, I want to deliver it myself. Shirleen would understand. If it wraps up early, I'll come to the reception."

It turned out that I did have one other thing to say. I tried to keep it in, but it just wouldn't stay there—stuffed into my heart like a wounded bird.

"Shania, let's say the system does work and that the path the others are taking will work out fine. Who attacked me? Twice? Because it sure wasn't Pashin."

Shania said nothing.

+++ Chapter 28

The United Church in North West River is one of those places that can make you believe in the good old days. Not only believe in them but think that they might be possible again. It was a small, wooden church with only one room upstairs—the sanctuary. There was a tiny vestibule suitable for one person at a time to take their boots off, but that was it. Inside the sanctuary were both real and fake stained-glass windows, the kind made with plastic fastened to the windows proper. Somehow, they didn't look hideous like one might imagine; even the plastic ones looked homey and nice. On the walls were several star quilts, made by the church sewing circle, that gave a plain and comforting feel. Although it wasn't as ornate as a Catholic church or as plain and graceful as, say, a Quaker church, it had a peace that was palpable.

I felt none of that peace. Instead, I felt a tremendous sense of hopelessness. Maybe it was time for me to let go of this thing. My guess was that the bad guys were in charge all the way up and all the way down. In which case, even if I was right, and Shania wrong, what difference would it make? I couldn't fight the big guns. The best I could do was wait until Monday, give the information I had to Renaud, and let him take it from there.

I settled into one of the pews at the back. I was alone. Nick had left me a message on the phone at home telling me not to expect him; the only time he could have a conference call with the lawyer he'd been set up with was this afternoon. Shirleen's service wasn't technically a funeral. It was a celebration of life, because they hadn't released her body yet. Her mother and some of her siblings sat quietly in the front pew. Unmarried and without children, Shirleen had paid special attention to her nieces and nephews, and I was glad to see that many were present and shined up for the event. I was surprised to read in the little memorial pamphlet that we were given at the door that she was 38. I would have thought that she was older than me. Despite a tendency to giggle, she was so old-fashioned in her clothing and her manners that she seemed to be from another age.

The low November light slanting through the windows cast lovely patterns on the walls. I sat in one of the pews at the back, which were quickly filling up, and pondered the sum of a person's life. Jay Tuck had had a full life by surrounding himself with all the chaos of community. Shirleen's life had been full in a different way, a way that appeared on the surface to be conventional and perhaps lonely. I supposed the two had the loneliness of single life in common. He had shunned church, for what may have been good reasons. Shirleen embraced church and an orderly life. She hated messiness, but she had a huge heart. All the love she could have showered a lover, a child, or a friend with, she'd given to making her community better. She'd hidden her activism, or she'd at least been quiet and humble about it. And she'd been firm in her truth. What she'd told Jenny about not giving up was surely true of her. I reflected on this while I waited, like everyone else, for the rest of the mourners to show up and for the service to begin.

I looked around to see who else had come in since I took my spot. I knew that Renaud would be here somewhere, although I couldn't see him. I did spot Shirleen's former boss, Jenny Black. I caught her eye and she smiled at me. Was she up or down? I saw her move to the front pew and talk to Shirleen's mother, Nuish. Their heads down, Jenny talking, Nuish shaking her head *no*. Johnny was up front too, sitting with some Innu kids, Zann, Kaitlyn, and Jeremiah among them. The kids were evidence of the quiet connections Shirleen had made with the youth of her community—especially those that might have been at risk.

I tried to keep my place by the aisle but was scooted to the side by Mrs. Nighthawk. There would be no denying the right of an Innu Elder to take whatever place they wanted. She was wearing a traditional Innu bonnet that looked like a tall beret with a beaded rim. To wear it to Shirleen's funeral meant that Mrs. Nighthawk held Shirleen in the highest esteem. After our last meeting, I must admit that I felt some apprehension in seeing her, although it was clear that she had chosen to sit next to me, since there were still vacant spots elsewhere. I greeted her, offering my general condolences.

"Yes. It's awful. I wonder where her niece Marilyn is? Have you seen her?"

Marilyn was the niece that Shirleen worried about. She'd had trouble with men and drugs, and Shirleen was forever grimly getting her out of one fix or another. I'd heard her say that Marilyn's ex-boyfriend had moved to Sept-Îles, and now maybe she could get her shit together. One more vulnerable person living on a knife-edge.

I shrugged at Mrs. Nighthawk.

She sat back in the pew and arranged her things disapprovingly. "Shirleen took care of that girl. You'd think Marilyn could show her some respect." She folded her mitts carefully, placed her scarf on top, and put the order of service in the slot on the pew in front of us. After she was settled, she turned her gaze to me. She struck like a hawk, fierce and true. "Shirleen never did anyone any harm to have this happen. She never gave up on someone or something, even when it became dangerous or people said that it was impossible." She said it in a soft but firm tone. I didn't misunderstand it.

There it was: the challenge. Oh, you could say that I was imagining things and that what Mrs. Nighthawk said was perfectly pedestrian. That she'd grabbed the first pew she'd seen and was making small talk. But you'd be wrong, and I knew it. This was a call and I would have to answer it. I knew then that I wasn't going to stop investigating, even if it meant my career—even if nothing changed.

"Thanks." Her bony hand shot out, grabbed mine, and squeezed.

Then the celebration of the secret life of Shirleen began.

The funeral (or service or whatever) was sweet. The hymns were those that you want to hear at a funeral: "Abide with Me," "The Old Rugged Cross," and my all-time favourite, "The Little Brown Church in the Vale." The church was filled with the reedy voices of old ladies that probably fill most churches in Canada, shy baritones, and stunningly off-key altos. Okay, one: me. But at least I take part. I think it's bad form to go to a funeral and not sing.

The minister didn't get too crazy and religious. That might seem like an odd thing to say about a minister, but this one was prone to hyperbole and much fire and brimstone. She'd been reproached a few times by the church ladies about it, and I guess she'd gotten the message. The only moment she fell back into her old ways was when she mentioned that most of us didn't darken the door except for funerals and Christmas, and we might regret that little oversight when we were on the pointy end of a pitchfork. All in all, it was fairly peaceful.

While voices said the inevitable about Shirleen—listing the committees she belonged to, her many connections on both sides of the river, the sadness of the sudden loss—I pondered my next move.

What did the deadline that the Big Eat four talked about have to do with the murders? If Pashin was set up, I had to consider Frank Andrews. I knew Pashin's mother had taken lots of photos, and Frank had access to her things, so it would be easy for him to plant one on Jay. He might have known that Tuck had been a priest, and that fact alone would cause the community to be suspicious. And what about the priest? I hoped that Pete had gotten some satisfaction from his interview with him.

On and on I ruminated; on and on the service went. Not true, it was short enough. I was just antsy to get going now that I was committed to action. By the last hymn ("Be Thou My Vision"), I'd decided that I would talk once more to Renaud and try to get him to see what I saw. Before leaving the church, I spoke to several members of Shirleen's family, saying the requisite things. Mrs. Nighthawk, I noted, was in what looked like fierce conversation with Shirleen's mother, speaking in Innu-aimun.

And there was Renaud. Standing just outside the door. I hadn't seen him come in, so I imagine that he'd arrived late and had stood in the entryway. That meant I could avoid going into the detachment.

"Hello, sir, lovely service, eh?"

"Yes. Shirleen would have liked it—especially the turnout."

"Sir, I found out some information last night that I think may have us take another tack with this investigation."

Renaud raised his eyebrows before answering. "Okay, Nell, we can talk at the reception over at Shirleen's mother's house. I might be a few minutes late—have to check in at the detachment. Oh, and Constable McLean told me to tell you that he met with the priest again. Father Ryan was in Natuashish the weekend of the murder."

Natuashish is on the north coast, a plane ride away, an alibi easily checked. I nodded in mute agreement, no closer to puzzling it all out.

✦

Shirleen's mother's house was on the reserve, not far from the detachment. I parked on the road behind a long line of trucks and cars. I wondered about the turnout. Would the North West River folk make it over? After all, Shirleen had chosen their church, but mothers were mothers. Everyone knew that.

The house was tidy, if not as persnickety as Shirleen's. It was too cramped for this sort of event, but folks from both sides of the river spilled out onto the lawn—the cool November air did not stop them. I found Nuish in the living room surrounded by women. I took her hand and told her how lovely her daughter had been and how she'd be missed. Nuish seemed to be in a cocoon of grief, my words not even landing. She nodded and I moved on and outside again. Shania was standing on the driveway, having just arrived. "Whew! That was tight, but the job is done and all are happy for the moment," she said to me as I approached.

I remembered something I wanted to ask her. "Do you know who Belinda Gardner is? I know that I know her name. She was the other name on that list of directors for Mokami."

Shania looked at me. "Belinda was Belinda Musgrave, remember? She took back her maiden name."

We stared at each other a second, the cogs turning in each of our minds. "Fuck" was all I could manage. Then I shook myself out of it. Sometimes my mind worked slowly and sometimes it zoomed along making connections.

"Shania, Renaud is coming by shortly. Tell him that I've gone into town to talk to Belinda Gardner. Tell him why, along with what I told you earlier about Mokami Trekking Adventures and Atik—they're connected. Got that?"

"You betcha."

+++ Chapter 29

I jumped into my car and set out for Goose Bay. As I drove, I tried to calm my mind. It wouldn't help anyone for me to go ballistic. I'd have to think this out as I drove. It seemed important to get everything in the right order. All I had were bits and pieces. Nothing that could lead to an arrest unless I could find the key piece. This was the first time I'd a solid connection between Musgrave and the scummy bunch from the Big Eat. If I could find out if Belinda was involved with this so-called company, it would be a way in.

What else did I know for sure? I knew that Fred had been dressed as the bubble-gum slut. And I knew that pink synthetic hair had been found at the murder scene. I wondered if Fred still had the costumes? Why had he bought two? And why would those guys want Tuck dead, let alone Shirleen? The Monday deadline floated into my mind. I knew that these were linked, but how? At least I could put to rest the idea of the priest's involvement. I still didn't like him, but it didn't seem possible that he had anything to do with either of the murders.

By the time I got to town, I had a plan of sorts. I made a quick trip to the municipal office to look at the records for new businesses. The woman working the front desk was a sister of Pete's and recognized me. She gave me a copy of the signatories of both Mokami Trekking and Atik Enterprises, bypassing the usual wait for forms. This in hand, I made a visit to Belinda Gardner. Her address was on the form. Belinda lived in a pleasant looking home in a small development just before the second post office: a ranch-style split-level with a neat and tidy yard. I went to the front door and rang the bell. Belinda answered within seconds, looking, as she had the few times I'd met her, like a whipped dog. I think she'd at one time been an attractive woman, but now had the curved shoulders of someone who'd given up. Maybe she was in her late 40s. Her fashion choices added to her general air of dowdiness. She wore dun-coloured slacks, a greyish shell, and an oversize sweater in a shade of cat vomit. Her hair was pinned back on both sides with barrettes that she'd likely had since grade school, her feet encased in old-lady slippers, her head dipped down. She seemed to expect me, like an executioner that she knew would show up one day.

"Hi, Belinda. I wonder if you'd mind answering a few questions. I came straight from Shirleen Gregoire's funeral and something just clicked about an investigation we're conducting, so I thought I'd check it out." I was almost certain that she and Musgrave weren't talking, but I still tried to be as vague as possible.

She motioned for me to take a seat on the couch in her tidy living room. Everything was in shades of pale muddy green and beige, decorated with cutesy signs that read *Home Is Best* and *A House Is Made of Boards, but a Home Is Made of Love and Dreams* and *Live in the Sunshine, Swim in the Sea*, which was odd because there was nothing sunny about Belinda. Maybe they were gifts. Along with the folksy signs were many candles, all with competing smells, and a large assortment of framed baby photos, likely of a grandchild. I sat on the edge of the couch and Belinda sat across from me in an under-stuffed chair.

"Can I get you a tea?"

"No, thanks, I'm good. I have a question about the enterprise you are involved with." I checked the document I'd just received. "Chesley McMaster, Murphy Lee, Dick Freemantle, Fred Goudge, and Frank Andrews."

She looked perplexed. "I'm not in any enterprise, and certainly not with any of those people. You must have some wrong information. What is this to do with anyway?"

"It's on the records at the municipal office that you're partners with the others at Mokami Trekking Adventures. I guess it's an ecotourism company. Ring any bells?"

"No. First of all, McMaster was my husband's lawyer in our divorce, which was not at all amicable. I hate him. I hardly know the others except that my ex-husband likes to get together with them, which doesn't make me like them any better. And I don't know anything about ecotourism, whatever that is. You're mistaken."

She looked animated, finally. It was almost worth it just to see that she had blood in her body.

"Well, your signature is on record." I handed her the form. "It's yours, isn't it?"

"It looks like mine, but I didn't sign this, or if I did, I didn't mean to. Al brought me all sorts of papers to sign for the divorce and settlement. Maybe he put this one in there by mistake."

"Yes, I suppose that could happen, but when it was filed, everyone else on this list must have seen your name. Why would he do that?"

"I'd better call my lawyer again. Am I in trouble? What has happened with the business?"

"Phoning your lawyer would probably be a good idea, because it looks like some fraud has been committed. I don't know anything about the business other than the names on this form. Was your husband in some sort of money crunch that you know of?"

"I really don't know. I mean, he makes a good salary, but he always complained about money. I just thought he was playing poor to get out of giving me a decent settlement."

I could tell that her energy was flagging. The burst she'd received in the first flush of realizing that it looked like her ex had done something sleazy had dissipated. I said my goodbyes and told Belinda that she should contact her lawyer right away.

I was in my car when my cell rang. Penny Leap.

"Hi, Penny. What's up?"

"Where are you?"

"I'm in town. Why?"

"I just found out that they released Pashin a few hours ago—just sprung him without so much as a call to anyone."

"Have you talked to him?"

"No. Here's the thing. I got a message on my work cell last night. Because I was talking to another client, it must have gone straight to voicemail, and I didn't check it till this morning. Pashin's voice was very quiet, but he said he wanted to talk to me or you or both of us today. He had something really important he wanted to tell us. That's why I went in. I tried calling you this morning but couldn't reach you. I called your detachment to let you know. When I got there, he'd been released. I just called Johnny, and he hasn't heard a peep. I don't know how they expected him to get home."

I sat there trying to order my thoughts. Why did they let him go, and why without telling any of us? I didn't like it. What did he want to tell us and had someone overheard him speaking to Penny?

"Okay, Penny. I'll call the detachment in North West and see if I can get Pete to look into Pashin's release. I'll check at the hospital. I'll call you back if I find anything, and you do the same."

Before I headed to the hospital, I phoned the detachment. Shelley told me that Sergeant Renaud was on his way to Goose Bay and that she wasn't entirely sure where Pete was.

"Listen, Shelley, get Pete by radio if you can, and tell him Pashin was released and is missing. Tell him to call Johnny Tuglavina."

"Who's that?"

"Never mind. Pete knows."

The hospital in Happy Valley was treated by many Innu, and indeed all the car-less of North West River, as a bus station. There was always someone going back to Sheshatshiu or North West River from the hospital if you waited long enough.

I saw a kid I knew from the school sitting on a bench near the front. It looked like she'd been there a while, so I took a chance.

"Hey, Louisa!"

"Hey, Miss, what are you doing here?"

"I'm looking for Pashin. Have you seen him?"

"No, Miss. I haven't seen him. I thought he was in jail."

"They released him this morning, so I thought he might have come here looking for a ride."

"Nope, and I've been here since 6 a.m."

"Awake the whole time?"

"Awake enough to see anyone coming in the door. I came in with my auntie and she's staying in. I didn't think she was till a few hours ago. You going back to Shesh, Miss?"

"Not right away, but when I do, I'll swing by, and if you're still here, I'll get you home."

"Aw, don't worry about it. I know my mother's coming in to see my auntie, so I'll go home with her. I turned down rides already—didn't like the way the drivers were looking." She grinned, and I grinned back, and we both said at the same time, "A ride with a drunk is a ride to the wrong place," in perfect sing-songy tones.

I went over to Emergency and checked with the staff there, although that was even more unlikely. No one had seen him. I crossed the street and went into Tim Horton's. The staff there said they hadn't noticed anyone like Pashin, but they couldn't be sure—so busy in the morning.

While I was so close by, I decided to drop in on the jail itself.

I recognized the guard sitting at the front desk.

"Hi Ralph, is it true that Pashin was released?"

"Well ..." Ralph looked up from his sudoku nervously. "I'm not sure I'm supposed to tell you."

"Ralph, as youth liaison officer, I'm supposed to have full access to information about youth prisoners under Sub-section 312 of the Criminal Code." Not technically true, but I didn't have time for Ralph to work the system in slo-mo. "What time was he released, under whose orders, and what arrangements were made for him to get back to Sheshatshiu where he resides?"

"Uh, just a minute. I'll get the discharge papers for you." Ralph shuffled through the files on his desk. "Here. He got out at 10:37. Staff Sergeant Musgrave signed the papers. I don't know if the kid was picked up or what have you. That's not our business here."

I bit my tongue. No point in getting the guards annoyed. I had to figure out another way. "Did he call anyone?"

"Listen, uh … Constable. I wasn't here this morning. I didn't start till an hour ago, but it looks like this was done by the book. He was allowed to call to have someone pick him up, and he signed this paper saying that he waived that right. That's all I know."

"But he called someone last night. He called his lawyer. Do you have a record of that?"

"No, I don't. Anyone in here is allowed to make one phone call a day to anyone local. No long-distance calls. I wasn't here last night, so I don't know if he did or didn't."

That's all I was going to find out from this guy. I turned on my heel and left the building. I stood outside the front door for a moment, zipping up my jacket, when I thought of something. I re-entered and went up to Ralph again.

"Ralph, I forgot something. I was supposed to talk to another person you are holding. Jaysus, with all this going on I've forgotten his name. Who have you got in here right now?" I knew they only had a few holding cells, and I was taking a chance.

"Pretty quiet here right now. Just Elijah Shiwak—some Innu from the coast. I don't know about that. Why do you need to talk to him?"

My mind went over possible connections. It came up with a vague hope. "Oh yes, Elijah. That's who I need to talk to. He worked in the school in Natuashish and I have to ask him about a youth program we're setting up there. Won't take me a minute, unless you want me to check with the sergeant? Only I guess he's getting ready for his trip about now, but I can check with him if you like."

And then I waited. And waited. Finally, Ralph responded. "Nah, that's okay, Constable. I know you're the liaison officer. Shiwak is supposed to be released later today, anyway."

He took me back to the cells and told me that if it was short, I could talk to Elijah through the door opening. "Fine." He left me there. I pitched my voice as low as it could be and still be heard, but I was banking on Ralph wanting to get back to his sudoku.

"Elijah, it's Nell Munro from North West River. I know Pashin was in the next cell. They released him this morning and I'm worried about where he is. Any ideas?"

"Hey, Miss. Sorry you found me here but—"

I cut him off.

"Elijah, I'm really worried about Pashin. Did he say anything to you when they came to let him out?"

"Ya. He told me to tell you or Miss Leap that he was going to go get purified. Not sure what he meant, but he thought you'd know. He was too scared to say anything with the goons around. He thought they might do something. He was worried all night. Just that: 'Tell Miss Munro or Miss Leap or Lonesome Johnny—whichever of those three and only those three—that I'm going to get purified. Got it?' That's all he said."

It didn't take me but a moment to puzzle it out. I hoped it would've taken longer for anyone else who may have heard. Where would an Innu kid go to be purified? There were only two ways to be purified from an Innu perspective: one was to be smudged, the other was with a sweat. The sweat lodge was about 15 minutes from here by car, but how would he have gotten there?

A few minutes later, after leaving messages for Penny about where I was headed and why, I was on the road to Caribou Lodge. I couldn't help but scan the sides of the road as I drove to see if I could spot Pashin. If he was released at 10:30 and started walking right away, it might take him three and a half hours to walk to the lodge. It was nearly 3 p.m. If he was scared he'd be followed, he might have taken one of the less-exposed snowmobile trails that ran near the road. There wasn't enough snow down for snowmobiles, but a kid could probably hike at a quick pace on these trails.

I pulled over to call the detachment while I still had cell service. I told Shelley to call Pete and tell him to meet me at Caribou Lodge and to tell Renaud, if he checked in, that was where I was headed. After I hung up, I thought that I should have told her not to tell anyone else where I was going. I tried phoning back, but no one answered. God, I missed Shirleen. I called Penny, who told me she'd reached Johnny and that he'd meet me there soon.

I turned down the road to the lodge and didn't see any signs of life around. I decided it would be smart to take a side road and park the car out of sight. I walked up to the lodge's buildings, sticking to the tree line just in case anyone was around. I didn't see any smoke coming out of the building that held the sweat lodge, but I did see a white, plastic bag near the doorway—just like the ones they give you when they boot you out of jail. It looked like it was full of something—clothes? It couldn't have been there long: no frost and too clean. I could feel my heart pounding in my chest. The building that held the lodge was an uninsulated, wooden shed. I could hear some movement and reminded myself that if I could hear those inside, they could hear me. I calmed my breathing, taking slow breaths in through my nose and down to my belly to quiet my nerves. I walked around to the back of the building, knowing that the sweat lodge itself was against the back wall. I heard a voice, the words in Innu-aimun—low. I couldn't make out who it was, but it didn't sound like Pashin.

While I crouched there behind the building, I heard a vehicle pull up out front, a car door slam, and then someone enter the building.

"Hey, Andrews? You in here?"

It was Fred Goudge. I heard him moving into the tent.

"Andrews—what the fuck have you got me into now? I didn't know that the kid was going to be here. What gives?"

"This should have been done before now, and we gotta make

sure it's done right. The kid was about to spill his guts to that lawyer. Musgrave got the word from one of the guards. Stupid cop screwed up big time. We coulda gotten rid of this dumb kid way back, but no. He told me that he'd have the kid released this morning, and I got one of my guys to watch by the jail and follow him. The kid lost him for a while—went into the woods—but my guy had his three-wheeler and followed his tracks. 'Just like hunting caribou,' he said. He saw him headed this way and realized where the kid was going. Those Crooked Knifers have been using the lodge for their stupid meetings. Only no one is around. All of them at that bitch's funeral."

"Why is he tied up? I'm not going to be part of another murder."

"Ya, you white folks only want the money. You don't want to get your hands dirty."

Goudge whined at that. "Come on, I was there when you killed Tuck. And me and Scottie scared that cop bitch, twice. We coulda gone to jail for that alone. Musgrave hasn't done a thing. Why does he get an equal share?"

"You're just the meat. Don't you know that? Musgrave and McMaster and even Lee keep us on the up and up. They're the insurance."

I wondered why Dick Freemantle wasn't mentioned in this all-star lineup.

"Now shut up. I don't want this fucked up. Nice and neat. It's going to look like he OD'd out of remorse for killing his lover. I got the fix here. Now come over and hold on to him in case he wakes up. Nice and gentle, we don't want any marks on him. Then we'll make sure it takes, and get the ropes off."

I tried to calm my heart and breath. I wanted to break in on their action, but I was unarmed. What could I do—shout at them? If I'd paid attention to one thing in my training, it was that martial arts didn't help much when people were armed. Didn't matter. I had to try. I moved around to the front of the building. Just as I was about to move, a hand grabbed my arm. I wheeled around to see Johnny, finger to his lips. He leaned forward, whispering in my ear.

"You might need this," and passed me a gun.

I slipped through the door and entered the vestibule. Unlike the last time I'd been here, it was empty—just benches for clothes and a bucket left tipped on its side. There was no way to enter the lodge without being noticed. I could see a line of light around the flap of the tent. I couldn't take any more time. Perhaps Pashin lay there now, his life slowly dimming.

"Police," I shouted. "Come out slowly with your hands raised." To add a little more confidence in my stance I added, "Constable MacLean, take the outside door. Walker, behind me."

Johnny, bless his heart, called out in a voice that did not sound like his. "I hear the backup vehicle now, Constable."

And miracle of miracles, he was telling the truth.

All of a sudden, the flap on the tent swung aside, and Andrews and Goudge came barrelling out. I stood my ground, the gun levelled at them as they stopped in confusion. Suddenly, they pretended they hadn't just tried to bolt. They hadn't realized that I was in the outer building.

Goudge looked terrified, and that worried me. A terrified man will take unnecessary risks. I could see Andrews taking stock of the situation. He wasn't as stupid as Goudge.

"It's okay, Officer. We were just about to call the detachment. My stepson called me for help. I don't know what the foolish kid was up to. Looks like he was going to kill himself and then called me after he'd taken something."

Man oh man, butter wouldn't melt in this super-cool dude's mouth.

"So why didn't you call before you came out here?"

Andrews licked his lips before answering me. "We were near here when he called, so we didn't think—just rushed here."

"Oh, that explains it." Andrews allowed relief to show on his face before I continued. "But it doesn't explain what I heard you and Goudge here talking about a few moments ago. Get out of my way so I can see Pashin."

Before I was finished, I saw Pete coming in the door, his gun drawn. I left him to it and rushed in to see Pashin lying on the spruce boughs. Too quiet.

+++ Chapter 30

I learned early on in my career that sometimes it is important to think before you act—most times. But sometimes, you must just act. According to brain studies, we experience a half-second delay between reality and our perception of it. That may not seem like much, but it adds to the feeling of time existing on two tracks during emergencies—a very slow track and a very fast one. Which is all to say that before I knew what my hand was doing, my mind had already taken in Pashin's grey skin tone, his laboured breathing, and his general unresponsiveness. *Unresponsiveness.* I grabbed my naloxone kit from my jacket pocket, and injected him within seconds. His response was immediate and violent, but I was ready for it.

"It's okay, Pashin. It's Nell. You've been overdosed with opioids and I've administered naloxone. You're going to be okay."

I hoped that that was true. His breathing had returned to somewhat normal if still jagged. His eyes locked on mine and I saw his body relax. I put him on his side and turned to see Johnny watching. I hadn't even heard him enter.

"Pete's got the goons in his vehicle. He wondered which detachment he should take them to? I've called the paramedics. They'll be here in minutes. I can stay with Pashin."

"Okay. I'll sort that out and be back to wait for the paramedics with you."

I left Johnny with Pashin and went out into the subdued lighting of the November afternoon. Andrews and Goudge were in the back of the police vehicle, and Pete was standing outside it.

"What do you think, Nell? We're smack between the two detachments. This is your call."

"Yep. Take them into the Goose Bay detachment. I'll meet you there. When you get them there, tell them they're both being charged with attempted murder, bodily harm, possession of controlled substances with the intent to sell, and resisting arrest."

Pete looked at me with one eyebrow raised.

"They were attempting to bolt when they came out of the tent. Don't worry about what will stick, throw enough stuff at them that it will make it tough for a judge to grant them a light bail. Get it? I'll bag the fix they left by Pashin, and you make sure they're searched well when you get them into the detachment. You won't find anything, but check for traces just in case."

"Yes, Constable Munro, I get it. I have an unopened evidence kit. I'll get it for you."

Moments after he left, the paramedics arrived. I told them what I'd administered and bagged the fix with the drugs I'd found tossed beside Pashin. I told them that he was to be treated if needed at the clinic, but he wasn't under arrest and I wanted him brought to the detachment in Goose Bay as soon as he was fully awake.

Twenty minutes later I entered the detachment. What was usually a bustling atmosphere seemed preternaturally quiet. Tina, the receptionist, who usually takes an unhealthy interest in her boss's business, had her head down and wouldn't meet my gaze even after I cleared my throat twice. I said loudly, "I'm going in to see the staff sergeant, Tina."

"Staff Sergeant Musgrave?" I announced myself before entering his office. He was sitting way back in his chair, which was tipped back to its maximum, and he had his hand up stroking his non-beard as if he were seriously contemplating something.

"Staff Sergeant Musgrave? I'm looking for Constable MacLean. I saw his vehicle outside. Is he here somewhere?"

"You bloody know that he is," Musgrave snapped, his voice an octave too high for pleasure.

"Pardon, sir?"

Musgrave leapt to his feet, placed his meaty hands on the desk, and pushed forward so that his face was dangerously close to spitting distance from my own.

"What do you want? I released that kid you were crying about. If he went right out and got into some trouble, what has that got to do with the detachment?"

"By trouble, Staff Sergeant, do you mean the attempted murder by your business partners?"

"I don't know what you're talking about. As far as I know, Andrews and Goudge were trying to help the kid. This nonsense has gone on long enough, and don't think I don't know you're behind it. You've gone too far this time, you little cunt. I'll see you stripped of your rank and discharged from duty permanently."

As he was spitting out those words, I heard the door open behind me and saw Musgrave's eyes go wide.

"I don't think that's a good idea, Staff Sergeant."

It was Sergeant Renaud, and he didn't look angry—he looked determined.

"This is your mess, Sergeant Renaud. I told you to keep this bitch under control, and now she's raving. I want her disciplined."

"Oh, I'm going to deal with her all right." He paused and looked quietly into Musgrave's eyes. "I'm taking her off the bogus stress leave and recommending her for a promotion."

Musgrave's mouth twisted into a rictus of indignation, but as he began to talk, Renaud stopped him.

"Staff Sergeant Musgrave, I'm arresting you on conspiracy to commit fraud, accessory after the fact on two charges of murder, one charge of abduction, and one of attempted murder. You have the right to retain and instruct counsel without delay. You also have the right to free and immediate legal advice from duty counsel by making free telephone calls to Legal Aid. You have the right to silence and anything you do or say may be used as evidence. Do you understand?"

Musgrave stared at Renaud.

"Staff Sergeant, you must answer."

"Yes, I understand."

"Do you wish to call a lawyer?"

"Yes."

"I wish to give you the following warning: You need not say anything. You have nothing to hope from any promise or favour and nothing to fear from any threat whether or not you say anything. Anything you do or say may be used as evidence. Do you understand?"

The rest of the rights were explained to a man who had probably done the same dozens of times.

✦

Two hours and a statement later, I was back in Sheshatshiu talking to Renaud in his office. We told each other in more detail what had happened in the other's absence.

"The reason I was late getting to the reception was that three very agitated women were at the detachment when I got there: Jenny Black, Elizabeth Nighthawk, and Marilyn Gregoire." Renaud explained. "Jenny and Elizabeth seemed certain that Marilyn was hiding something, so after the funeral they went and found her. Those two make a fierce team and they wouldn't let up till she agreed to make a statement. Marilyn told us that she had been coerced by Frank Andrews to get her Aunt Shirleen out to the boat ramp at Terrington Basin under false pretences. She swears that she didn't know that Andrews was going to hurt her aunt, but that will be for the courts to decide."

"But the accessory-after-the-fact charges? How did you link Musgrave to the murders before I gave my statement?"

"Sometimes just straightforward police work gets the job done, Constable." Renaud grinned at me. "Dick Freemantle came in right after the women left. He'd heard wind of what was going on and decided that discretion was not the better part of valour in this case. It appears that he didn't know that Andrews murdered Jay Tuck and arranged for the murder of Shirleen till Goudge phoned him in a panic this morning. I tend to believe him. It won't keep him entirely out of trouble though because of his involvement with the shell companies. Freemantle undoubtedly knew that the creation of two bogus companies in order to move speculators' money was not only morally wrong but possibly fraudulent. It might be considered money laundering, but that's for the courts to figure out. Apparently Goudge's fears had been festering since Tuck's funeral, and he was sure that Pashin knew something. I gather that Goudge let slip something to Freemantle about the fact that everyone knew that he, Goudge that is, had been at the dance till 2 a.m., so they couldn't link him to the death, and Musgrave wouldn't let anything happen to him or he'd be up the creek himself. Freemantle thought it was mighty odd that Goudge was worried about an alibi for the murder of Tuck, and Goudge shut his mouth tighter than a hummingbird's arsehole when Freemantle asked him about it. That got Dick thinking about how you'd told him that you'd been threatened, and he decided that some bad choices were being made. He knew that he was going to be in a helluva mess one way or the other and thought that it would be prudent to cut his losses by throwing Musgrave under the bus."

"Okay, but what I still don't get is why Pashin was threatened in the first place. What was he going to tell either Penny or me this morning?"

"Perhaps he should tell you that."

I turned my head. Johnny stood in the doorway of Renaud's office. Behind him I saw Pashin—looking frailer than normal but with a light in his eyes that I hadn't seen the last few times we'd met.

"Hi, Miss." His voice was soft but strong. "Is it okay if I sit? I'm a little—"

Renaud gestured to one of the chairs. Pashin sat down slowly and then looked at the three of us.

"I already made a statement, but I wanted you to know, Miss. It's all my fault. I know that Johnny says it isn't, but it is. If I hadn't told Shirleen what I'd overheard, she'd be alive and so would Mr. Tuck. After he died, I was so scared—scared to tell anyone else. Then Shirleen died, and I knew it was from what I'd said. Mr. Tuck tried to get me to be quiet, but I was sick of what was going on."

My heart broke to realize the burden that Pashin had been carrying. He was a victim of the silence that had infected the citizens of Sheshatshiu because of their lack of trust in law enforcement. And hadn't that lack of trust just been confirmed when one of our own had been partially responsible for the murders?

"What did you overhear, Pashin? I know it's hard to say it, but telling your story will heal you in the end."

"I'd broken into Frank Andrews's house to find my grandfather's drum. My mother had put it there when she married that asshole. I hid when I heard Andrews and someone else come in. They were talking about some deadline and how a cop was involved. Problem was, I didn't know which cop. All I knew was that it was a male cop that must have been high up. And the white-sounding guy told Andrews that they were going to make way more money than Andrews does with all the drugs he sells."

"That must have scared the shit out of you."

"Ya. No. It wasn't anything I didn't already know about Andrews. That man has always been a sleazy shit. I told Shirleen, because I'd told her stuff before and because I knew that she'd want to know, as part of Crooked Knife. She must have told Mr. Tuck, and then he tried to get me to hold back on the play, but I got mad at him. I was sick of how slow everything was going. He must have tried to reason with Andrews. I didn't believe Mr. Tuck. I didn't think anyone would care about a play a bunch of kids were doing. I should have listened to him."

Pashin stopped for a moment, and a long, juddering sigh came out of him. "I don't know what happened with Shirleen. She must have tried something, knowing her. Last night, well, it was like Mr. Tuck was talking to me—like Hamlet talking to Yorick's skull—telling me that I had to speak up. I called Miss Leap and I guess someone at the jail alerted Musgrave. When they let me out, they wouldn't let me phone anyone, but made me sign some piece of paper saying that they'd offered. It was such bullshit, but I hoped one of you would understand where I'd try to go. It was the only place I could think of. I took the back road out of town and then a snowmobile trail. I thought I was being followed, but what could I do? When I got there, I just waited in the sweat lodge building for you or Miss Leap to arrive, trying to keep quiet, but then some guy with a balaclava on came in and hit me over the head with something. Next thing I knew was you, Miss, hovering over me."

I sighed.

"Pashin, I know you aren't going to believe me yet, but you did nothing wrong. From everything I've gathered about those sleazebags, they were going to make an example of those involved with Crooked Knife no matter what. It was just bad luck it was Jay Tuck—though he probably would say, why not him? And it was brilliant of you to go to the sweat lodge. If you hadn't, they would have gotten to you earlier, and you'd be dead and we wouldn't be able to prove anything. As for Shirleen, well, she died a warrior to her people. Now it's up to you and the other kids to keep on with what those two would want from you. I know you know what that is."

Pashin sat there, his head in his hands. I knew it was going to take a while. I hoped he hadn't lost hope.

"Pashin?" It was Johnny. "I have a message from Pien Nuna. He told me to tell you that your grandfather came to him in a dream and told him that you were ready to begin. He said that you'd know what that meant."

A Sunday in January

+++ Chapter 31

It is another Sunday morning and I have nothing to do. No crimes to see to, no plays to oversee, no funerals to attend. I am on a break, and Sergeant Renaud has assured me that my one-week vacation is secure. Nick and I aren't in Cuba, although we did consider heading there. We'd decided on a quieter retreat, so we headed to our cabin in Butter and Snow. There'd been several snow dumps a few days ago, so we'd come by snowmobile. Two snowmobiles. When we'd first moved to Labrador, I had tried being a passenger, but flailing around on the back while someone else decides which hills to crest and which ones to swing around is a lousy trip. Nick's snowmobile hauled the komatik full of our gear, and I had a carrier fastened on the back of my seat for Bean. He'd take turns riding in it and running alongside us. We realized in the early days that he'd run until his heart burst if we didn't make sure that he was contained for at least part of the trip.

Nick looks at me as I sit in a rocking chair by the fire, Shirleen's favourite place to enjoy the view. We won't own the cabin properly until Shirleen's estate, such as it was, is settled, but Shirleen's eldest sister, the executor, had approved it in principle and written up an interim lease charging us $4 a year so that we could be here fair and square. This was our second and longest stay.

"More coffee?"

"Yes, please. You're going to make breakfast, aren't you?" Nick nodded. "And then what shall we get up to?"

"I thought we'd go back to bed for a little while. Then maybe out for a snowshoe and a boil-up while we still have light."

"Perfect."

We haven't changed much. After the crime-scene barriers came down, the family took the things they cared about: a few knick-knacks, some small pieces of furniture. They left her rocking chair for me, which melts my heart every time I consider it. On our first trip, I brought some Hudson Bay blankets, a few oil lamps, and art by some of the kids at the school. I had a big photo done of the cast and crew of the play, which I framed and hung in pride of place above the table.

Nearly two months have gone by since Shirleen's funeral and they'd been busy ones at the detachment. Some of the consequences were immediate. Frank Andrews is on charges for both murders, as well as the attempted murder of Pashin. Fred Goudge is on charges for the murder of Jay Tuck, and the attempted murder of Pashin. Murph Lee is on a charge of conspiracy to murder Jay Tuck because of his part in providing Fred Goudge with an alibi for the evening of the dance. Andrews, Goudge, and Lee are joined by Chesley McMaster and Dick Freemantle in the various charges associated with the shell-company scam, although the last two swear that they knew nothing of the murders. Of course, none of them, except Andrews, managed to keep their mouths shut; they were all so busy ratting each other out. Al Musgrave is up on three charges of accessory after the fact. It is still unclear how much Musgrave knew about the murders, but there's little doubt that he was complicit in the attempted murder of Pashin. One of the guards at the jail came forward with the instructions that he was given regarding the careful monitoring of Pashin's calls and his subsequent release. As well, Musgrave has charges against him for the fraudulent shell-company scam, including forging his ex-wife's signature. They had set up the ecotourism company as a way to launder the money they'd make from Atik Enterprises. Atik Enterprises would raise all the money through their power line-widget scam. Nick explained to me that nothing actually needed to be made—just some prototype and maybe a bogus manufacturing company in China that looked like it was ready to make the widgets. That's the deal with a mega-power company: everyone tries to skim off some of the dough floating around. They were paying off the Innu "partners" a handsome amount and going to rake in the money in grants and investments from other greedy folks. All the partners knew that once the reservoir was flooded, it would be smooth sailing.

Shirleen's niece Marilyn is also up on charges related to the death of Shirleen. Marilyn had been both a client of and a pusher for Andrews in the recent past. Andrews had coerced or blackmailed Marilyn into delivering Shirleen into his hands. Shirleen's autopsy had shown Rohypnol, also known as the date rape drug as it makes the victim unable to resist without knocking them out completely, in her system, which explained how they'd overdosed her on insulin without a struggle. Only time would tell if Marilyn would be offered some clemency for coming voluntarily into the detachment on the day of Shirleen's funeral. If being press-ganged by Jenny and Mrs. Nighthawk could be called voluntarily.

According to a statement made by Fred Goudge, Andrews killed Tuck because he wanted to scare the Crooked Knife Society prior to the flooding of Otter Falls. After that, it wouldn't matter if the Innu community could prove that it had been duped into signing the Aurora Agreement. Andrews was scared that Crooked Knife was gaining influence on the reserve. He was suspicious that Pashin had overheard something; neighbours had seen Pashin leaving Andrews's house when he'd retrieved his grandfather's drum, and so he set him up as a prime suspect for insurance. Andrews had slipped a photo that he'd found of Pashin into Jay Tuck's pocket to muddy the waters. Goudge swore that the murder weapon was a hunting knife that Andrews had, which has not been found to date. The crooked knife left beside the body of Jay Tuck was a warning. The murder of Shirleen had been further insurance. Turns out that Andrews had had a plant in the Crooked Knife Society. He blackmailed this woman into spying, and in return he wouldn't complain to Family Services about her being an unsuitable mother.

Shirleen had tricked the woman into revealing that she was passing on information to Andrews. When the plant confessed to Andrews that her cover had been blown, he disposed of Shirleen as if she were nothing more than an annoyance. No knife had been left, it was thought, because he'd been so convinced that Musgrave would stop the investigation. Clearly, Andrews thought that he could do anything once Musgrave was involved. As for Father Ryan, he was in the clear for the murders. Pete told me, however, that based on what I'd found out regarding Ryan's past as a suspected pedophile, he was in contact with the Archdiocese in St. John's. I'm proud of Pete for going the extra distance.

Initially, in the long conversations I'd had with Pashin since everything happened, no matter what I told him he continued to hold himself responsible for Tuck's and Shirleen's deaths. The fact that a cop had been involved only furthered his paranoia, but he'd started to come around as of late. I put him to work on the play. I had him do rewrite after rewrite until it was perfect. The drama group had a stunning debut with *A Northern Hamlet*. It was full of pathos and humour too. The play would travel to St. John's in the spring for a festival there and then possibly to British Columbia for an international festival of Indigenous art.

When Pashin and I weren't fine-tuning the play, we talked. We talked about how easy it was to have a failure of nerve, but if we could remember to keep acting on behalf of those more vulnerable than us, we could dispel our hopelessness. We agreed that it seemed that the machine called *progress* was winning out over the one called *basic sanity*, and we'd have to be good with the small wins. Learning to stop judging ourselves was hard work and it meant giving up on an approach that said that things were black or white, all or nothing. The machine wanted us to believe that success was counted by the number of bodies you could stand upon to reach your goal. When it seems that the AT-AT Walkers are arrayed against us rebels, I remember to keep my temper and keep believing in our cause.

Speaking of mega-evil, the mega-dam project at Otter Falls continues to grind on, impervious to the harm that it causes Labradorians. We haven't given up the fight, but what can be gained becomes smaller day by day. As Roberta, my mentor in slow activism has taught me, if all we gain is an example for other eco-activists around the world as to what *didn't* work, it will still be worth it. The Land Protectors, the River Keepers, and the Crooked Knife Society have begun to join forces whenever it is deemed a good idea. We think that Jay Tuck and Shirleen Gregoire would have been proud.

Nick's book on the debacle of Otter Falls is nearing completion. He is still mired in the justice system—once they have their claws in you, it's hard for them to let you go. But as the business with Musgrave has been deeply embarrassing to both BECorp and the RCMP higher-ups, it looks like something might budge soon. Nick has meetings with the Canadian Civil Liberties Union in late January, which will get things on the boil.

For now, we'll spend this time at Butter and Snow, at the cabin Nick calls our fortress of solitude. I watch him make me a second cup of coffee, the dog eyeing us from in front of the fire, the day and the week laid out ahead of us under a fresh blanket of perfect snow, and I can be happy here in the wild beauty of Labrador.

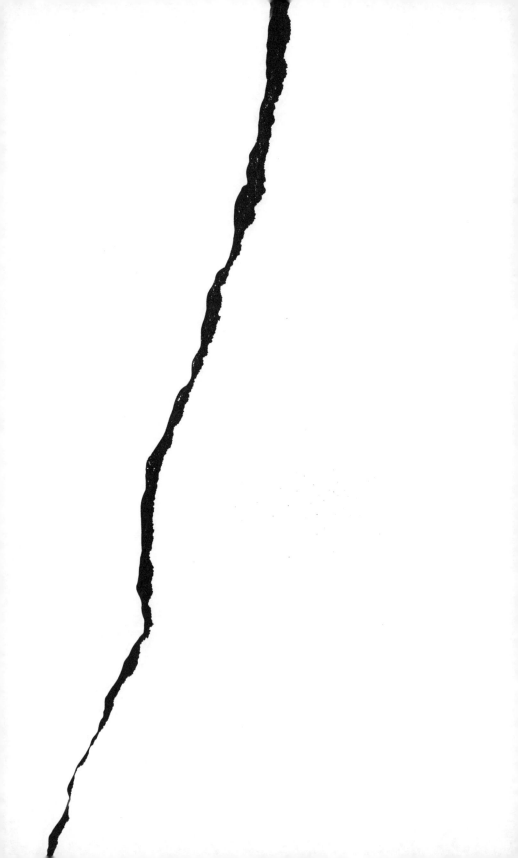

Acknowledgements

Writing *The Crooked Knife* helped me understand a place that has confounded and entranced me. Here are some of the people who guided me on this journey:

Thanks to Kate Juniper, an editor both fierce and gentle, who helped me say what I wanted to say.

Thanks to the team at Boulder Books, especially Gavin Will and Stephanie Porter. I'm so happy to work with a gang out of Newfoundland, who know the jigs and reels of publishing.

I am grateful to Mallory Burnside-Holmes for being the first editor on the team. Thanks for your excellent brightening and tightening of the manuscript. And thanks to copy editor Iona Bulgin for your sharp eyes! Thanks to Tanya Montini for your inspired design.

Huge appreciation to Willa Creighton for her expert help in navigating social media.

Thanks to my friends in Labrador—especially Robin Goodfellow-Baikie, Liz Dawson, Eldred Davis, and Roberta Benefiel. Thanks to the Sheshatshiu Innu School for always welcoming me and allowing me to have the most fun work ever. Deep gratitude to the Grand Riverkeepers and the Labrador Land Protectors, an amazing group of loving activists.

Thanks to all the people who were kind to me in Sheshatshiu and North West River, even when I didn't know what I was talking about.

Thanks to Katherine Greener for being a first reader. Thanks to my newest sister Judy McInnes and her husband, Jim, who helped with some of my stickier policing questions. All errors are mine. Thanks to Annie Abdalla (Trinkar) for keeping me grounded, and to Ren Skelley for being delighted. Thanks to Sue Goyette for talking me off the ledge once or twice.

Boundless thanks to my teachers Dzongsar Jamyang Khyentse Rinpoche, Pema Chödrön, and Tsoykni Rinpoche for patiently teaching me about the dance of interdependence.

Thanks to the Canadian Babes: Cindy Littlefair, Debra Ross, Julia Creighton, Marion Stork, and Molly deShong for always knowing when to laugh and when to cry.

I owe so much gratitude to Gwen Davies, my dear writing friend, who has kept the faith, meeting Wednesdays to write for over 20 years. Her encouragement and skill as a reader are invaluable.

Thanks to Linda Jackson, who was around for the very first inkling. And much more.

Thanks to my sister Jude Morrison for believing in my dream. And to my boys, Jesse and Calvin, for understanding my kind of crazy and for making me laugh. Thanks to my brother Don Morrison for his cheerful passion for all things northern, and my sister-in-law Anne Budgell for walking the path ahead. Thanks to my stepmother, Stella Morrison, for her wit and wisdom.

I am so grateful to both my parents, Mo and Bea Morrison, who were such lovers of the written word. What a gift that has been.

Thanks to my dearest pal, Kerol Rose, for asking me "what's your story?" and daring to listen for the next 45 years. We are two blossoms on one branch.

And last and most, my fella, Ron Budgell, who brought me to Muskrat Falls in Labrador and asked me to listen.

About the Author

Photo credit: Marion Stork

Jan Morrison was raised in the back of an avocado green station wagon. Jan is an air-force brat, and her family was either being posted across the country or exploring the back roads on summer holidays. This vagabond life has carried on into Jan's adult years, and she enthusiastically embraced an adventure that took her from Nova Scotia to Labrador. While working with Innu youth in Sheshatshiu, Jan, a playwright, poet, and psychotherapist, was inspired to write *The Crooked Knife*, her debut novel. When not writing, Jan is in her garden or rambling the shoreline near her home in Prospect, NS, with her fella and dog.